Scoundrel in My Dreams

Celeste Bradley

St. Martin's Paperbacks

This is a work of fiction. All of the characters, organizations, and events portrayed in this novel are either products of the author's imagination or are used fictitiously.

SCOUNDREL IN MY DREAMS

Copyright © 2010 by Celeste Bradley.

All rights reserved.

For information address St. Martin's Press, 175 Fifth Avenue, New York, NY 10010.

ISBN: 978-1-61664-899-2

Printed in the United States of America

This book is dedicated to people who adopt unwanted kittens and puppies from shelters across the U.S. All my animals are rescues and I love them even more for it. Think first before you buy.

I must acknowledge the help of three great brainstorming partners! Darbi Gill, Robyn Holiday, and Joanne Markis. I couldn't have written this trilogy without you.

I must again mention the inspiration of little Frankie Jean Baca-Lucero, soul-sister to Lady Melody. Thanks, everyone!

Prologue

*The mony stopped coming from the mother. I can't keep
her no more. The father can take her now. Don't know
his name. He's a memmber of Brown's.*

Once upon a time a child was left on the doorstep of a
stuffy London gentlemen's club with a note pinned to
her coat. Since the question on the minds of most of the
members of Brown's was 'Where did I leave my teeth?'
only three were young enough to be sowing oats of any
kind, wild or otherwise. Aidan de Quincy, Sir Colin
Lambert, and Lord John Redgrave.

Aidan and Colin were quick to pin this foundling
on their absent friend Jack. It is always easier to blame
someone who isn't there, isn't it? Yet as Aidan grew to
love that tiny cherubic hellion, he began to wonder . . .
could little Melody be his?

Forced to face his past and seek out the lovely widow
Madeleine Chandler, Aidan brought her back to Brown's
to get to know her discarded child and to become his
bride. The problem was that Madeleine had a secret, a
past that made lying to Aidan seem like the best chance
of escape.

Chaos and mayhem ensued, of course, when their
pasts collided and the truth was revealed. By the time

peace reigned once more, Sir Colin Lambert was beginning to have doubts of his own.

Therefore, Colin set off to Brighton with little Melody to find Chantal, the lovely actress who had held his heart captive for years. However, Chantal had fled. Colin hired her seamstress, the saucy Prudence Filby, in order to find Chantal before she married another.

Travel and misadventure ensued, bandits and giants went to war, and little Melody adored every moment. Colin, however, began to fear finding the woman of his dreams now that he had feelings for flame-haired, hot-tempered Pru. Torn, he knew that for Melody's sake he must find Melody's mother and wed her at once, even though his heart belonged to Pru. Fortunately, Chantal was as deceitful as she was beautiful and her claim to Melody was false.

This happy discovery led to one inescapable conclusion.

By the process of elimination, Melody must be the child of Lord John Redgrave, heir to the Marquis of Strickland.

When Jack arrived home from tending to his uncle's sugar plantations in the West Indies, he was going to have quite a surprise waiting for him.

For the only woman he'd ever loved had long since married another man.

Twenty years later . . .

"Button?"

With a noise between a chuckle and a sigh, Button ceased his narrative and looked down at the dark head resting upon his shoulder. "Yes, Melody?"

Melody sat up straight, which made her taller than he, even seated on the sofa. She wrinkled her nose apologetically. It made her look far younger than her three-and-twenty years. "I know I'm interrupting again, but that's simply not how it was. Mama never married someone else."

Then, as if the merest mention of marriage was more than Melody could stand, she shot a single panicked glance at the exquisite Lementeur wedding gown hanging only a few feet away. The sight of that shimmering confection of lace and beaded silk only made her bury her face in Button's shoulder again.

"Never mind. I'm sorry." Her words were muffled by panic and Button's superfine wool surcoat. "Please continue."

Button tipped her chin up with one finger to gaze into dark-lashed eyes like summer sky. "Mellie, if I finish this story, will you promise to put on the wedding gown that I painstakingly designed myself and then charged your poor father an obscene amount for?"

Melody shrank back. "If I get dressed, I'll have to . . . to . . ."

Button raised an implacable brow. "If you can't say it, you certainly won't be able to do it."

Melody tried to take a deep breath, then another, but she rushed the process and lost her breath altogether. Her eyes widened as she paled and she shot him a gaze of pure panic. Button plunked his palm on the top of her head and matter-of-factly pushed her head down between her knees as if he did that sort of thing often. Considering all the brides who clamored to wear an actual Lementeur on their momentous day, he probably had.

Melody's breathing eased back to the sort of rhythm

she'd never had any trouble with until this day. She sat up and pressed both palms to her flaming cheeks. "I don't know what's wrong with me."

"I don't, either," Button said patiently, although not quite as patiently as the first time he'd said it several hours before. "You love him to tiny little bits. He adores you. You are clearly meant for each other."

She shut her eyes tight and shook her head swiftly. " 'Meant for each other'? What does that mean? Meant to live together forever, making each other uniquely miserable, like half the couples in Society? Meant to know precisely how to hurt each other the most?"

Button frowned. "He has never hurt you!" Then, "Has he?"

"No." Melody sniffled. "But he could. He could, he could—" Her face began to crumple. "He could *leave*."

Button put his palms on either cheek to stop the disintegration. "No crying. It will melt your face."

Melody stared up at him for a long moment, her cheeks a bit smushed and her brow crinkled. "Button," she said finally, through lips pooched out from the gentle pressure, "you're a bit mad, aren't you?"

He smiled and released her with a quick kiss to her forehead. "Mad like a fox. If you cry, it will take hours for the redness to fade."

Then he tucked her beneath his arm once more. "Here is how matters will proceed. You will listen to the best and last story of the complicated courtship of your parents—"

"I know you said it was the basis for Uncle Colin's book, *The Queen in the Tower,* but I don't believe a word of it is true." She gazed up at him seriously. "There are no such things as elves."

Button ignored her and continued. "You will listen to this story and you will find yourself entirely reassured that your own rather event-filled courtship was nothing out of the ordinary for your family. You will gladly get dressed in that marvelous frivolity of a wedding gown and you will make it look exquisite and it will return the favor. You will walk down that aisle without the slightest hint of reluctance and you will marry that young man and make him—and yourself!—eternally happy!" He glared at her fondly. "Is that understood, little Milady?"

She gazed back at him sadly. "I suppose you ought to get started." She sniffled and snuggled closer. "I think this might take a while."

He squeezed reassuringly as he began again. "Once upon a time there was a man who thought he'd lost everything. . . ."

It all began in a castle far away. . . . Oh, very well, it was only a country manor in Surrey. A young woman tugged her cap down over her hair and smoothed her dressing gown with nervous hands as she tiptoed down the dark hallway in the guest wing.

Without a candle—and why would she need a candle when she'd lived in this house every moment of her entire life?—the only light came from the moon, streaming through the window at the end of the hall. The chambermaid had forgotten to pull the draperies closed at sunset, an understandable lapse with the house so full of guests to tend to. The house party had raged for days and the staff was worn quite thin.

For this particular young lady, however, only one guest mattered. Lord John Redgrave, heir to the Marquis of Strickland, handsome, dashing, and still so pitiably distraught over the battleground death of his cousin, Blakely.

She stopped outside the door assigned to Lord John and took a deep breath. "Jack," she whispered, just to practice her speech one last time. "I know that you're sailing away tomorrow to tend to your uncle's plantations, but . . . I love you."

Ridiculous. She sounded childish and pathetic even to her own ears. Yet how else was she to let him know her feelings before he went so far away she might never see him again?

Her trembling hand touched the chill iron of the door latch and with the merest of clicks, she was in Jack's room.

The moonlight came, too, pouring in through the wide bedchamber window like blue and silver magic. Sprawled in the pool of light, tangled in the snowy bed linens, Jack lay sleeping in the middle of the wide bed.

Naked.

Her mouth went dry and her heart began to hammer a warning.

Jack lay on his back. As she moved closer—and she couldn't seem to help moving closer—she could make out every dip and plane of his broad muscled chest. One arm was flung wide, as if reaching for her. The other lay lax across his rippled abdomen, his hand resting just above his navel.

The linens covered much of what lay below that, except for one muscular thigh and knee, so she let her gaze travel back up his long, muscular body to his face. She'd always loved the angled planes of his sensitive face, even before he went to war, but now the desolation he'd witnessed had refined the easy sanguine features of old into a honed, more rugged version of her Jack.

His jaw and the planes of his cheekbones were sharper and more defined. His mouth with its sensual lower lip had not given a single smile since he had arrived. Tragedy had worn his brow and given him slight creases on either side of his beautiful mouth. The war had taken the lighthearted boy and brought back to her a dark and troubled man.

She loved him all the more for it. It had been easy to adore him before. Everyone did. Now, however, he was left to himself. The young man who was so happy to be entertaining and delightful was gone.

At present, he scarcely spoke at all and when he did, his words were terse and startling, as if he no longer had the patience for the banal and trivial conversation of Society. His gaze was distant instead of laughing, his dark brown eyes now smoldering with something battle born and much too momentous for the tender constitutions of the other guests. They shunned him as if avoiding an improperly tamed animal. To her, however, his darkness drew her like a moth to a black flame.

He had not cut his hair in far too long, but she loved how it fell straight and midnight dark nearly to his shoulders. It made him seem untamed and a little dangerous, as if he cared nothing for the standards of Society. Her hands twitched to brush it back from his brow as he slept, to let the glossy strands of it run through her fingers. His jaw showed dark stubble, even in the moonlight. It would feel rough to her touch, like sandpaper on the steel angle of his jaw.

She licked her lips and moved closer to the bed. She'd studied his face for so long she could draw him in the dark. She had longed to see more.

Now was her chance.

His body was long and tall, flung across the mattress at an angle. Broad, powerful shoulders narrowed down to his hips, giving his torso a catlike leanness she'd not noticed in his clothes. His chest was broad and sculpted. She could clearly see the dips and bumps of more muscle cording his upper arms and strapping across his ribs, rippling over his abdomen. A patch of dark hair covered his chest from one flat nipple to the other, then narrowed to a dark trail over his taut belly down past his navel. Her eyes followed it in fascination. Her fingers itched to explore as well.

The corner of the sheet concealed his groin. She let out a faint sigh, half in disappointment, half in reprieve.

One thigh was hidden beneath the covers, but the other leg bent outward, muscled and long, ending in a large shapely foot. The bed was huge, one of the largest in the house, yet he filled it by himself.

He was so different. He no longer seemed aware of the handsome exterior he used to wear as confidently as a fine coat. Now his awareness was turned inward, consumed by loss and tragedy, a witness to death and destruction on a scale she could not even imagine in her sheltered, decorous world.

She saw scars, new and angry, darkly ominous on skin gone silvery in the moonlight. A starburst pattern on one shoulder. When had he taken a bullet? Why had she heard nothing of it? A diagonal slash across his opposite ribs—a bayonet had struck dangerously close to his heart. Another such slash on one muscular thigh, as if he'd been mounted while the other man was on foot.

This was a new Jack, harsh and deadly serious, with danger emanating from him even in sleep. He was like a lethal weapon, hammered hard by war.

Beautiful.

Men weren't supposed to be beautiful, but there was no better word for the way he looked, bare and muscled and unembarrassed in his magnificence. He was splendid and virile and entirely male, while she—

Her hand reached, but she drew it back, ashamed. Her romantic fancies seemed even more foolish against this physical confirmation of his ordeal. This man could not possibly take an interest in an inexperienced creature such as herself. Her adventures had all happened on the pages of books. Her own tribulations consisted of enduring her shallow, social-climbing parents and her vindictive sister.

She was being absurd, like a child wishing to own a pet tiger.

She shouldn't be here. She should turn right around and run back to her room and keep her silly girlish fancies to her silly self.

She bit her lip. This was no place for her, here with this beautiful, unclothed man. His barely covered form sprawled before her, so male, so potent. Fascination and fear twined through her belly, vying for supremacy. Touch . . . or flee?

Without her truly choosing, her feet decided upon fear. With only a few running steps, she had one hand on the door latch. As humiliating as it was to realize it, she knew her proper place was back in her silly girlish bedchamber, in her silly girlish bed.

With tears of helpless fury at her own weakness, she pressed down on the latch—

A deep moan came from behind her. Words, muttered and intelligible, but clearly full of anguish.

She turned.

The man in the moonlight had changed. All sign of peaceful repose was gone. Instead, she saw him tense and twitch, the muscles in his chest and belly going tight with strain. A meaningless cry of protest came to his lips, his voice full of pain and loss.

She drew closer to the bed, unaware of her moving feet, only responding to the pain she heard, the horror she saw etched in his tensing, twitching form.

She licked her dry lips. "Jack?" Her whisper went unheard beneath the gasping sounds of his nightmare. Now sweat began to gleam on his skin, silver in the moonlight. His hands fisted in the sheets. She heard threads pop as they tore.

Should she fetch someone? But who? She dared not alert her parents to her presence in a man's bedchamber. One of the staff? What could they do that she could not?

Wake him. "Jack!"

He was too lost in his dreadful dream to hear her.

Shake him.

She had to. She couldn't bear to see him wracked with such agony. He would know she'd entered his room . . . but she would tell him she'd been woken by his cries.

And hope he didn't realize that her room lay in a different wing.

One trembling hand reached out to him. Naked man, bare skin, where . . . ? Hesitantly, her hand came to rest on his shoulder. She tried not to think about the heat of him in her palm, about the intimacy of skin to skin. She gave his shoulder a quick, brisk shake. "Jack! Wake up!"

A thrashing hand brushed hers away. Chewing on her lip, she moved closer, lifting her wrapper and gown and bracing one knee on the mattress. She leaned down and shook his shoulder again, hard. "Jack!"

He arched his back and cried out. She overbalanced and fell forward, landing across his broad, naked chest. Even that impact did nothing to penetrate his nightmare, though the heat of him went straight through her body.

"Blakely—" he gasped.

She ached for him. He called for his cousin, the one who died in battle. His best friend. No longer thinking of her own embarrassment, she pressed his trembling body down with her own and smoothed his face with her hands. "Shh. Jack, it's all over. You're back now. Shh. You're safe and sound."

The awful thrashing eased a little. Encouraged, she continued to soothe away the rictus of pain and horror from his beautiful face. The moonlight dimmed away. The clouds were thickening. The darkness made her braver still. She dropped quick kisses to his cheeks. "Shh. Come back to me, Jack. Come back to England."

With every passing moment, his tension began to ease. The hot gasping of his breath began to lessen. Against her breasts she could feel his pounding heart begin to slow. She clung to him, stroking her hands through his damp hair, calling to him, whispering his name, kissing his cheeks, his forehead, his tensed and grimacing lips.

Then, as if by accident, their lips began to cling. She didn't even realize it at first. It felt so natural by now to lie with her body sprawled across his, her hands in his hair, her mouth on his. When his hands came up to wrap about her face and the kiss gained in strength and commitment, she had spent a little too long pressed to his long, hard naked body, a little too long smoothing his damp, muscled neck and shoulders with her hands, a little too long breathing in his scent, sharing his breath, touching and kissing and pressing. . . .

When he rolled over onto her and deepened the kiss, it didn't occur to her fogged senses that there was a single thing wrong with that.

Lord John Redgrave, newly minted heir to the Marquis of Strickland, woke alone but more rested than he had been in weeks.

For the first time in a very long time, he'd slept without nightmares. The woman he was to marry had come to comfort him in the night and her sweetly hesitant touch had taken them all away.

As powerful as a goddess, she had even driven off the battleground memories masquerading as graphic dreams. No ghosts of blame and regret could linger in the shadows, not in the shimmering light of her giving body and hot, eager kisses.

For the first time since the war had stolen his untainted soul and given him back nothing but black guilt and sorrow, Jack had enjoyed the carefree sleep of a man with a clear mind.

As Jack rolled his head on the pillow he was caught by the scent of her. There was the softly floral smell of her hair, which reminded him of the way it had felt spilling over his bare chest. There was the clean, sweet smell of her skin, just a hint of woman with a top note of scented soap.

And there was the scent of her sex, on the sheets and on him as well. His fingers tightened on the covers and he breathed deeply of the night before. Her body had been a celebration of soft mounds and sweet wet places, of open arms and welcoming thighs. Heat flashed through him, reigniting the ember he'd thought had gone cold forever.

Heat . . . and simple warmth as well.

He kept his eyes closed for a moment longer, savoring the memories—the taste of her soft, inexperienced mouth, the way her trembling hands had caressed him as her dark hair spilled across his chest like warm silk, how she'd clung to him when he'd carefully entered her at last. . . .

Sitting up, he flipped back his bed linens to reveal the telltale smear of her virginity on the sheets. "Hmm." Mingled embarrassment and pride of possession twined through him.

My woman. Mine.

He smoothed the covers back again. He probably ought to speak to her father before some overeager maid tattled on them both.

When he had returned to England some weeks ago as a shadow of himself, dreading taking his dead cousin's place as heir, Jack had tried without success to take up the strings of that life. Now, it seemed almost possible, if he could so with her at his side.

With her hand in his, perhaps he could at last face his uncle, the marquis, the man who had been father and more to him, and not feel the ghost of Blakely behind him, watching Jack take the place that had been rightfully his.

Perhaps, with a loving and generous bride at Jack's side, the war would someday slip into the past where it belonged and he could see a future untainted with gunpowder and death.

With something almost like a smile teasing at the corners of Jack's mouth, he washed and dressed quickly. Matters had most definitely taken a turn for the better.

Matters couldn't be worse.

"I don't understand, sir." Jack tried to keep his anguish hidden, but his voice growled ever so slightly on the "sir," causing the jowly Mr. Clarke to shoot him a wary glance. "She cannot possibly wed the Earl of Compton. She's engaged to *me!*"

Mr. Clarke harrumphed indignantly but avoided Jack's desperate gaze. "That was a sentimental promise given by a young girl to a soldier going off to war." He wrapped his fingers around his own lapels and rocked back on his heels, lifting his chin pompously. "There was no *official* marriage contract."

"A sentimental promise," Jack was trying very hard to remain calm, "is a promise nonetheless. For you to insist that she wed some hoary old goat simply for your own financial gain—"

"But Jack, I *wish* to marry Compton." Amaryllis's voice, light but decisive, preceded her into her father's study.

Jack turned even as his heart began to pound eagerly. Then her words penetrated his fervent haze. He stared at her, stunned. She stood framed in the doorway, a cool and perfect version of the sweetly passionate girl he'd made love to the night before. Now her cloud of nearly black hair was swept artfully into a knot, with only small, tempting tendrils free to caress her cheekbones. Those restless, roving hands that had driven him wild only a few hours ago were clasped calmly before her. If he'd roughened her neck with his beard stubble while he'd lost himself in her, there was no flush of pink remaining upon that flawless ivory skin.

"Darling—" He stepped forward, unable to stop himself, yet when her gaze met his he saw nothing in her eyes for him. She tilted her head and gazed at him as if nothing untoward had occurred at all. His steps faltered, then stopped.

Amaryllis crossed the room to stand with her father. The two of them faced him coolly, as if he were an inconvenient caller or, worse, a tradesman outstaying his welcome.

Everything he'd felt the night before came boiling up within him, threatening to spill from his lips— except that somewhere on those fields of fire and blood and death he'd forgotten how to use the glib tongue he'd been born with.

When he'd come home from the war midsummer, his friends had encouraged him to attend this house party. They'd hoped, as he had, that seeing the girl he'd loved would remind him of the man he'd been before he'd left for war. As the family had abandoned London for a house party in Sussex, he'd followed her here. Once arrived, however, he found it impossible to join in, found it difficult to remember why the old amusements had been amusing. He felt as if he were in a glass bubble, trying to reach out, unable to touch anyone. His very presence merely seemed to make people uncomfortable.

He'd felt this very coolness from her every day since he'd arrived at this house party. He'd begun to wonder if she was purposely avoiding him or if she was simply distracted by her new role as hostess while her mother lay ill. He'd tried to speak to her, tried to remember the easy teasing banter they'd once shared, but his brain felt like a stranger's brain and his tongue a stranger's tongue. If he wanted to say something, he couldn't remember what, and if he could remember, he didn't know how to make it fall from his lips in a normal manner. He felt like a foreigner in his own world, new and raw and underinformed.

And at the moment, entirely confused. When she'd come to him last night, offering comfort, it had been the first moment of true connection he'd felt. He'd taken the comfort she'd offered, taken it greedily and thankfully, for were they not already engaged?

It seemed the answer was no, they were not.

Amaryllis averted her eyes from his wondering gaze and lifted her chin. "The Earl of Compton is an admirable catch," she said in a distant tone. "I think we shall do very well together."

"You said . . . I came back. . . . You promised—" Blast it, his mouth was not connected to his brain! He took a deep breath, but she was already answering his blathering.

"I'm terribly sorry if you received a wrong impression from my friendship," she said carefully. "I intended no such confusion." The words sounded a bit rehearsed.

Perhaps he ought to rehearse himself, for he could find nothing to say except for the one thing a gentleman never ought to say.

"I compromised you!"

Her eyes widened and her mouth opened, but Jack never had the chance to hear what she had to say in response, for Mr. Clarke had had enough. He stepped between them, looking very much like a deeply offended bulldog.

"Now see here, my lord, if you're going to spout lies, I'm going to have to ask you to leave!"

It's not a lie. He pleaded to her with his eyes, helplessly inarticulate. *Tell him!*

She said nothing. He felt the breath leave his lungs as the truth finally struck. She had her eye on a bigger prize now. A prize who, though old, was rich and titled, something Jack would not be until his uncle breathed his last—which could take many years.

Yet he could not let it go, could not walk away. That night, that single night of humanity when he'd thought his soul lost forever—how could he let that go without a fight? However, when he protested, the dams of sanity cracked ever so slightly.

"You cannot do this!" he shouted at them both. "I will not stand aside!" He turned his fury on her, making her take a step backward in alarm. "How can you—after what we've shared?"

He was to have no answer to that. Amaryllis simply stood there, color high in her cheeks, blue eyes flashing with contempt, as two sturdy footmen took him by the arms. He fought them, unable to stop himself, all the fury and rage of the battlefield taking over his mind. In his blurred and shattered memory later, the only things he clearly remembered were the way the gravel scraped his palms as he sprawled on the drive in front of the house, the way every window and doorway of the house was filled with the shocked, voracious eyes of the guests and staff, and a single final glimpse of those wide, horrified blue eyes, crying as if she finally realized what she'd done.

When he returned to London, the battle haze continued. He drank and brawled, brawled and drank, until the night two months later when he ended up sitting on the edge of a rooftop, his boots dangling over empty space and an empty whiskey bottle in his grip, contemplating heights and weights and drop velocities and how long it would take to reach eternity.

Even when his friends managed to talk a bit of sense into him, it was only enough to send him off to sail the seas, trying to forget the woman who had shown him his single hope for salvation, only to snatch it away again.

One

Jack walked slowly off the gangplank of the *Honor's Thunder,* a simple valise hanging from one hand. The sailors glanced up to watch him pass, a few nodding respectfully, but none exchanged a single word with him. There was no reason for them to. He was not really the captain. A salty fellow with many more years at sea had that esteemed title. Nor was Jack truly the owner, although he would be someday. He was simply "milord," and only spoken to when necessary.

When he stepped at last upon the soil of England, where he had not walked for more than two years—or had it been three?—the ground seemed to lurch beneath his feet.

I have sea legs.

It would take a few days to regain his land legs, he recalled dully. Land legs. *Eng-land legs.*

Would that those legs could turn around and stride back onto the ship. He had not returned in a long time because he did not wish to. Even now, it was only a cryptic fragment of a letter from his old friend Aidan de Quincy, the Earl of Blankenship, that prompted Jack to leave the ship at all.

The letter had awaited Jack right here in the East India Docks of London, pinned up in the dockmaster's office in appalling condition. The man had handed it to Jack with an apologetic shrug. It was crumpled and so stained with seawater that the ink had run illegibly through most of the paper. If Jack had not recognized the signet pressed into the wax seal, he'd scarcely have been able to tell from whence it came. The letter looked as though it had followed him halfway around the world, only to await him at home.

When he'd unfolded the stiffened paper, only a few startling words had remained.

"Return at once" and "your [something unreadable] awaits you here" and last but most alarmingly "you cannot flee from her forever."

Her.

Aidan could not mean *her*. Not the woman who still kept Jack awake long into the night, standing alone on the deck of the ship while the stars hung almost close enough to touch. Not the woman whose soft sighs and sweet whispers still filled his ears, keeping him from hearing any inviting hints from other women.

It was impossible that Aidan meant *her*. Jack had never told anyone what had happened at the Clarkes' house party nearly four years ago and he was quite certain that the Clarke family themselves would never speak a word of it.

Yet even the slightest possibility had pulled Jack away from his numbing routine, had compelled him to step foot upon the chill, unwelcoming shores of England.

Damned bloody coldhearted England.

As Jack walked down the docks through the wisps
of dawn fog, managing to counter his sea legs and main-
tain his dignity in this at least, he refused to see her in
the mist. Those whorls of shimmering fog did not remind
him of the sweet curves of her body in the moonlight.
The color of the brightening sky did not bring to mind
the cloudless blue of her eyes.

As he walked on and the hour grew later, the morning breeze did not make him recall the nearly black
silk of her hair brushing over his skin as she trailed
kisses down his body.

No, he would not think of *her.*

After all, he had not thought of *her* in years.

The door to Brown's was untended, standing open in
the morning sunlight to reveal a dark rectangle of shadowy interior. Jack blinked slowly at it, more weary than
he could recall being in a very long time. Numb and
weary and damned bloody cold, yet here he stood, home
again.

Brown's Club for Distinguished Gentlemen was the
closest thing he had to a home. Some ancestor had
been a founding member, and although the membership tended toward the silver haired and stick wielding,
Jack had sponsored his friends so they could all enjoy
the quiet surroundings and excellent service of Brown's.

The estate of Strickland, on the other hand, was a
fearsome place and one to be avoided. It was large and
luxurious and contained the one man whom Jack could
never bear to face again. The old marquis was a fine
man, a good and just master to his people.

It was Jack who counted as the villain there.

So in the brief time he'd still been able to stand England, he'd spent his days at Brown's, with the friends who still remained. Aidan and Sir Colin Lambert had walked by Jack's side as boys and stood with him still, though he lately returned their friendship with nothing but distance and silence.

The rented cab pulled away in a clatter of hooves and creaking wheels, leaving Jack standing on the walk, gazing up.

Go on. Walk in. Learn the meaning of the letter. Your ship has been instructed to wait for you. Once you know what it is that "awaits you here," you can simply turn around and leave again.

With feet that felt as leaden as in a bad dream, Jack climbed the steps and entered the open door.

In the entrance hall of Brown's stood a group of people. Jack hesitated at the door, his grip tightening on the handle of his valise. "People" meant strangers, and strangers had a disturbing tendency to speak to him, to ask him questions, to force him to search for sensible replies in the haunted corners of his mind. Even *how do you do?* became an impossible test—for he had not the assembled wit nor the will to lie, but the truth would only make them back away from him and look for the soonest possible excuse to leave the room.

Baggage lay piled just inside the door. Someone was arriving. Or leaving.

There's a coincidence. So am I. Arriving and leaving, as soon as possible.

Then Jack spotted a tall, broad-shouldered man with dark hair and blue eyes. Aidan. Jack next saw Colin's fairer head, only slightly shorter, and heard his teasing voice.

Two women, one dark haired, one fiery red, stood with Jack's friends. The women were both quite pretty, noticed a distant corner of his mind. Then, more slowly, the truth rose to the surface of his mind.

Women. In Brown's Club for Distinguished Gentlemen. Moreover, the women were most certainly attached to Aidan and Colin. Either that or someone really ought to slap Colin a good one, for his hand rested intimately low on the flame-haired woman's hip. The pretty brunette with the large brown eyes turned her limpid gaze adoringly on Aidan.

My, how things have changed. Go away for a few months—

Years.

Fine. Go away for a few years and the world turns on its head.

At that moment, the two couples moved slightly apart and Jack saw her.

Jiggling eagerly on little booted tiptoes, with her head tilted back so far that her tiny tricorne hat threatened to slide from her dark curls and her wide blue eyes bright and shining with excitement, was a beautiful child of perhaps three years. She was dressed rather improbably as a pirate, right down to a tiny wooden sword thrust into the belt of her striped trousers.

The sight of her struck Jack like a blow from a real sword, directly into his chest.

Oh. Her.

Though Jack made no sound or movement, the four adults noticed him at last. The dark woman stepped forward and began to speak, something about the child. It was simply noise lost in the roaring in Jack's mind. *I know those eyes.*

He held up a hand and they all went very still. "I know who she is." He dropped his valise and crossed the hall to go down on one knee in front of the little girl. "You look just like your mother," he said softly.

She pulled off her silly, adorable miniature eye patch and blinked her startlingly blue eyes at him. Then she reached out to stroke his thin face with her pudgy baby fingers. "You're Cap'n Jack."

It was as if Jack's heart began to beat again in that moment, hesitantly, rustily, then growing in strength and rhythm.

No one touched him. Ever. Even his friends satisfied themselves with a quick clap on the shoulder, and that only rarely. Her tiny fingers were sticky and scented with lemon cake crumbs.

Jack would not have drawn away for all the world. He remained motionless for her inspection. "And you are?"

She put her other hand on his face, framing his darkness with pink softness. "I'm Cap'n Melody."

Melody. Of course. Any other name simply wouldn't do. "Hello, Melody. I am your father."

Melody tilted her head and gazed at him for a long moment. "I like ships," she said finally. "Do you have a ship?"

He nodded again. "I have many ships." Somehow, her childish questions seemed perfectly simple to answer.

"Can I see them?"

"Certainly." *Anything else? Shall I slay a dragon? Fight off the monsters under the bed? Glare at your suitors until they shake in their boots?* He stood and held out his hand. "I shall show you my flagship, the *Honor's Thunder.*"

"All right." She took his hand and walked him to the door, then turned to wave at the assembled pairs of wide eyes. "I'm going to go see Papa's ship. Bye!"

Wilberforce, who seemed entirely unchanged by the passage of anything as feeble as mere years, helped Melody into her little coat, then opened the door for her and Jack, bowing silently as they passed from the club.

Outside, the afternoon had advanced. Jack blinked at the brightness of the day. When had the sky become so brilliantly blue?

He looked down at the tiny pirate by his side. She looked back up at him.

Blue, like a summer sky.

One night . . . one night that he could not erase from his mind, no matter how far he had sailed or how long he remained gone. One dazzling night of true unity before she'd tossed him aside to wed a richer man—

The former Amaryllis Clarke, now the Countess of Compton, was going to tender her explanations, and this time she was going to tell the truth.

"Papa! I can see the house! It's a big house!"

It was quite possible that no one in the world could be as excited as three-year-old Melody could be excited. She jumped on the sprung carriage seat. She hung from the window. She even forgot her rather loathsome rag doll for two consecutive minutes.

"Yes, Melody. The Earl of Compton has a very large house." Jack picked up his tiny daughter's doll from the floor of the carriage with two fingers and put it back on Melody's seat. Gordy Ann looked like a tatty cravat tied into knots and then dragged behind a mule team for a year or so.

Yet Melody's love for her knew no bounds. Jack could hardly complain, for that expansive circle of love now included him as well.

I rank somewhere after Gordy Ann and before berry trifle. Well, perhaps I am tied even with berry trifle.

It was an acceptable place to stand. After all, he was rather partial to berry trifle himself.

At least, he had been long ago when the world had consisted of colors other than gray and tastes other than sand.

Beside him, Melody bounced on the seat and sent him a gleeful look over her shoulder. "Papa, I can see the door!" Her big baby blue eyes sparkled.

Things were looking up. His world of gray now included the color blue.

They were her mother's eyes exactly. Eyes like summer sky, like blue topaz, like the egg of a robin. Amaryllis's eyes could tease and flash and twinkle, turning unwary fellows into brainless wax in her hands.

Moreover, those eyes could turn as cold as the shadows of a glacier, like the ones he'd seen in the north seas. Like the one he carried inside his chest.

Tiring of the unchanging view from the window, for they still drove slowly up the lengthy winding drive, Melody scrambled over to the other seat to fetch Gordy Ann and then returned to Jack. Without hesitation, Melody climbed into his lap and leaned contentedly against his chest. Looking down, Jack tried to decide if he ought to put his arm about her for safety. She looked secure enough, so he let her be.

Tirelessly affectionate, Melody was like a candle flame, trying to thaw that glacier inside him. Yet even a tiny thaw might become a summer, given time enough. He tucked his arm about her, just in case the carriage hit a pothole.

He was a little surprised that she wasn't intimidated by him. Most children were, as were most adults, now that he thought upon it. Melody, however, had simply adopted him as part of the strange and unlikely family of Brown's Club for Distinguished Gentlemen and had instantly accepted him as her very own papa.

He'd known she was his at once, for she looked exactly like the only woman he'd ever loved. Even without such a reference point, Melody had seemed to simply know him.

She called him Papa to his face and Cap'n Jack to everyone else. Melody was his child and his responsibility, yet over the last three days she had become something much, much more than that. Melody was the first person in a very long time to make him feel anything at all.

Which made him doubly furious that Amaryllis could abandon his child to halfhearted foster care and go on her merry way!

Anger was also something new to his gray world. Interesting thing, anger. Anger meant that he cared about something. Each new/old emotion unfolded before his numbed soul like a letter written by him but long forgotten. Familiar, yet entirely untried.

The carriage rolled to a smooth halt. Jack looked

through the window to see a vast and luxurious house. His view was limited mostly to the semi-circle of costly marble steps that led to the richly carved front doors. A flurry of liveried grooms came forward to hold the horses and to open the carriage door.

Jack was unimpressed. Strickland was older but every bit as luxurious, with five times the estate of this place. Amaryllis had married well. She was a wealthy countess. If she'd waited a little, she could have been an obnoxiously rich marchioness, who might or might not deign to notice a mere wealthy countess.

Amaryllis had never been a patient sort.

Jack and Melody were admitted to the house at once and installed in an ostentatiously formal parlor. The room was so grand and gilded and dripping with crystal that the usually irrepressible Melody clung to Jack's leg and stuck a corner of Gordy Ann into her mouth, gazing about her with wide eyes.

Jack didn't sit. He remembered that much about anger. Anger was done better standing.

In an almost-but-not-quite-rude amount of time, the door opened and Amaryllis drifted in. tall and elegant, hair as dark as fine mink, eyes like cool blue pools. Perfect features, inviting figure, exacting fashion sense. Her gown was as black as a mourning gown, but the cut was perfection.

She was every bit as lovely as the last time he'd seen her, when she was furiously demanding that her father throw him from the house, but now her liveliness was replaced by a layer of acquired ennui.

She watched him closely for his reaction, though she pretended stylish lassitude. "Jack? Is that really you?

Heavens, what in the world brings you to this dull old house?"

Jack waited curiously for some feeling to emerge, but the sight of Amaryllis left him entirely cold. Except for the anger, of course.

"I've come to speak to you about our child."

Amaryllis flicked a bored glance in Melody's general direction, then focused on Jack with a calculating gleam. "I don't have any children, darling. Everyone knows that."

Without another word, Jack turned and walked Melody to the door of the parlor. He pointed at the bottom step of the grand winding staircase. "Sit."

Melody sat, clutching Gordy Ann close. She gazed up at him with those eyes—couldn't Amaryllis recognize her own features in miniature?—and her bottom lip slowly emerged.

Jack gazed at her, nonplussed.

She thinks you're angry at her.

Oh.

"I'm not angry at you, Melody."

Big blue eyes blinked. And dampened.

Oh God. Alarm was a new feeling. Definitely one for the list.

"Melody, I am angry, but I am angry at the lady in the parlor. I am going to say some rather rude things to her now and I don't want you to have to hear them. If you sit here with Gordy Ann, I will come out in a few moments to fetch you."

As he watched, the lower lip began to retreat and the eyes blinked back the moisture. "You're angry at the lady?"

"I am."

"Gordy Ann doesn't like the lady."

Oh damn. "Gordy Ann might like the lady better after a while."

Melody nodded, but Jack had to admit that Gordy Ann didn't look very forgiving.

"Will you stay here?"

Melody nodded again, this time seeming her usual self.

Jack left her sliding Gordy Ann up and down the polished banister at the bottom of the stair and returned to the parlor.

Amaryllis had arranged herself attractively on a sofa. There was plenty of room for Jack to join her, but he remained standing.

"How can you deny you had my child?"

Amaryllis blew out a breath and abandoned her seductive pose, instead reaching for a chocolate from a box on the table next to her. "I repeat, I don't have children, Jack. Despite my husband's initial hopes, I'd never ruin my figure so." She shrugged. "It isn't so difficult to manage. A few herbs, a bit of this and that."

Frowning, Jack sent an assessing glance over that figure. He was no expert, but Amaryllis looked exactly the same as she had four years ago. Possibly slimmer.

She was watching him look at her. "Do you like what you see, handsome Jack?" She ran a fingertip along her neckline, ending at her cleavage. "You used to like it quite a bit, if I recall."

"I don't recall, actually." He narrowed his eyes. "Amaryllis, no more games. Four years ago, you came to my bed. The next day you announced your engagement to another man. Nine months later, you deposited our child with a nurse and left her there. Two months ago, you ceased paying that nurse, whereupon she abandoned our child on the doorstep of my club. Go on. Admit it!"

As he'd spoken, her face had undergone a journey from amusement, to surprise, to outright confusion. Now she gazed at him with her jaw frankly slack and her eyes blinking uncomprehendingly.

Then she shut her jaw. "Four years ago—" She closed her mouth, blinked, and then laughed out loud. "God, you've become so droll, Jack! It's a silly joke, but it has brightened an otherwise deadly day immeasurably." She chuckled. "A secret baby! Good lord, what a thought!"

Jack gazed at her, his anger turning to furious bewilderment. "Amaryllis, how could you abandon her? Why did you stop paying the nurse?" He gestured angrily at their luxurious surroundings. "Or is all this riding on debt?"

At that, her eyes snapped. "Of course it isn't! Debt? The very idea!" She stood, angry herself now, and advanced on him. "I'll thank you not to spread such rumors!"

He shook his head, disgusted. "Heartless! How could I—" He stopped. Rubbing his open hand over his face, he turned away from her. "You disgust me!"

"Leave my house!" Amaryllis's lovely features twisted into shrewish ugliness. "Take your foundling brat and get out! Or shall I have you tossed out on your arse, *again*?" Her lip curled. "After all, it was so very amusing the first time!"

Again.

In Jack's mind, the past and the present collided. He'd dreamed of her for so long! Yet the woman before him was a wicked, selfish shell of the girl he'd loved. With a single silent cry, the past slipped away, slaughtered by the woman of the present, by the cruelty gleaming from her sky blue eyes.

She seemed to sense that he was reaching the limit of his battle-honed temper.

With a toss of her head, she tried to regain her former ennui. "For your information, Lord John, you and I were never lovers. You are intruding on my mourning with your nonsense. I think it is high time you left."

Mourning? The black gown. Jack swallowed hard, tamping down his rage. There were polite things one said in such situations, weren't there? "Your husband?"

She rolled her eyes. "How I wish. No, it was my father. His heart, eight weeks ago."

Jack reeled in his fresh, unaccustomed anger and took a step back. Her denial was complete. Raging at her would get him nowhere. He bowed. "My apologies," he said stiffly. There was nothing more here for him or for Melody. "I shall go. Give my sympathies to your mother and sister."

Amaryllis plunked back down on the sofa and took another chocolate. "Mama died a year ago. Laurel wasn't fond of Papa anyway."

Jack turned and walked slowly from the room. Amaryllis was nothing like the girl he'd once loved. And although she was full of spite, her surprise had seemed entirely genuine. She'd sincerely had no idea what he was talking about!

In the hallway, Melody looked up from her little spot on the stair and blinked Amaryllis's blue eyes at him.

Could Amaryllis have *forgotten* that night?

That night . . . that one night still ranked as the only moment in the last few years that he'd felt even remotely human—that one night when the world was not cold and gray and grim.

That night that might as well have not existed, for he had nothing to show for it now. Even his memories were now suspect, tainted by Amaryllis's malice. He had remembered a girl who had never truly existed, painting her with his own need, his own dreams.

Amaryllis had looked at Melody like she was some sort of unpleasant subspecies, as if at any moment the little girl might lunge at her with grubby paws extended, intent on soiling her gown.

No, Amaryllis was no one's mother.

Which meant that he, Jack, was no one's father. Melody was not the product of that magical encounter. Melody was just a foundling, simply an anonymous lost child dumped on the doorstep of a gentlemen's club with a cryptic note pinned to her coat.

Lost in his swirling thoughts, Jack took Melody's little hand and walked her down the hall toward the great doors.

They passed a dark-clad woman in the hall without truly registering her presence. She dropped the book she carried as Jack passed. Quite automatically, he bent to retrieve it and pressed it back into her hands. "Pardon me, madam."

Melody waved at her, opening and closing her pudgy fingers in the manner in which tiny children waved.

How in the world was he going to break it to Aidan and Colin that the little girl they loved so much was of no connection to them whatsoever?

* * *

Miss Laurel Clarke, clad in black mourning—but not for the parents she'd grown to despise!—never wed, never asked, stood in the hallway of her wealthy sister's house and watched the man and child walk away from her to the door. Her shaking hands held a book with a grip that turned her knuckles white with strain.

The world had just spun wildly on its axis and had come down in an entirely different shape.

Memories. Fear. Pain. Then at last, the tiny furious wail.

The midwife who wouldn't meet her gaze. *Born dead. Poor little mite. It happens.*

She'd lived on, although she'd thought perhaps she might die. Yet in truth, it was but a half-life, for the heartbreak of Jack Redgrave's betrayal and her family's cruelty was nothing compared to the loss of her child.

Now, the man in the doorway, the man who couldn't be there, had just walked past her as if she didn't exist. He knelt before the child at the open door. "It looks like rain," he said quietly. "Are you buttoned up?" He stood and extended his hand down. "Come along, Melody."

Blue eyes.

Melody.

Just like hers.

Melody.

Born dead.

"I heard her cry." The words slipped from Laurel's numb lips like a whisper, like a battle roar, like the last words of a defiant prisoner.

She'd heard that cry. She'd believed that cry. So she'd named her child, despite all the argument and disbelief.

Melody.

Two

Once she could move, Laurel followed his lordship and the little girl out of the house at a run, but the carriage with the Strickland crest was halfway down the drive before her own feet touched the gravel. Laurel stood in the middle of the drive, one hand pressed to the stitch in her side, her heart pounding with more than exertion, and watched Melody leave. Matched black horses kept up a smart trot, taking Laurel's baby away from her with every revolution of the carriage wheels.

She lives! Joy shimmered like rising bubbles in champagne.

He took her! Fury flared hot and crackling like wildfire.

Jack had compromised and abandoned Laurel, had stolen her child, had let her mourn all these years for them both!

Oh, the loss! The oceans of tears, months and years of aching emptiness, the painful, creeping realization that she was all alone, that she would never love anyone, never have anyone, that the rest of her life was to mean nothing but more of the same . . .

The bloody thrice-damned bastard kept Melody all along!

Melody lives!

Rage burned.

Elation glowed.

The bewildering combination of emotions left Laurel nauseated and shaking. Damn that enervating shock! If only she'd moved faster, she could have snatched her daughter away from that betraying rotter forever!

Her daughter . . .

Jack had not asked to see Laurel. He had been leaving the parlor where Amaryllis usually held court to guests. Why?

In the past few years that she'd lived as a dependent in her sister's household, continually reminded of her indebtedness to such a kind and tolerant relative, it had never occurred to Laurel that her sister might know the secret that their parents had tried so hard to keep.

Laurel turned and hurried back into the house, her heart pounding in her chest.

In the parlor, Amaryllis pretended unconcern. "Heavens, why the urgency? It was only Jack, after all." Yet Laurel could see that her sister was hiding something.

"Amy, for someone who lies on a regular basis, you are rather terrible at it." Impatiently Laurel moved to block her sister's view of herself in the mirror over the hearth. "Tell me, what was Lord John Redgrave's business in this house? Why did he bring you the child?"

Amaryllis sulked at Laurel's tone and toyed with the fringe on a silken pillow. "He had some silly idea, that's all. Nothing to concern you."

Laurel gazed at her sister, a chill disbelief growing in her soul. She had always believed Amy innocent of evildoing, for she had been away on her honeymoon when matters had turned dire. Laurel had been certain that their parents were as concerned with keeping their actions from their elder daughter's knowledge as they were committed to hiding them from the world at large. This belief, this faith in Amy's innocence, had been what had allowed Laurel to live in this house and act as her sister's companion and virtual slave.

Of all the world, only Amy had not betrayed her.

Now doubt trickled past that wall of trust, a trickle that fast became a flood when Amaryllis shot one shamed, guilt-ridden glance up to meet Laurel's gaze.

"You knew." It was not a question.

Amaryllis's fingers began to pull the threads from the fringe, one by one. "Not . . . not in the beginning. There were rumors among the servants. At least that was what my maid told me. Until Papa died two months ago, I knew nothing for certain. Then someone came to me, trying to blackmail us over your . . . indiscretion. Gerald sent her packing, of course. I suspect he made a mistake there, for she knew rather a great deal. She knew you had a little girl."

Ice would be warmer than Laurel's heart. "You knew my child lived."

Amaryllis shook her head quickly. "No, I didn't! Not until half an hour past, when Jack brought her in to show her to me."

Laurel advanced a single step. Amaryllis must have seen something new in Laurel's face, for her arrogant and often domineering sister cringed away from her. "Laurel, I swear to it! I knew nothing about a living child! The servants' rumors told of a stillbirth!"

Watching closely, Laurel noticed that Amaryllis's left eyelid had a tendency to drop. "Amy, I know that you are lying."

Amaryllis looked away, but then her shoulders stiffened. "I don't know what you're so angry about. Mama and Papa were simply trying to save you from yourself! And save us all from a terrible scandal! I'd think you'd be relieved it all went away so quietly."

"Relieved." Laurel's gut churned as she gazed at the stranger wearing her sister's face. "You thought I'd be relieved to think my child was dead."

Amaryllis tossed her head defiantly. "Well, yes, of course! No one knew a thing outside the family. It all worked out rather nicely, until Jack walked back through that door and asked me—"

"Nicely." Laurel held up a hand, halting her sister's lying, betraying words. "I'm leaving," she said flatly. "My portion awaits me untouched in the Bank of England. It isn't much, but it will get me and my child far from you evil, wicked people. You and bloody Lord Jack Redgrave!"

With that she turned and strode from the room, her black skirts fluttering with new purpose and new power. Amaryllis's voice rose behind her, but Laurel cared not a whit for the words that followed her down the hall.

"You ungrateful wretch! You can't leave! You daren't! Who will manage the house? Laurel, who will plan my dinners and balls? Laurel!"

Her heart hammering with a new rhythm, Laurel heard nothing but her daughter's name echoing again and again in her mind.

Melody.

When Jack arrived back at Brown's Club for Distinguished Gentlemen with Melody, the front door of the club opened before the marquis's carriage attained a full stop before it. As Jack stepped down and swung Melody to stand on her little booted feet next to him, the club's head of staff was already waiting for them at the top of the stairs. Wilberforce was as inscrutable as always, but Jack spied several expectant faces hovering just through the entrance.

Everyone would want to know what he had learned. Jack felt a dull dread at the thought of what was to come. Melody had found a family at Brown's. Within those walls she was surrounded by loving uncles and aunts and a full dozen doting grampapas. Even the servants were her willing devotees. Jack would have to be the one to tell them all that Melody was not theirs to keep.

He spied a boy's face, the thin twelve-year-old features twisted with concern. Poor Evan. He was half protector, half prey to Melody, spending his days fleeing persistent games of house and tea party and yet never far from his tiny Mellie's side, always ready to make her flash her dimpled smile. Unlike the others, Evan had not wanted Jack to make the journey to visit Amaryllis. The boy had seen enough tumult in his short life to know that sometimes change was not a good thing.

Evan had been quite right about that. Jack took Melody's little hand in his and helped her make the big steps up the marble stairs. At the top he held on for a moment, loathe to let her small fingers slip from his grasp. Then she ran forward to deliver a nonstop account of their trip to Wilberforce, who bent attentively, focused on every chattered word.

Jack walked past Wilberforce, into the front hall of the club. The occupants tried not to crowd around him, but he could see that they were eager to hear what had transpired. His friend Aidan stood a little apart, his usual cool expression on his face, but Jack knew him well enough to know that his sensitive soul was perhaps in the most danger, for Aidan had been the first to assume parentage for Melody and the first to fall headlong in love with her.

Aidan's bride, Madeleine, stood at his side, supporting and being supported, as always silently in tune with her husband, as he was with her. Jack observed it without truly understanding it. He could not imagine a woman who would look into his own soul and like what she saw, much less love it.

He saw Colin, his oldest friend and boyhood companion, leaning against the ornately wood-paneled wall near the grand staircase in apparent unconcern. Such indifference was a mere mask, for Jack knew that Colin profoundly adored Melody and would have gladly claimed paternity. Jack also saw that Colin's hand was entwined with that of his wife, Pru. She made no pretense at cool nonchalance. Pru bit her lip with deep concentration and Jack could see that her knuckles were white next to Colin's larger ones.

Young Evan's scowl was deepening by the moment as Jack's silence stretched on. Even the giant underfootman, Bailiwick, picked up on the growing tension in the hall. Beyond him, Jack could see the other, older members of the club, gray haired and wrinkly and bent, more patient perhaps, yet just as eager to have their suspense ended.

Then Melody danced through the door, hand in hand with Wilberforce, and the thrumming tension was concealed by smiles and cries of welcome. Though they'd been gone scarcely a day, Jack watched as the tiny girl gave every single person a heartfelt greeting, as sincere as if she'd been absent for weeks.

Evan, who always knew when he was being shamelessly used as a babysitter, didn't even wait to be asked this time. Glancing warily around at the adults, he took Melody's hand.

"C'mon, Mellie. Cook made lemon seedcakes for tea today. I know he saved you one."

Melody, having dispensed easy-hearted love upon all present like a spring rain, was tempted away by the cook's pastry prowess and swung down the long hallway on the end of Evan's arm. Even as Melody's constant chatter faded, all eyes were turning back, pinning Jack like an insect in a display.

Through the heavy numbness that consumed him once again, Jack could only shake his head sharply. He saw Madeleine press her fingers to her mouth. Aidan made no sign of response, but Jack saw the devastation behind his eyes. Colin put his arm about Pru, who was openly distressed.

Bailiwick, great lout that he was, was the only one brave enough to question Jack directly. "But ye said she were yours, milord! Ye said so! Ye said she looked just like 'er mother!"

Jack raised his gaze to meet the younger man's. "The lady denied it. That is that."

Madeleine stepped forward. "But she could be afraid! Does she know that all we want is for Melody to be happy? Does she think we condemn her?"

Jack turned his gaze on the slender, dark-haired beauty. The loss in her brown eyes was nearly enough to pierce the deadening fog in which he stood, but he had no more words. Words came harder by the moment, in fact. When Colin moved forward, still holding flame-haired Pru to his side, Jack could only gaze at him dully. Colin's words sounded as if they came from a very great distance, called out across a desert whose wind stole half the sounds.

One by one, they all began to accept the truth. Jack could see their eyes go from bright disbelief to leaden grief. They knew what it meant that he was not Melody's father. They all knew that if no one in Brown's held blood claim to their darling girl, then the only honorable thing to do was find Melody's true family and return her to them.

They didn't want her! Jack wanted to shout. *They left her and never returned!*

Deep inside him, a caged beast of grief pounded at bars of iron suffering. Even if he'd wanted to release it to howl at the fates, Jack had no idea how. Everything he felt, everything he wanted to say, remained trapped within him, just like before. The crack that Melody had effortlessly opened in his shell was swiftly closing, scarring over like a wound left unstitched.

The others followed Aidan and Madeleine sadly down the hall. Even Wilberforce moved as if his feet were weighted with lead, though the butler's spine remained as ramrod straight as ever.

Jack remained by the door. Every moment in a crowd was like sand scraping into raw skin. The combined focus of everyone's eyes on him had stolen the breath from his lungs.

Now the hall was empty. Just like him.

He'd prized having a child. Even just for a few days. Now the years stretched out before him once more, endless and gray with gritty restlessness. He could go back aboard his flagship and sail away, though he couldn't imagine it would be any better than it had been before.

He could stay here and face Society again. *I'd prefer to go back to sea. At least there the sharks smile like they mean it.*

As he turned rather helplessly in a circle in the hall, he noticed a heavy envelope awaiting on a silver tray resting on a table near the door. He could see the waxen crest of Strickland on the paper from where he stood. After a long moment, it penetrated his consciousness. The letter contained bad news.

The wax in which the seal was pressed was black. The Marquis of Strickland was dead.

Long live the new marquis. Alone.

Three

The envelope weighed in Jack's hand, the expensive paper thick and heavy, like the news borne within.

Slowly he broke the seal and read the letter. It was from his uncle's steward, a good man but one of few words.

My lord,

His Lordship the sixth Marquis of Strickland expired at quarter past eight this evening, June 20 of the Year of Our Lord 1816. Greetings and deepest sympathy to you, Lord John Redgrave the seventh Marquis of Strickland.

The paper crackled loudly in the silent hall as Jack's fist closed around it. Another man might have thought of his new title, or of his new wealth. All Jack could form was one single thought.

I have no one.

His parents were long gone. His cousin was gone. His uncle was gone, the man who had stood in the stead of Jack's father for all those years of his boyhood when he'd been most needed.

This blow, coming so soon after the loss of Jack's

all-too-short-lived fatherhood, nearly knocked him to his knees.

I have no one.

The world, like the marbled hallway, echoed with emptiness.

And then came a knock.

The force of her knock left Laurel's fingers tingling. All the long ride into town, her body had vibrated with tension. Now the accumulated effects had her wound as tightly as a spring. If someone did not answer this door soon, she rather thought she might have to knock it right down.

With the fury simmering inside her, it was not even an outlandish notion. She felt as if she could very well rip aside any barrier that kept her for even one more moment from her child.

When the door opened to reveal Jack Redgrave himself standing there, greeting her like a blasted butler, Laurel felt as though she'd taken a step on a stair that wasn't there.

Heavens, he's so thin! He's still Jack, though. Still so beautiful, damn his soul.

Seeing him face-to-face brought back so much that she'd determined to forget, all the hours that she'd watched him, worshiped him, waited for him with so much more eagerness than Amaryllis ever had, then the sweet, hot hours of that night.

Followed, of course, by the icy betrayal and finally by the horrific pain and loss. All of those feelings were tangled up in the sight of his face, wound into a wiry, spiky ball of fury.

Her momentum did not falter for long. After a startled glance up into Jack's face, she pushed past him into the hallowed halls of Brown's itself, the sacred place of men and whiskey and smelly tobacco.

The woman on the doorstep wore black from the pointed tips of her boots to the crest of the net veil over her bonnet. The sight of such an apparition on the heels of the black seal on the letter rocked Jack back on his heels a bit. If he were a superstitious man, he might start losing sleep about his own near fate.

Before he could blink back his surprise and greet this visiting Lady of Doom, she pushed past him and strode into the entrance hall of Brown's. Well, that determined it. He would never make a satisfactory doorman for a gentlemen's club. He was much too inclined to get out of a lady's way.

Still, he ought to help Wilberforce and at least learn the harridan's purpose. Closing the door on the noise from St. James Street, Jack turned to greet the woman.

"Madam?" He even bowed a little, although not much. He was a marquis now, come to think of it. The bowing would soon be going the other way about.

His air of bemusement seemed to offend her. Her spine straightened with a snap and she lifted her chin. "Where is she?"

Jack frowned. He truly had not grasped the difficulties poor Wilberforce endured. Madwomen in mourning probably showed up on a daily basis, and here Jack had thought Wilberforce had nothing to do but stand by the door and look stern.

Jack tried stern. He frowned down at the woman from his great height. "Where is who?"

If Jack was not mistaken, sternness offended her even more than bemusement had. The woman ripped her black lace gloves from her hands as if preparing for battle, then unpinned her black straw bonnet and whipped it from her head to flutter to the floor behind her. Dark hair gleamed, pulled tightly back from her brow, and blue eyes burned ice cold in her small, pale face. This stranger, who looked remarkably like Amaryllis except for the unholy fury in her eyes, advanced upon him. *"Where is she?"*

Jack drew back in surprise, then peered closer. So familiar . . .

"Bramble?"

He used to tease her with that name, saying she was too thorny to be a mere laurel bush. Impossible. Laurel was a mere girl when he saw her last—and even then he scarcely noticed her beside the more flamboyant Amaryllis.

Flinching at the old nickname, Miss Laurel Clarke— for it was indeed Laurel, all grown-up—turned a particularly enraged shade of marble white. Lips stretched tightly over her teeth, she grated out a noise of pure fury. "Where is she, Jack? Where is Melody?"

Jack stepped back once. "Melody is upstairs in her room. Why—?"

Instantly Laurel turned and lifted her skirts high, going for the stairs at a run. Shocked, Jack quickly followed.

"Laurel, what is this?" She ignored him, taking the stairs fast, her dainty booted feet flying.

"Laurel, is this Amaryllis's doing?"

Laurel cast him a single disbelieving glare over her shoulder and kept on, taking the next story at speed. "What floor?" she snapped out.

Jack frowned. "The top story. Lady Madeleine built her a nursery—" He was losing ground. He picked up the pace, catching up to Laurel as she took the last steps up the staircase and rounded the banister into the hallway Aidan shared with Colin and the elderly but still spry Lord Aldrich.

She paused there with one hand on the polished railing, out of breath and panting. When Jack stepped closer to her, she whirled on him. "Get out of my way! I'm taking her out of this place right this minute!"

"What?" Alarm raced through Jack. "What do you mean? Has Amaryllis finally decided to confess? Did she send you to take Melody back to the Compton estate?"

Laurel made that noise again. Then she placed both palms on his chest and physically shoved him backward. "Get. Out. Of. My. Way!"

Jack didn't budge, which seemed to add to her rage. She stopped pushing and brushed a dark curl out of her eyes with the back of one hand, all the better to glare up at him with so much hatred that then he did step back a little.

"Where are your rooms?" she demanded.

"One down, directly below here." She was so different from the girl he'd known. "What possesses you, Laurel?"

She snarled, then turned toward the first door on her left. Thrusting it open, she ran inside. "Melody!"

Jack waited for Laurel to come back out of the unoccupied room. When she emerged, however, she simply pushed past him and made for the next door, which happened to be that to Colin's new quarters with his wife, Pru, and her young brother, Evan. Jack blocked Laurel's grasp for the latch with his hand. She backed out of his reach, shooting him a glare of hatred.

"What do you want, Laurel? What business have you with Melody?"

"Business," she snarled. "*You* have no business with Melody. I am taking her out of this madhouse and you will never be able to manipulate her or me ever again!"

"Manipulate?"

"Melody! *Melodyyy!*"

A piping little voice called from Aidan's quarters, "Papa?"

"Stay put, Melody," Jack called back. He didn't know what Laurel was talking about and he certainly didn't know why she was looking daggers at him, but he did know that her wild demeanor and shouting would frighten Melody, who had already borne enough today. Holding both hands out soothingly, he advanced on Laurel.

"Calm yourself. Simply listen. . . ." Using his size to herd her away from Melody, he maneuvered Laurel back down the hall. Not down the stairs. No, better keep this to himself for the moment. There was no need to get everyone's hopes up again until he understood why Amaryllis had changed her mind and sent her sister to claim Melody after all.

Over Laurel's shoulder, he spied the door to the attic. It would provide a quiet place to talk and one where her excited state would not alarm anyone. Keeping his voice at a soothing murmur, he had Laurel by the elbow and through the door in a moment. Up a narrow flight of dusty stairs, and then they were in the main room of the attic, a vast cavern of roof beams above and discarded furniture all around them.

Her skin was flushed and he could feel the heat of her body through the thin black stuff of her sleeve. The sensation of touching her both alarmed and confused him. Surely that was only because he'd kept to himself for so long.

Once at the top, Laurel shook off his grip and backed away from him, glaring at him in the light entering through a large, dirty window to the rear of the attic.

Laurel clapped a hand to her elbow and rubbed it, but not because he had hurt her. His firm grip had been implacable but not harmful. She massaged her arm to erase the sensation of his large, warm hand upon her flesh. Even the brief seconds of contact had reminded her. One tingling touch and she lived it all again. Flashes through her mind, moments from those hot, sweating hours of large, talented hands roaming every inch of her, driving her higher, making her shudder again and again, lost in pleasure like nothing she'd known before or since.

So he has big hands. What of it?

All the more reason to hate him, for he could do more damage with a single touch than any other man could do with hours to study the problem.

Now Jack had her here, alone in this attic, and was gazing at her with those dark eyes, like the wells of his soul, dark and impenetrable.

Unless one knew how to look into them.

Still, they lied. They must, for he could never be the man she'd once thought him and have the capacity to ruin her life the way he had.

Enough of this. She took a step back toward the stairs. He held out one hand to stop her. She backed away from his touch once more, unwilling to test her own fortitude.

"I'm taking her and we're leaving this place and you shall never see us again, you foul *blackguard*!"

Jack's brow creased. "I gathered that. Why?"

Betrayed fury welled up in Laurel. "Why?" She flung herself at him, fists raised, instantly forgetting her vow to stay away from him. With an animal cry containing echoes of every single moment of pain he'd caused her, she beat at his broad chest. "Bastard! You rotten, black-hearted, soulless—"

He pulled her into his arms and held her tightly to him. "Laurel—"

She couldn't strike while trapped inside his embrace, which was of course his intention. She could only struggle wildly while feral noises ripped from her throat. Jack, Mama, Papa, Amy—all the people Laurel had loved most in the world, all had cut away a piece of her heart until all she had was pain and black, swallowing loneliness!

Well, no more!

So she struggled and thrashed and it was quite possible she did a certain amount of biting as well, but she could not break his unyielding embrace. His arms remained tight about her as she enacted years of soul-shattering loss with her flailing fists and her kicking feet and curses spilling from her lips that she hadn't even realized she'd known.

At last, as her fury dulled into exhaustion, her mind quieted enough to realize that through all her violence not once had he retaliated. Not even with a harsh word. He'd simply stood there, like a granite figure, and held her while she rioted.

With her breath still catching in odd little sobs, she spread her palms across his chest and pushed firmly. "Let me go," she whispered.

He didn't respond. She took a deep breath and spoke more firmly. "Release me."

When his grasp did not ease in the slightest, she risked a glance up. His face was turned to one side and his eyes were closed. If his body was granite, that face was glacial ice. His jaw was clenched so hard that the tendons on his neck were distended. Something was wrong. . . .

Then she felt it, hardening against her belly. She recognized that hardness. For one endless night, she'd had it for her very own. Memories of his largeness, his heat, his silk-sheathed steel in her hands, in her body, in her mouth . . .

She dampened instantly, her body betraying her yet again. For all her hatred, all her pain, she had never entirely convinced herself that that night had been anything but ecstasy. If anything, that was one of the betrayals—to give her the knowledge that such sweet pleasure could exist and then take it away forever.

For a long breathless moment, an instant that felt like an hour, they remained pressed together, no longer in struggle, no longer in combat. Her fury spent, her will weakened by exhaustion and memories, Laurel even let her forehead drop to rest upon his hard chest. All by themselves, her fingers spread against that chest, feeling the warmth of him through his weskit and shirt, tracking the thudding of his heart through touch.

Her own heart skittered wildly and the dampness between her legs gave way to a dull throbbing, as if she was
empty and ached to be filled. The silence stretched about
them, winding around and around like a spider's silk,
keeping them pressed together, breathless, waiting. . . .

Jack's mind rioted, though he kept his body still
from sheer will. This was Laurel he held pressed to his
body, held tight to his growing erection. When last he'd
seen her, she'd been a girl, a near stranger, a someday
sister—

How was it then that his body knew her? How was it
that he stood here, holding her, *wanting* her with an
intensity that kept his jaw clenched and his gut trembling and his cock turning to iron?

Odd shreds of memory tangled in his mind. Laurel,
in braids, laughing as he teased her. Amaryllis sneering as her sister, red faced and mortified, daubed at a
tea stain on her bodice. Amaryllis, sweet mouthed and
giving, rolling naked beneath him.

Laurel, gazing at him with blue eyes filled with longing he'd been too young and stupid to see at the time.

Amaryllis, crying as he was thrown from the house,
even though she'd been the one to spur the ejection.

Something isn't right. Think.

He couldn't think. His mind was helpless in the
maelstrom of his sudden, inexplicable lust, a black,
gaping void of *need*—

Need for his former lover's sister?

Appalling. Dishonorable. Utterly impossible, except
for the undeniable fact of his painfully erect cock and
the responsive softening and melting of her body against
him. His hold tightened. Her face lifted as he opened
his eyes to gaze down at her tearstained face. Blue eyes

locked on brown. Her lips parted and her breath warmed his mouth—

"Papa?" Melody's high little voice piped up the stairs. "Are you there?"

The latch of the door below rattled. Jack watched Laurel's face as the sweet vacancy of lust left her eyes and reason—or what passed for it today—returned. She pushed hard at his chest. "Melody!" she called. "Mel—"

The door below began to open. Battle instincts took over. Shielding Melody was second nature. With a single decisive movement, Jack thrust Laurel into a side chamber of the attic. She stumbled to a stop, then turned to stare at him.

"No!" Her eyes widened and she rushed forward, trying to stop him. "Jack, no! She's my—"

He slammed the door shut on her words and twisted the key that stood in the lock. One hand slid the key into his pocket as he turned to greet the cherubic little face peering through the crack of light at the bottom of the stairs. A dull pounding started on the heavy oak door behind him, so he masked it by trotting briskly down the stairs to where Melody waited. No danger of her pursuing her curiosity any further.

Melody wouldn't enter the attic. Ever.

Four

"He did *what*?" In the quiet dressing chamber, Melody's voice was nearly a shriek. "I cannot believe it!" She lifted her head from Button's shoulder to stare at him in horror.

Button nodded. "It's quite true. He told me himself."

Melody looked ill. "But that's ghastly! How could he do such a thing?"

Button patted her hand. "He didn't do it to be horrible. It was a . . . mistake. A mistake that rather got out of hand in the days afterward."

"Days? Afterward?" Melody gaped. "You mean he kept her in there? For how long?"

Button pursed his lips. "I could tell you, but then I'd be forced to skip all the good parts. Besides, you should have a little more faith in your father."

"No! It's too horrible!" Melody folded her arms. "I shall never speak to him again."

Button smiled. "Be sure to tell him that when he walks you down the aisle in an hour." He tweaked her nose. "Now, my fine, fierce Melody, do you want to hear this story or not?"

"Not!" Melody flounced, but it was a rather poor effort, since she was already sitting down. She let out a long breath. "Oh, well. I suppose."

With his arm about her shoulders, Button coaxed her into a more comfortable position, leaning into him once again. He dropped a quick kiss on her head, taking care not to muss her bridal hairdressing. "Now where was I?"

"My father tossed my mother into the dungeon and walked away."

"Your father was trying to convince your rightfully upset mother that she should listen to him."

"I wouldn't listen to someone who locked me up!"

Button chuckled. "Well, there is a definite resemblance of temperament, now that I think about it, for pretty Laurel had much the same reaction. . . ."

Laurel pounded on the thick oak door until her fists began to numb. Jack didn't return. Finally, she turned to lean her back against the barrier and slid down it to sit with her arms about her knees.

Trapped. Locked away. Imprisoned.

Again.

She tried to keep her anger paramount, so that she wouldn't have to feel the chill growing in her belly. Four walls. A window. A door she could not open. It was all terribly, nauseatingly familiar.

A good girl from a good family shouldn't know about imprisonment. A girl like she had once been couldn't conceive of a time when her very existence depended upon a tray of food passed through thrice a day.

Good girls from good families shouldn't suddenly become with child, either.

Please, Mama, don't lock me in! Papa, please, please let me out! I'm sorry. I'm so sorry!

It hadn't been the pregnancy that had enraged them as much as it had been her refusal to identify her lover. She'd kept the secret, waiting for Jack, believing that he would come back for her.

Yet months had passed. Months when the idea of climbing down three stories clinging to nothing but an ivy vine consumed weeks of thought. She'd never been brave enough to try it then, not with her body growing larger by the day, but now she dried her eyes and gazed thoughtfully at the large window at the other end of the room.

She wasn't helpless and pregnant now.

Unfortunately, the window opened up onto nothing but the street far below. Mentally, she recounted the flights she'd climbed in her rush to find Melody. The main floor. One. Three turns around the landing. Four. The attic stairs. Five. She swallowed hard, gazing at the very narrow ledge running beneath the window. It was only a little wider than her palm and slick with soot and bird droppings.

Perhaps . . . not.

She shook her head and extended her gaze out over the street. There were carts and a few carriages driving by, but the drivers were intent on their horses. The sound of clopping hooves covered her calls.

She waited for the carts to pass, then turned her efforts on a young man carrying a sack on one shoulder as he unloaded a stopped cart at a storefront. Her loudest cry finally caused him to glance up. He tipped his cap back on his head, flashed her a smile, and answered her frantic wave with a blown kiss.

Cheeky devil. He thought she was flirting with him!

It was no good. The street was too noisy and too far away. People tended to mind what was in front of them, not above them.

Casting a last reluctant glance at the crusty ledge, Laurel withdrew back inside the room, latching the window shut against the late-afternoon chill.

She couldn't climb down five stories, but then again, she wouldn't have to. Jack would come back, and when he did she was going to kill him! At least twice! Then she was going to lightly step past his battered body and stroll directly out the front door!

Pressing her fingertips hard against her eyes, she refused to let tears of frustration and remembered terror come. That didn't stop the memories, however.

Jack. Handsome and dashing, full of laughter. He'd fallen under Amaryllis's spell at once, just like every other young man who met Amy, but unlike the others, he hadn't ignored Laurel's existence. Or worse, mocked her for her shyness and her fondness of reading.

Plain Jane, the suitors had called her. Wallflower. Once they'd realized that it amused Amaryllis to mock Laurel, they'd let loose the full force of their imaginations to come up with witty little jests at Laurel's expense.

Fortunately, those imaginations were almost universally limited. Only Jack had come up with a name both teasing and admiring.

She'd just stalked out of the parlor yet again, having had enough of Amaryllis's admirers for the day. Her mother had ordered Laurel to attend to Amy, for Mama hadn't felt well enough to sit in company. Though Laurel was but sixteen to Amaryllis's eighteen, any female presence would do in a pinch, to keep the forms of propriety.

"Propriety can go hang!" Laurel muttered under her breath as she marched from the room. "Dandies! Ought to call them candies, for they've all got sugar floss for brains!"

A bark of surprised laughter behind her had made her whirl, one hand over her mouth in horror. Oh, heavens, if Mama learned of this!

Then Laurel saw him, leaning one shoulder on the paneling of the wall outside the parlor. On his narrow, handsome face was a flash of teasing smile and gleaming admiration in his dark eyes.

So brown they're nearly black.

And . . .

He's looking at me. At me!

And although she stuffed it deep as soon as it seared across her mind . . .

He's beautiful. I want him.

"So sharp!" He'd lazily lifted off from the wall and sauntered closer, one corner of his lips still twisted upward in amusement. "Don't you know laurels aren't supposed to have thorns?"

She never directly addressed Amaryllis's guests if she could help it. Her shyness made it impossible to say anything sensible, so she preferred to hide her timidity in a stony silence. She liked to think it was interpreted as cool superiority—although she suspected that she never quite carried it off.

Now, however, she tossed her head and looked the bold fellow in the eye. "Are you lost? I know it's a confusing route to the front door." It was all of twenty steps. "Perhaps I may show you out?"

That smile flashed again and her belly warmed. Or perhaps slightly lower. She found her gaze lingering on his bottom lip and forced her eyes back up to meet his knowing ones.

"Thorny little Bramble, as sharp as tacks. Who would have thought it?"

She'd lifted her chin. "My name is Miss Laurel Clarke. And we have not been introduced. You overstep, sir."

He'd leaned closer and reached to tug on one of the long dark braids she wore to show her scorn for Amy's elaborate hairstyles. His warm fingertips brushed the side of her neck. Did he see her shiver?

"I won't tell if you won't," he whispered huskily, then laughed when she blushed furiously. "Come on, Bramble, show me the library, will you? If I have to outwait the brainless brigade in there, I'm going to need something to read."

"You read?" This time she hadn't meant to sound snappish. She'd simply been surprised.

"Oh yes. For months now." He tickled her ear with the end of her braid. "And you can call me Jack. See, introductions tidily managed. No duennas needed."

She reached her hand up to pull her braid from his grip. Their fingers brushed and she felt her cheeks pinken again as a rush of heat swept up her body. Jack.

This fellow was trouble on the hoof, she'd thought deliciously.

Too bad she hadn't realized how true that was.

Jack pulled the door to the attic stairway shut and turned. Melody stood in the middle of the hallway, gazing at him with little frown lines between her wispy brows.

"Papa, why are you playing in the attic?"

"I'm not! I mean, the attic is no place to play. You know that, don't you, Melody?"

She eyed the attic door warily. "The bad man took me to the attic. He took me to the roof!"

Where the villain, Lady Madeleine's deranged and brutal late husband, had dangled Melody's tiny body over the edge, threatening to fling her to shatter on the street below. Jack's fists clenched. If the bastard hadn't died on the cobbles himself that day, Jack would surely make it happen now. He hadn't been here to protect Melody then and he should have been. If he'd not been so lost in his own misery, he would have known of her existence much sooner.

I'm taking her out of this place right this minute.

Laurel. Jack rubbed one hand over the back of his neck. He didn't understand Laurel's reasons, but he didn't doubt her rage—er, her sincerity.

And she was truly enraged.

Which meant that he'd just locked a deeply furious woman in the attic. That suddenly seemed like a very bad idea.

Too late.

Wincing at the thought, Jack took Melody's hand and walked her down to his rooms. He was going to have to deal with Laurel sooner or later. He wasn't a man to put things off, but he needed to make sure that Melody was kept far away from anything so disturbing.

The first step—put Melody to bed. From the moment Jack had arrived back at Brown's, Melody had insisted that he and he alone should have this duty. Colin had taken this rather well, considering he'd been the irreplaceable one until then.

However, although Colin might not be present,

Colin's stories were still entirely necessary. Jack didn't know much about Colin's pirates, but he'd had plenty of adventures at sea. Each night the tales grew a little longer and more detailed. Melody's ability to listen, wide-eyed and breathless, did wonders for his strange inability to speak.

Everyone at Brown's blinked in mystification but allowed Jack to take over this bedtime ritual.

This sounded easy enough, but he'd learned in the last week that though generally cheerful and full of fun, Melody was not what one would call easy. Always busy, always in motion, usually in danger, but never easy.

Well, perhaps when she was asleep.

An hour later, Jack gazed down at the sleeping child. She wasn't his. The thought didn't want to stick to his mind. It kept sliding away, as if unable to take purchase in his brain.

She isn't mine.

Yet, apparently, she had something to do with Laurel.

It certainly explained Melody's resemblance to Amaryllis, although now that he'd seen Laurel again, he wondered why he hadn't thought of her in the first place. Melody was so obviously like her—clever and curious and prone to displays of affection.

None of which applied to Amaryllis.

Lifting Melody's limp, warm body and draping her against his shoulder, he stood to carry her to her own room. Madeleine and Aidan had set up a nursery for her in their chambers. After Jack had tucked Melody into her small bed, he straightened to assess the latest additions.

There was a little chess set on a side table. That was new. Jack lifted a piece to examine it. The knight had been carved as a pudgy pony with large expressive eyes. Each piece was a charming toy, and the kings and queens were absolute treasures of detail.

Another gift from Lord Bartles and Sir James, Jack had no doubt. Those old codgers were shameless in their efforts to win "favorite grampapa" in Melody's estimation. Soon there wouldn't be any room in the nursery for all the bribes—er, *presents.*

Full night had come while Jack put Melody to bed. Now the clock chimed half past ten. He blinked. His stories were most definitely becoming longer. Odd. He had probably spoken to Melody tonight more than he'd spoken in the last year.

Why was it she was the only person he could order his thoughts into speech for? He certainly hadn't been able to muster any such basic skill with Laurel.

Laurel.

Oh, hellfire, what had he done?

You're still at war. Still making peacetime decisions with wartime extremity.

Still mucking up in a grand fashion, that was for sure.

Yet compared to his previous crimes, kidnapping was next to nothing. He was not the man his friends thought him to be.

He was barely a man at all.

Sinking into the overstuffed chair that Madeleine had added to the room, he didn't even pause to think what he might look like lounging on the puffy pink seat cushion.

Rubbing one hand over his eyes, he tried mightily to remember the last time he'd seen Laurel. She hadn't been at that final, humiliating house party.

Or had she?

Think.

He had been so lost in darkness, so under the rubble . . .

His friends commanded him to attend the house party, to see his girl, so he'd gone. He'd had the most amazing night of his life, which left him feeling almost human again. Then his heart had been ripped out once again.

Then came the two foggy months, lost in the bottle, flailing in the darkness. Colin and Aidan had convinced him that suicide was selfish. Too many people needed him to be a good master for his ailing uncle. Jack had responsibilities. This realization stabilized the darkness, but he remained lost in the gray. Until Melody.

And now Laurel had come to take her away.

Outside the door, Colin and Aidan lingered in the upstairs hallway.

"He's putting her to bed right now," Colin told Aidan quietly. "Poor bastard. I've never seen anyone look so shattered as he did when he came through the door of the club."

Aidan eyed Colin for a moment. "I have."

Colin looked away. "I'll be all right. It's Pru and Maddie I worry about. And Jack."

Aidan nodded slowly. "I hate to see Maddie so sad, but she's been through many difficult times, as has Pru. Jack . . ."

Colin rubbed a hand over the back of his neck. "Jack walks a bit close to the edge as it is."

"He was getting better the last few days." Aidan let out a slow breath. "I thought having Melody was almost like . . . redemption for him."

Colin gazed into space. "A life for a life, you mean."

Aidan looked down at his hands. "We don't know that."

"No." Colin didn't meet his friend's gaze. "We don't know anything of the kind. Not for certain."

Across the hall, in the rooms occupied by Colin and Pru, the door was slightly ajar. On the other side, Pru pressed a hand over her mouth, her eyes wide.

A life for a life?

Five

Upstairs in the attic, outside the locked chamber, Jack hesitated. Should he knock? Feeling foolish, Jack tapped on the door. Pressing his ear to the door, he could barely hear her reply with a derisive snort.

"Oh, please do come in." Not even the thick oak could dampen the irony in her tone.

The heavy key was warm from his pocket. His face was warm from a combination of embarrassment and shame, mingled with a dash of irritation. That made three more emotions in one moment than he was accustomed to feeling at all.

He turned the key and pressed the latch, pushing the heavy door open slowly. He was barely able to duck the flying splinters of porcelain as a piece of crockery exploded against the door frame next to his head.

"Oh, pooh. I missed." She sounded deadly calm. Seething.

Jack hesitated behind the safety of the door, then shook off his own cowardice. He'd done this. He had to face the consequences.

The consequences began to fly rather quickly right about then. He held his arm up to protect his eyes as more pottery shards took flight. "Damn it, Laurel!"

"You wanted to come in. Come in, then."

"Stop."

"Oh, I wouldn't dream of actually hurting you, Jack."

He stepped into the room, only to duck wildly as a cracked plate spun through the air toward his head. "Oy! I thought you didn't want to hurt me!"

Laurel paused, one hand poised to lob a handleless teapot his way. "I don't want to hurt you. I want, as a matter of fact, to *kill* you." The teapot arced through the air, narrowly missing his shoulder as he twisted out of the way.

She glared at him. "Stop moving."

He held up both hands placatingly. "Laurel, I know I was wrong to put you in here—"

In a blur of motion, she reached down to a pile of discarded crockery at her feet and flung a soup tureen at him, grunting with the effort. This time Jack kept his stance, knocking the bloody thing away with his forearm.

That hurt.

He must not have shown it, however, for her eyes widened in surprise and she hesitated in her next barrage. That was her first mistake. Like a soldier springing an ambush, Jack was across the room in an instant, pulling her away from her arsenal, pinning her flailing arms to her sides.

"Let me go!" She kicked wildly, but her skirts protected him.

He held her close, her back pressed to his chest, his arms wrapped about hers, keeping her immobilized.

She smelled exceptionally good.

Irrelevant. Except that it reminded him of something. . . .

Laurel struggled against tears as she fought his grasp on her. Weeping did no good. She ought to know, having shed enough tears in the past four years to thoroughly test the premise. Staying angry—that most definitely showed promise. She'd never felt such a towering rage in her life, or at least she had not allowed herself to acknowledge it before.

But this man, this most unbelievable blackguard, had stolen so much—

Her body began to tingle in response to his size and strength.

No. She broke from his hold even as a long-held sob broke from her throat. Clamping her jaw against another such self-betrayal, she backed away from him, hands outstretched behind her.

Anything she could reach, anything, a teapot, a broomstick, a fireplace poker . . . she would happily brain him with, and then she would take her baby and disappear, leaving Lord John Redgrave broken and bleeding in her past.

He stood before her now with that same distant and puzzled look on his face. She'd remembered him wrong somehow. The laughing young man of her girlhood had become a figure of sly manipulation in her memory, of course, but her vengeful memory had conveniently misplaced the broken, grieving man she'd spent that single night with. She could see that man now, a ghostly figure still wretched, still lost, as if his shadow were permanently attached to the hollow, distant fellow before her.

She shook off the image in her mind. She must cling to her fury. Only rage made her strong enough to do what she must do. Understanding and empathy were worthless, weak emotions that had landed her in this pickle to begin with.

No, in this case she would be like Amaryllis. She

would keep her eye on the main chance, dealing the best hand to no one but herself.

For her daughter, she would do anything, even emulate her heartless sister.

"Give her to me." Was that her voice, that maternal growl? "Take me to her *now.*"

"What do you mean to do?"

Her chin lifted defiantly. "Run. Run far away and never come back. By my reckoning, you have lost all rights to our child!"

Our child. Shock echoed through Jack. Ours? But—

Laurel went on. "This attic stunt is only the latest of your sins, my lord, and whatever future you envisioned with Melody, I shall—"

He held up one hand to interrupt, still reeling. "Wait—"

Something came to hand at last, a long stick, a laundry paddle, leaning in the corner of the room. The dry, elderly wood drove splinters into her hand as she gripped it tightly behind her back. A true weapon, at last. Could she kill a man?

She could kill this one.

Well, she could quite happily knock him unconscious and then step on him a bit.

He stepped closer. Taking a firm grip on the paddle, she inhaled deeply. One more step . . .

He took the step, his hand at his brow in evident confusion. Now, strike *now*—

The paddle swung. He saw it a moment too late and ducked, but the blow landed hard on his shoulder. Battle instinct took over and he ripped the paddle from her grip and rushed her. Pinning her with his body, he pressed her to the wall and secured her hands safely over her head.

At this intimate distance, however, more danger lurked. The feeling of her pressing to him, the way she writhed against him in her struggle, the scent of her body and the feeling of her breath upon his skin as she fought him . . .

I recognize her.

Then, from somewhere deeper and darker . . .

I need her.

He held her still and made no move, but there was nothing he could do to suppress his desire. His cock hardened to iron, trapped painfully within his trousers. His heart pounded, the sound loud and alarming in his ears. His skin went hot and his vision narrowed. *Need. Want.*

Now.

He could feel her struggles slow. He could hear her furious cries fade to small, broken noises of protest.

He could smell her desire.

Dropping his head, he hovered over her upturned face, his mouth an inch from her lips. Her eyes were huge and deep, pools of sky that a man could fly into. He needed to know . . .

When Jack kissed her again after so long—oh God, it had been so long!—Laurel wanted to fight him, to push him away, to bite his invading mouth. Yet even stronger than the urge to cause him pain was her deep, aching need for his kiss.

His mouth was hot and hard and familiar and strange. When she opened her lips to get a better taste of that strangeness, she felt a growl tear through him and rumble into her.

He raised her trapped hands higher and pinned them both in one large fist. Laurel had to rise to her tiptoes, which only brought his mouth harder onto hers. He wrapped the other hand around her jaw and angled her face to deepen the kiss. It was scorching and wet and she kissed back just as hard. Thrusting tongues warred and tangled and her moans went unheard into his mouth. The will to fight left her body and she shamelessly let herself fall into the kiss.

Jack's hand left her face and slid down her neck, testing her pulse and teasing at the sensitive place where her neck turned to shoulder. Then his big hot hand covered her breast, pushing it high.

There was nothing she could do. She was trapped, pinned . . . blameless. Anything that happened from this point onward could not be her responsibility. The cry that rose in her throat at that thought was a noise of pure animal arousal.

His hand tightened on her breast when he heard her moan. Then his hand slid down her body, over her buttock, and down her thigh. His mouth left hers for a moment and she let her head fall back, panting and ashamed and shaking with need. When she felt his hand slip beneath her gown and slide over her knee and up her inner thigh, she closed her eyes and relaxed her stance, letting her knees widen. She hated him. He'd ruined her life. Her need for him was mortifying, insane, and entirely beyond her control.

His hard, hot hand cupped her mound and his mouth fell back onto hers. As his tongue slipped back between her lips, his long finger followed suit below.

He knew what to do to a woman. Laurel was well aware of that. His touch was sure and firm, gentle but not to be denied. He took her with his hand, stroking his finger deep into her, then sliding it out slowly, dragging the wet length of it upward against her clitoris. Then he stroked down and in once more, setting up a rhythm that matched the way his tongue invaded her mouth again and again.

It began within her, starting from that single spot and spreading outward. First heat, then chills until she shook from it. She made noises into his mouth and he swallowed them, taking them as a signal to increase the speed of his touch. She hung from his grip, impaled first by one finger, then by two together. The long thickness of his fingers opened her. She tightened convulsively around them, increasing the friction, increasing her own pleasure.

Then his wide thumb began to circle her clitoris, round and round, gently but relentlessly. It was too much for her. His strength, his big hard body pressed against her, his mouth owning hers, his hand penetrating her, claiming her, conquering her. It was too much heat, too much sensation, too much *Jack*. She uncontrollably pressed her thighs together until he had to force his foot between hers and press his knee forward to part hers wider.

Pinned. Helpless. There was nothing she could do.

The relief was enormous.

When her orgasm struck her, she shattered like an icy pond hit by a boulder. Her knees buckled as she screamed her release into his hot, demanding mouth. He pressed her hard against the wall with his muscled body, keeping her upright as her body convulsed from the powerful shocks of pleasure ripping through her. His fingers continued their invasion, not letting up, dragging her pleasure on and on and on until she collapsed limply in his grasp, whimpering into his mouth, shimmering aftershocks causing rhythmic tremors to run through her.

Jack released her hands and let her arms fall as he took her weight onto his chest. He wouldn't think about what he had just done. He *couldn't* think about it.

I am not that man.

Withdrawing his other hand from beneath her skirts, he slipped his fingertips into his mouth for a taste of her.

Then he knew it was true. He knew the taste of this woman like he knew the sight of his own face in the mirror. Her voice had matured, her body ripened, but the simple salty-sweet nectar of her body would always mean one thing to him.

That night.

He'd made love to Laurel Clarke that night. It was she who came to his room to soothe away his nightmares. It was she who gave herself so unselfishly that night.

It was her blue eyes that wept when he was thrown from the house—

After proposing to her sister.

It was Laurel.

Laurel, covering his face with tender kisses to ease him from his death-wracked nightmare? Laurel, stroking small, cool hands all over his naked skin, coaxing the tension and horror from his body?

Laurel, soft and giving, passionate and wild, writhing beneath him? Crying out his name as he lost himself in sweet, hot, exquisite *life*?

He could only stare at her. "Laurel?"

For all the melodrama that had ensued after, Jack had never been able to bring himself to regret that night. That moment, that shimmering affirmation, that coming together of souls, was the only reason he had not thrown himself from the rooftop of Brown's years ago.

He'd never told anyone about it, not even Aidan or Colin. That one evening, when they'd found him up on the roof, whiskey bottle in his hand, contemplating the convenient distance to the cobbles, they thought they convinced him to live for his duty as heir, for his responsibility to his uncle's dependents, to carry on the family legacy of good stewardship.

All excellent reasons to live. Not, however, as good as the tiny flicker of hope that single night of warmth and tenderness had given him.

If someone could touch him so, if someone could embrace him and trust him and give to him so very freely . . .

Well, then, there might just be something inside the man that he was that was worth saving after all.

Oh, God, what have I done?

Again?

He released her and she stumbled away from him.

"You . . ." His voice was naught but a hoarse whisper. "You and I—"

Laurel lifted her chin. "I should have known you would forget me."

"Never." Jack looked into her betrayed blue eyes. "I simply didn't remember you . . . quite right."

She blinked. "Whom did you remember in my stead?" Then, as he stayed silent before her sarcasm, her eyes widened. "Amy? You thought I was *Amy*?"

"Bramble, I'm sorry—" He reached for her. Laurel moved a safe distance away, then turned to face him, her face flushed, her eyes wide, obviously realizing how terribly, awfully they'd got things wrong.

"Laurel, you gave Melody away—"

"No!" Her eyes went ten shades of stormy. "I did not abandon her. She was stolen from me. They told me she died!"

"They?"

"My mother and father. The midwife. I swore that I heard her cry, but they told me she was stillborn, that I was mad with grief and the pain of childbirth. I believed . . . I should have known I could never believe them. I should have known I could never believe my sister. Everyone *lies*." She looked down at her gown and stroked both hands down her skirts. "All these years of mourning and she lived here all that time."

Jack shook his head. This at least he was not guilty of. "Only a few months. She was left here at the club. We don't know by whom."

Laurel's eyes widened. "Where has she been?"

"We don't know."

She pressed her hands over her heart. "What if it wasn't a kind place?" Her words came fast in her distress. "What if she was frightened, or struck, or worse? Did they feed her well? Did they keep her warm?"

Jack could only shake his head.

Laurel turned away from him, her arms wrapped tight about herself. "I mourned my daughter! I shall never mourn my parents. Never! How could they do this to their own grandchild?"

Jack watched her. Laurel's concern was truly for Melody's happiness. If he could reason with her now . . .

"So you will not take her away?"

She swung about, her face white. "I will take her so far away, Jack. I never want to see you or my sister or a single stretch of English countryside again for the rest of my life!"

"But—"

She stepped forward. "You ruined me and you didn't even know my name! You lock me in here and then you—" She waved a furious hand in the direction of their moment against the wall. "You are no sort of father! You are no sort of man!"

Her words struck deep. Jack could only stand before her, mute. She was quite right. He had no defense for his actions. At any rate, the wall around him was too high to climb with ordinary words. He felt as if she was too far away to hear him anyway. Or perhaps he was the one who was in the distance.

So he did the only thing he could think of. Even as he did it, he knew that it was the wrong thing to do.

Taking out the key, he looked at her. "I cannot allow you to flee into the world unprotected. I cannot allow you to take Melody away from her home." With that, he stepped backward out the door, drew it shut, and locked it. The small click of the locking tumblers did nothing to drown out her gasp of protest.

He locked her in the room, yet it was beginning to be clear to him that he was the one in the cage.

Lord Aldrich shuffled down the hallway of the top floor, making his way back to his rooms at the end for a nice little evening of peace and quiet. He adored his new bride. No doubt about it. Aidan's mother, the former Countess of Blankenship, had been the love of Lord Aldrich's life since he was young enough to think in terms of things like "the love of his life."

Nevertheless, his darling bride's bloody-minded stubbornness—er, charming strength of spirit—did tend to exhaust a man.

A sound behind Lord Aldrich made him pause in his headlong, if shuffling, race toward his longed-for evening of port and silence. He turned to peer through his thick spectacles toward the far end of the hallway.

Someone was exiting from the attic stair. One of the younger lads, by the black hair and straight back. Blankenship? No, it was Redgrave. The Marquis of Strickland now, since that letter had arrived earlier today.

Lord Aldrich was old enough and sensitive enough not to congratulate young Strickland on his advancement upon the death of his uncle. Still, a few words of sympathy might be in order. Such a strange duck, this Captain Jack, as wee Melody called him.

Turning, Lord Aldrich began to shuffle back down the long hall, his slippers making only the slightest *wiff-wiff* noise on the thick carpet runner.

Strickland paused to dust bits of stuff from his sleeves and shoulders. Then, without noticing Aldrich, Strickland took the stairs down to the next level at a businesslike pace.

Aldrich paused at the attic access door. Pushing on the latch, he opened the door and peered in.

The light from behind him fell onto nothing but the bottom steps of the stairs leading upward. Aldrich listened carefully, for his hearing wasn't nearly as bad as people supposed it to be—as he preferred people to suppose it to be. It did cut down on tedious social conversation.

No, not a sound. Just an old attic, dusty and stuffed with things nobody wanted.

As he turned to head back to his room and his port,

something gritted beneath the sole of his slipper. Bending slowly and laboriously, he had time to ponder the vagaries of his age on the way down. At last, he was able to brush his trembling fingertips across the carpet.

Sharp little shards pricked his fingers. He brought them close to his eyes and peered closely at them.

Broken crockery. Lord John, Marquis of Strickland, had just been brushing bits of broken crockery off his suit.

In Lord Aldrich's long life's experience, broken crockery usually meant a woman. A very angry woman.

How entirely intriguing.

Grunting, Aldrich aimed his shuffling pace toward his port. He'd almost forgotten how exciting things were at Brown's.

In her attic prison, Laurel tossed restlessly on the nest of linens she'd piled in one corner of the room. Her sleep had come late and scantily. Now having finally fallen asleep, she cried out in a dream that wasn't a dream at all but a memory.

From the moment he rolled Laurel beneath him, she was Jack's. His to hold, his to kiss . . . his to do anything he pleased with. She'd loved him for so long. Now, at last, her devotion was to be rewarded.

And what a reward! She'd never felt like this before. His hot mouth on hers, the taste of him as she took his tongue inside her, sucked upon it, slid hers against it, following his every hint, following so closely she quite forgot they were two separate beings at all. His thoughts were hers. His wants were hers.

As his mouth moved from her lips down her jaw, down her neck, she felt the harsh brush of his stubble on her skin. The difference excited her. He was so large and powerful, so broad and muscled and masculine, so different from her own soft skin and fragile form. Wrapping her hands over his naked shoulders, she measured the breadth of her man. She felt small and weak beneath him, yet powerful in her vulnerability. She was the one he desired. She was the one he kissed.

It was her nightdress he pulled down, setting her breasts free for his mouth to devour. She gasped as he sucked her virgin nipples into his mouth, one after the other. They grew hard and pointed for him, the way that they did when she climbed from the warm bath into the chill of her bedchamber. The wicked thrill that shot through her made her pant his name again and again.

He sucked harder, tugging at her, letting the edges of his teeth slide against her tender hardened nipples until she whimpered aloud with pleasure-pain and shoved her fingers into his hair to hold his head close.

Another part of her was aware that her demure nightdress had become nothing but a wad of muslin about her hips. Her breasts were bared to his mouth, and her belly and thighs were naked to his roaming hands.

She felt his hand between her knees, large and callused and hot. Oh, sweet heaven, his touch was like fire! Her skin burned as she parted her tender untouched thighs for his exploration, opening to him in total trust. He stroked them, sliding his hands firmly over her flesh, over and under, thighs, hips, buttocks, ever nearer to her damp and aching core. She writhed, trying to bring her wet center closer to his touch, until he threw his heavy leg across her thighs, pinning her still.

Only then did he begin to toy with dark curls there. Large hot hands, delicately teasing. Feather touches, soft and tantalizing, until she begged breathlessly for more. She wanted so much. She wanted things she had no name for. She wanted it all, and she wanted it from Jack, only Jack.

Always Jack.

Even as he continued to suck and roll her nipples in his mouth, he at last let his fingertips slide up her slit, which had grown exceedingly wet and slippery with waiting for him. The invasion of his rough, gentle fingers made her yelp out loud with pleasure.

His other hand, gentle but implacable, came to cover her mouth and keep her silent. Gratefully she cried out into his muffling palm. She had no sense of self-preservation. She wished to sigh and moan and cry out her pleasure as his fingers teased up and down her slit, dipping into her virgin hole, slipping up the smooth valley to her clitoris, where it stood swollen and rigid, thrusting out between her lips as if begging for his attention.

She lay pinned and gagged, helpless to move, as he devoured her breasts and rubbed small, skillful circles around her clitoris. How wicked that it excited her so! The pleasure, the helplessness, the heat and weight of him, his hot mouth, and his hard, persuasive fingers proved too much for her untried senses.

This man was and yet was not her Jack. The darkness that filled him came out in his kiss, in the urgent roughness of his touch. His need and his bottomless wildness made him dangerous.

This untamed side of him excited her further. She writhed and bucked and cried out beneath his hand as

she was swept away by her first ever orgasm. The pleasure rocketed through her, radiating from her wet, hungry core, convulsing her with ecstasy. She screamed
into his covering palm, a wild, senseless thing quivering helplessly in his controlling hands.

She toppled as if from some high cliff, falling into
bliss as small, wicked shocks of pleasure continued to
bombard her from within.

At that moment, he thrust a thick finger into her,
hard. His thumb pressed to her swollen clitoris, rubbing more firmly than before. His large, callused finger slid into and out of her, fast and relentless.

She was swept mid-fall right back into the climb of
ecstasy. This time she was one step behind, powerless
before his urgency, flailing beneath his restraint, as he
ripped yet another orgasm from her, much to her surprise.

It tore from her throat in an animal howl, muffled
by his heavy hand over her mouth. Just as she peaked,
a second finger joined the first, thick and urgent in her
tight hole. The stretching ache was scarcely of note
beneath the pleasure. If anything, it drove her senses
higher, losing her thoughts in the madness of her ecstasy.

He pulled his mouth from her breasts and put it to
her ear.

"Come!" he demanded harshly.

She came again, a third time, at his command. At
that moment she was naught but an empty shell, a ves-
sel filled with aching, throbbing pleasure and need for
him. Her wordless cries shrilled as she was lost, swirling in a hurricane of rapture.

As she grabbed double handfuls of bed linens in her

fists and arched her body, helpless in the throes, he rolled between her thighs.

Still lost in her panting, pounding heartbeat state, she was barely aware as she felt his thick erection press to her wet, swollen core. He replaced his hand with his mouth, kissing her deeply as he held her head in his two large hands.

She wrapped her arms about him and kissed him back.

Six

Up and down St. James Street, in White's and Boodle's and all the other gentlemen's clubs, the staff sedately served breakfast to those few men who stayed the night in their luxuriously appointed chambers. In richly paneled rooms, still hushed and peaceful, gentlemen snapped open their news sheets and placidly perused yesterday's events, both political and social.

In a certain formerly exclusive gentlemen's club, just a few doors down St. James from those hushed and peaceful halls, came the pitter-patter of tiny feet.

"Can't catch me!"

Then came the *clomp-clomp* of growing masculine feet.

"Got you!"

And then, sadly, came the great pounding of giant feet. "Oy! Wait for me, you two!"

Wilberforce, head of staff at Brown's Club for Distinguished Gentlemen, winced slightly at the great thudding above his head as he passed beneath the grand staircase into the entrance hall.

"Eeeee!"

Wilberforce leaped to one side with admirable agility, considering his ponderous dignity, just in time to avoid the two young bodies shooting down the banister at dangerous speed.

The broad curve at the base of the stairs put an end to that nonsense. Wilberforce gazed down at the tumbled bodies newly arrived on the floor and, after assuring himself that there were two gangly legs and two chubby legs, two scrawny arms and two pudgy arms, and two unbroken skulls, let his gaze turn sourly up to the top of the steps. His youngest and largest underfootman, a gigantic lad of nineteen named Bailiwick, stood there gazing wistfully down the banister at the childish tangle below.

"C'mon, Billy-wick!" caroled little Melody from where she sprawled on Evan's belly. "You try it!"

Bailiwick bit his lip and glanced warily over his shoulder. Then, even as he reached slowly for the banister, he spotted Wilberforce glaring up at him.

"Do not." Wilberforce never raised his voice, yet somehow the clipped syllables rang through the domed hall like bullets. "Even. Think. Upon it."

Bailiwick snatched his hand behind his back, eyes wide.

"Wibbly-force!" Melody grinned up at Wilberforce. "That was fun. I fell on Evan."

"Well done, Lady Melody. Master Evan is much softer than the marble of the floor and much less likely to turn one into broken bits." Wilberforce was no more able to be cross with Melody than any other member of Brown's staff. Even if he assembled his most daunting lack of expression, the one that made giant Bailiwick tremble, it only made Melody giggle. This, of course, only made Wilberforce melt into a gooey puddle.

Fortunately for Wilberforce, such a change was not discernible to the naked eye. All the staff remained satisfactorily terrified.

Young Evan, however, was catching on. Wilberforce gazed at the young boy flatly, but even as the lad considered him in turn he was having trouble suppressing a grin.

"I held her tight, all the way down, Wibbly—er, Wilberforce," Evan assured him. "I made sure she didn't hit the floor."

Wilberforce tilted his head slightly. "I trust this incident will not be repeated."

"No, sir. We only wanted to try it the once."

Melody somersaulted off Evan and rolled into Wilberforce's shins. She lay across his gleaming shoes and looked up at him with one finger in her mouth. "I'm hungry."

Wilberforce bent slightly to gaze down at his Melody-covered feet with both hands clasped behind his back. "I believe Cook is baking lemon seedcakes at this very moment, little Milady."

Large blue eyes widened appreciatively. "Can I give one to Papa?"

"I'm sure Cook will be thrilled to select the very finest example for his lordship's consumption."

Melody giggled at the big words. Then she clambered to her feet and dashed away down the hall to the servants' stair. "Bye-bye!"

Evan stood and dusted himself off. "You know she just finished breakfast."

Wilberforce cocked a brow infinitesimally. "And you did not?"

Evan snickered. "There's always room for lemon seedcakes." He turned with a careless wave of his hand. "See you, Wibbly-force!"

Wilberforce remained standing in the hall. Outwardly, he seemed ever the portrait of stern serenity. Inwardly, he was somewhat less so.

Only last evening, Lord Bartles had bid him good evening with an absentminded, "Sleep well, Wibbly-force."

Dignity, old man. Always dignity.

As the morning sun finally penetrated the dingy attic windows enough to denote the coming of day, Laurel opened her eyes and blinked at the unfamiliar ceiling of whitewashed beams and angled eaves. For a long moment of sleepy confusion, nothing came to mind. Not her room at Amaryllis's house. Not her old room at her childhood home. The sloped ceiling almost looked like . . .

An attic.

Reality flooded her sleepy thoughts, waking her with a cold start. *I am locked in the attic of a gentlemen's club.*

Righteous fury swept her. *I am going to kill Jack.*

Oh yes. Kill him dead. Truly dead. Stomp him a few times, then don gay florals and dance on his grave while reciting dirty limericks at his funeral. That kind of dead.

Vulgar irreverence helped quell the panic enough for her to rise from her bed of piled linens and roll her head stiffly on her sore neck. *I'm starving. I'm so hungry I'm imagining I smell—*

"Food!"

There, set out on a small side table that she hadn't noticed last night, was a covered tray. Laurel dashed eagerly across the room in her bare feet, only afterward thinking in alarm of the shattered pottery on the floor.

It was gone. The entire attic was clean swept. In fact, if she wasn't mistaken it was much neater in general than it had been last evening when she'd been rooting through the crates and boxes for projectile weapons.

Looking down at the table in front of her, she realized that it and the rather fine little chair beside it had not, in fact, been present at all last evening.

"Elves." Or servants, although servants who participated in kidnapping were just as guilty as Jack, in her opinion.

She lifted the shimmering cover of the silver tray and grunted at the plenty offered there. A large loaf of fine white bread. A thick wedge of cheese. Gleaming red apples in a circle around them. Fresh and plentiful. Plain, but she evidently wasn't meant to starve.

"Well," she said to the empty room. "It seems as though I am not leaving here anytime soon."

The walls did not reply but only seemed to inch a little closer. She closed her eyes. Thinking about it would help nothing. Eating, however, would keep her strength and her courage up. Gazing down at the plate, she realized that there was nothing there with which to eat. No fork or knife. Not even a spoon.

No servants then. Oh, a loyal servant might do his master's bidding and partake in kidnapping, but even the lowest chambermaid knew how to put together a tea tray. This little meal was Jack's doing and Jack's alone.

Picking up the large wedge of cheese in both hands, Laurel took a wide bite and chewed angrily.

Men!

After her meal, she covered up the remaining food for later. Dusting her hands, she decided to inventory the contents of the room thoroughly, if for no other reason than to keep her sanity. She might find almost anything in these piled boxes. Perhaps at the bottom of one of them lay a key for this—

Frowning, she looked around at the room. What was it for? There was a large main attic for storage, so this wasn't truly needed for that. It made a handy gaol. Did this gentlemen's club often keep prisoners?

Four whitewashed walls. A door. A big hearth, but not one equipped for cooking. A large grimy window. And . . . She walked closer to one of the walls. Hooks, in the wall, a few feet apart. Yes, in the opposite wall as well. Hooks for . . . string? Twine? Parallel lines . . .

Laundry lines?

She was locked in a laundry.

Giggles bubbled up that were half panic and half absurd coincidence. In a way, it was all because of the laundry, wasn't it?

It was the washerwoman who had turned Laurel in nearly four years past. Three months with no menstrual cloths to beat against her board and the woman had drawn the only logical conclusion about her ladyship's younger daughter.

The washerwoman was a respectful woman and not inclined to gossip; at least that's what Laurel's mother had claimed. Laurel rather thought a bit of coin must have changed hands as well as information, for the laundress soon retired with her butcher husband to a cottage in the country.

Laurel remembered the entire confrontation clearly,

although with a gloss of horror and humiliation that had not dulled in the slightest over the intervening years.

"You wicked, selfish girl! How could you have done such a thing to this family?" That was her father, who was much kinder than her mother.

"You *slut!*" Mama had never been one to mince words. "You dirty, filthy creature! Who is it? Who is the foul blackguard? Your father will call him out at once and put a bullet in him! I shall see to it myself if he misses!"

Intersperse the above with several hearty and well-aimed slaps and one might get a sense of the moment. Throw in being dragged to her room by her braid and locked tightly away and the picture grew more clear.

Then color it in with six months of imprisonment and stark isolation as her belly grew and her soul shrank until she was reduced to the basest pleading. Not that it did an ounce of good.

All of that was nothing compared to the thirty-six hours of terrifying labor, which she was completely unprepared for. How could an innocent girl know anything of the grueling contractions and rending pain? Laurel had thought she was dying. Then she'd wished she were dying.

Then that faint wispy cry . . . and then the midwife's brusque pity.

Until the moment that the midwife told her that her daughter was dead, Laurel had somehow believed that Jack would return and set everything to rights. Right up until the moment when she'd been left alone with her empty womb and her broken heart, she had *believed*.

Like a silly child listening to fairy stories.

Or like a gullible idiot, robbed and left for dead.

She'd kept Jack's secret—the secret of Jack. Through the blows and the insults and the imprisonment, she'd held her tongue and believed. Her parents had never even entertained the notion of Lord John Redgrave as their daughter's despoiler.

He'd been Amaryllis's suitor and he'd been gone for months. And anyway, he'd never paid any attention to Laurel that they were aware of. They'd forgotten him as soon as he'd been thrown from the house.

Much the same way Jack had forgotten her.

In his rooms, Jack finished tying his cravat and turned away from the mirror. Melody lay on her belly in the middle of the carpet, little stocking feet waving in the air.

"Do you have a papa, Papa?"

"I had one once. He's dead." It did not occur to him to speak less than frankly. Melody seemed to appreciate truth.

"Do you have a mama? Uncle Aidan has a mama."

"She is also dead." Everyone was dead. Everyone except for him.

And now, apparently, Melody.

I should marry Laurel. Dull surprise struck that he had not thought of it before this moment.

How terrifying, he thought with distant panic. *I am no sort of husband.*

His first decision was to lock Laurel in the attic—not an outstanding first effort! Yet he had no choice. Melody was obviously hers. He could not rightfully keep them apart. Yet to keep Melody—not alone, after all!—he'd be willing to wed a caged tiger.

Pondering that very tiger, upstairs in her cage, Jack

absently stepped over Melody in order to reach his surcoat where it hung on a peg in his wardrobe. When he
turned back, shrugging it on, he happened to glance
down at the little pile of things that lay on the carpet
before her.

Tilting his head, he peered closer. It didn't look like
much. A rock, a feather, a tatty hair ribbon. And a dirty
white skinny braid tied in a pink ribbon?

"Is that horsehair?"

"Uh-huh! That's from the mighty Balf-zar! He's a
lightning horse!"

After a moment racking his memory, Jack recalled
some mention of a large white horse purchased for the
underfootman Bailiwick so that he could ride with
young Evan. "And the feather?"

"That's Pomme! He's a pirate!" She held it up and
watched mournfully as it sagged, all stiffness gone from
the much-abused quill. "It was beautifulest in his hat."

Colin's bride, Prudence, had told a story about a theater troupe led by an outrageous character named
Pomme. Intrigued, Jack knelt on one knee and picked
up the stone. "Where did this rock come from?"

"It's not a rock," Melody confided. "It's Uncle Aidan's heart." The stone was rather heart shaped, now
that he looked at it. Melody went on. "He gived it to
Maddie and Maddie gived it to me."

So Aidan really did have a heart of stone. Jack
grunted, amused.

The ribbon, it turned out, was from Maddie as well,
and as Melody chattered on, Jack realized that it was
finding that very ribbon that had given Aidan the clue
that Maddie was trapped in the attic by her mad late
husband.

Jack ran the ribbon thoughtfully through his fingers. So many adventures. Danger that he'd not been able to protect her from. High times on the road that he'd not been part of. He was glad that she'd spent the last several weeks wrapped in laughter and love.

He only wished he could have been part of it.

Still, if he could not add to the treasures, he could at least give Melody something to keep them in. Standing, he brushed absently at his trouser knees. Now where did he put that . . .

Ah. Rummaging on a shelf stacked casually in books, he found a seashell from a beach in Jamaica, a gold coin from a sunken ship, a tiny porcelain snuffbox from China, and there in the back, yes. Pulling it out, he turned to hand it to Melody.

She squealed when she saw it. "A treasure chest!"

It was just a carved wooden box, really, but it had taken his fancy for the very reason that with its domed lid and intricate little iron latch it looked exactly like a wee pirate treasure chest.

"For wee pirates," he told her, as she squatted down immediately to pack her treasures away. The poor feather suffered a few more indignities before the lid could close completely, but if Melody didn't mind, Jack was sure that Pomme fellow could bear it.

Jack glanced back at the jumbled pile of his accumulated bits from all over the world, then back down at Melody's gathered little pieces of her short little life. The resemblance was unmistakable.

Our child.

Yes, well . . . he'd delayed facing the tiger long enough. It was time to go back to the attic and learn the truth.

Seven

There was no flying crockery this time. When Jack unlocked the attic chamber door, he found Laurel standing by the enormous grimy window, gazing down at the street below through a single carefully cleaned pane.

He should greet her. That's what people did. "Good morning."

She flicked him a dismissive glance and said nothing. By the stiffness in her shoulders and the way her folded arms pressed tight to her sides he was fairly certain she was not at all calm on the inside.

Well, neither was he. "*Our child.*"

"Yes, our child." Her tone was acid. "Or are you preparing an argument to deny it?"

He hadn't realized he'd spoken out loud. That was an alarming development. Imagine his chaotic thoughts actually turned to utterance! He'd be locked up in Bedlam for certain.

"No. I mean, yes, I'm not denying anything."

Another cold glance. "So polished. How *do* you do it?"

Embarrassment was as foreign as most other emotions, so Jack didn't take her tone personally. He was here for a purpose. "Melody—"

"It makes me ill to think you didn't even know it was me."

Jack opened his mouth, but the tumbling thoughts in his mind would not come out. *I knew. Somewhere inside, I knew you were not Amaryllis. I suppose it was the only truth I could accept, for if you were Amaryllis then what I needed would not be so wrong, or at least would be easily repaired. And I needed it so very badly. I think if I had not had that night, I would not have lasted till morning. There was a pistol in my belongings. I'd come close before, after the nightmares. . . .*

But none of that would spill from his lips.

Blast it, he must try! He must make her understand!

He looked at her fully for the first time since he'd entered the room. "You . . . saved my life—that night."

She didn't turn her head, only gazed out the window. "And to repay me you ruined mine."

He looked away. "Yes, I did."

Laurel knew what he wanted. She could feel it coming off him in waves, like heat from sun-bleached stone. His awkwardness aside, she understood him perfectly, as always. He wanted her to forgive him so that he could keep Melody.

However, Laurel would believe nothing that came from his lips. Nothing. She had heard it all before, the promises, the pleading, then the rages and the punishments. She knew intimately how one could be convinced and imposed upon in captivity.

"I want to leave," she told him coldly.

"Where . . . do you wish to go?"

She closed her eyes. "Far, so far away. Somewhere that I can breathe, and live and be free. Somewhere that no one wants to own me, or push me, or use me. I want to wake up my baby every day and see her laugh and smile and play and know that she can never be taken from me again." She opened her eyes and turned her head to meet his gaze. "Will you give me what I want?"

"I . . . cannot."

She rolled her shoulder high and dropped her forehead to rest on the cool glass. "Then I have nothing more to say to you."

Jack stared at this Laurel, who was nothing like the Laurel he'd known. She was so wary, like a wild creature in a cage. So filled with rage, in fact nearly brittle with it, as if a single word would shatter her damaged walls and turn it loose upon them both.

Yet he had to make her listen. He had to come out of himself to reach her, to make her understand that Melody was *home*.

"I suppose you're wondering . . . This is my club. We live here, ladies and all. For Melody, you see. It's all for Melody."

No response. He went resolutely on. "It was a secret at first . . . or they thought it was, Aidan and Colin. They kept Mellie in their rooms and snuck food . . ." It made her sound like a pet in a cage. Best not approach *that* topic too closely. He went on, stumbling and feeling more and more as though his thoughts might start spilling out his ears before he could lay them upon his tongue.

"The staff . . . the members, too, all those old codgers, they're all mad for her. . . . Melody does that to people. She makes them . . . It's uncanny, really. . . . If you knew her—"

She spun on him then. "Well, I don't, do I? I don't

know my own daughter!" She advanced upon him, each step stiff with rage. "Everyone here, ladies and codgers and *servants,* they all love *my daughter*!" She sneered. "I'm so bloody happy for them I could spit!"

She spun on her heel and stalked back to the window, pressing both hands open on the glass. Jack could imagine how it would feel, cool and hard, like ice on her hot palms.

She was right, of course. It was horribly unfair that the lowest footman at Brown's had more knowledge of Melody than her own mother did.

So Jack went on, doggedly determined, clumsy words and all. It was hard when she was so icy and silent, but in a way it was easier as well. She couldn't possibly think any worse of him, after all. He kept trying. He would be willing to do anything to keep Melody.

He had to keep her. Without her he would go back into the darkness, never to return to life.

"If you would vow to stay in London—we could . . . share her."

"If I cooperate with you, you mean. If I give in and do things your way, you'll deign to give me a bit of time with my own child."

"Well . . ." This wasn't going well. He probably ought not to mention the marriage part quite yet. "Yes."

"No. I won't share her with you. I won't stay in London. I won't allow you to dictate my life to me. I will take her and I will flee so far from you that you'll never so much as get a glimpse of our skirts!"

"That's not . . . You're not being—"

"What? Rational? Obedient? A proper lady?" She snorted. "If I were a proper lady, Melody would never have been born. Or don't you remember my mouth on you, your hands on me?"

Oh, he remembered all right. The briefest reminder sent heat flooding into his trousers and blank lust flooding into his already-compromised thoughts.

"I—" *Think! Not about damp white thighs and the silken fountain of her hair streaming across your body!* "I . . . I can't let you." She had admitted she had nowhere to go. He couldn't allow Melody to disappear like that!

"I will take her, Jack. I shall take her away forever, the first chance I get." She turned and began to walk slowly around the perimeter of the room, always at a distance from him. He rotated to match her. "If you think that I am too weak, or too stupid, or too spineless to fight you, then you have a serious surprise in store. I am clever, remember? Laurel and her books. Laurel and her serious clothes and her sensible hair, thinking circles around everyone who came to our house."

Except for me. I used to be able to keep up with that Laurel.

She would stomp me now, even in the simplest game.

Laurel kept walking, even as he kept turning to follow her with his gaze. So slow, so stupid—he didn't even realize that she was steps away from the unlocked door until she made a dash for it.

Fortunately, his physical instincts were as battle ready as ever, despite his locked mind. In the merest instant, he had her pinned against the closed door, her bosom pressed to his chest, her hands pinned on either side of her head.

She went very, very still. Some part of Jack's mind wondered why she didn't struggle. The rest was fully occupied with the sensation of soft breasts pressed to his chest, with the scent of her hair in his nostrils, with the sweetness of her breath against his lips. . . .

When his cock leaped to attention, he released her. He kept one hand pressed to the closed door, of course. However, she only backed away from him, back toward the center of the room. Her face was white with fury.

One touch, two very different reactions.

No, he really ought not to bring up his wedding plans just now.

He gazed at her, one hand covering the lower half of his face, watching the past rearrange itself behind her eyes, even as it did in his own mind.

"How could you have not known?" She swallowed visibly. "You must have known."

He shook his head slowly. "It was dark. We didn't . . ."

"Speak." She blushed hotly and looked away. "No."

That scent. He'd detected it a moment before when he'd held her close. That light, lemony-sweet, as tantalizing as the smell of molten candy from a confectioner's . . .

Amaryllis wore musk. It was a wicked, sensual scent, meant to drive men wild. "You wear scent—"

"Verbena," she murmured. "It isn't scent. Only soap."

Only soap. Why did that simple fact make his blood heat all over again?

Because now you are imagining her wearing only soap.

Lust was so strange and new. Yet every sense tingled with something wondrous and familiar.

"Jack, if you are not going to let me out, will you please go away?"

"You can leave now. Simply agree to my terms."

"To. Hell. With. Your. Terms."

"I'll come back. Please, think on my . . . offer." He'd almost said *proposal*. Flying crockery would be the least of his worries then!

When he left, locking the door behind him, Laurel pressed both hands to her trembling belly. Her arousal, so instant, so complete, even after all this time, was the worst possible thing that could happen.

How could she want him still? How could she ache for the man who had ruined her life?

Even as she pondered that unthinkable fact, she knew that if he pinned her against the wall again, she might not again be able to resist grinding her body into his like a wildcat.

Bloody hell.

Below in the club, in the card room that had been set aside as a drawing room for the ladies, Lady Lambert paced the room, fingers clenching and unclenching at her sides.

"It is the right thing to do!"

Lady Madeleine watched her with dark, sad eyes. "I can't believe this of you, Pru. I know you love Melody as much as I do."

Lord Aidan de Quincy, fifth Earl of Blankenship, stood with one hand on the mantel, gazing into the coals. "Leave her be, Maddie. She's quite right. We must do our duty and find Melody's true family as soon as possible."

Pru shot Maddie a hunted look, but her jaw thrust out stubbornly. "It isn't merely duty. It is a terrible thing to be alone in the world. Losing our family almost destroyed Evan and me. If there's the slightest chance that Melody has family—"

"We're her family!" Madeleine's voice was a whisper of agony.

"*True* family out there in the world, then we must bring them together at whatever cost to us." Pru stopped in the middle of the room and gazed unseeing into the middle distance. "Someone out there must love her, must want her, is possibly searching madly even now. Perhaps . . . perhaps they won't take her away completely." Her determined face crumpled just a little. "Perhaps they'll let us see her, now and again."

Sir Colin Lambert had been silent until now, standing with his back to the window and watching his wife try very hard not to crumble. "I agree with you, Pru, and so does Maddie, in essence. Only . . . what's the urgency? Tomorrow, next week—"

Pru turned on her husband. "Next year? The year after? It is our duty to do our best for Melody. Do you call that doing our best?"

Colin sighed. "You're right, of course. It's just that Jack—"

Aidan grunted. "Yes. Jack."

Madeleine looked up at her husband with worried eyes. "He seems much better now. He actually replied when I bid him good evening last night. And I heard him telling Melody quite a long story when he put her to bed."

"He is better," Aidan replied, "because of Melody. I can't help but worry that he'll withdraw again if he loses her."

"I don't think there's any doubt." Colin let out a long breath. "And this time I'm not so sure he'll ever come out. With his uncle gone and Melody—"

Pru chewed her lip. "I know. Although sometimes

I wonder if he is good for Melody, there is no doubt that she is good for him. Yet we must at least make a start."

Aidan lifted his head. "We could try to find Nanny Pruitt."

Pru's eyes widened. "The woman who left her here with nothing but a vague note? She thought one of you was the father. I hardly think her information will be dependable."

Madeleine straightened. "What if . . . what if we never find them? What if we do as Pru says, if we do our best, and it still doesn't work? Can we keep her then?"

Aidan smiled. "Of course we can."

Back to her normal efficiency, Madeleine stood and shook out her skirts with a snap. "Then I vote we begin at once."

Pru frowned at her. "You don't think we'll find anything, do you?"

Madeleine lifted her chin. "No, I don't. If Nanny Pruitt didn't know any better than to leave Melody here at Brown's, then I say the sooner we find out for sure the better. Things will be back to normal in no time and we'll all be satisfied that we did our best."

Pru's frown slowly cleared. "I suppose . . . yes, I think I can live with that." She turned to Colin. "You and Aidan must begin immediately!"

Colin bowed his head. "Yes, my queen." He glanced at Aidan. "We ought to bring Jack along. It might help him to be involved."

Aidan regarded Colin sourly. "Anything rather than be stuck with you all day."

"Inbred blue blood."

"Social-climbing upstart."

Pru and Maddie exchanged a knowing look. "If you two have finished measuring your . . . noses," Pru said dryly, "then we ought to get started."

Maddie jumped to her feet. "I'll get the satchel that Melody came with. I kept everything."

Aidan frowned. "Colin and I have examined those things over and over again."

Maddie stopped to give her husband a pert look. "Then you'll examine them one more time, won't you?"

Aidan smiled, a wry twist of his handsome mouth. "Yes, my queen."

Pru dusted her hands as she left the drawing room with Maddie. "My heavens, but training men is a full-time occupation!"

"Ah, but the rewards are worth it," Maddie replied airily.

When the women were gone, Aidan and Colin lost their smiles. Colin rubbed the back of his neck. "We've never actually looked for Nanny Pruitt before."

Aidan nodded, his gaze still on the door where Maddie had just passed. "I know. Because we were afraid we might actually find her."

Eight

As Maddie and Pru hurried down the hall, they passed Bailiwick showing admirable hustle as he escorted the new chambermaid to Wilberforce's office.

"Now, be quiet and respectful," Bailiwick reminded Fiona in hushed tones. "And don't you be thinkin' you can flash one of your smiles at Mr. Wilberforce and he'll go soft on you—"

"Soft ain't usually the problem." Fiona smirked at Bailiwick.

Bailiwick stopped short and gazed down at the dark-eyed, dark-haired buxom beauty who unknowingly held his shy heart in her hands. "D'you want the job or not?"

Fiona rolled her eyes. "I'll be a proper miss, right enough. Don't get your knickers in a twist." She reached up and poked Bailiwick in one massive arm. "You're different than you were on the road. Back then you liked my smiles." She pursed her lips teasingly. "Almost as much as you liked my mouth."

What Fiona called the road, Bailiwick called the single most adventurous period of his life. For a brief span of days, he'd been spy, warrior, and hero combined. Mounted upon the mighty Balthazar—although one might debate who held the reins in that partnership!—Bailiwick had raced across the English countryside, facing hardship, hunger, and bandits in search of Sir Colin and Melody.

Well, it had really been Balthazar who had driven away the bandits from Fiona and her traveling cohorts, but Bailiwick would never admit that in the face of Fiona's flattering admiration and delectable gratitude. It had taken all of Bailiwick's gentlemanly honor not to accept more than a few—oh, very well, *several* breathless kisses in reward for his bravery.

The memory of those lips had driven him mad in the weeks since, yet even more he had longed to hear her voice and see her smile at him saucily.

With those very lips.

Bailiwick looked away. "That were the road. This be *Brown's*."

"Where I'm the only girl on staff." Fiona smiled slyly. "You'd best be nice to me, Bailiwick-with-the-fine-horse, or I'll step out with some other fellow here at Brown's." She sashayed ahead of him and tossed him an arch smile over her shoulder. "Perhaps even this Mr. Wilberforce of yours—"

Fiona faced forward again, just in time to stumble to a halt before the tall, imposing figure of Brown's head of staff himself.

"You must be Fiona." Wilberforce never raised his voice or altered his tone, yet somehow even Fiona heard the disapproval dripping from every syllable.

She dropped a quick but correct curtsy, eyes downcast and blush rising. "Yes, sir. I be Fiona. Thank you for the job, sir."

"Hmm." Wilberforce regarded her for a long moment, then turned to Bailiwick. "Young man, I allowed this hiring because you have shown yourself to be exceptionally devoted to our members and because you pointed out to me that our ladies could use a bit of feminine assistance."

Bailiwick nodded. "Yes, sir. Thank you, sir."

Wilberforce blinked slowly at him. "Therefore, it follows that you would never recommend someone who did not have our members' best interests at heart. You would never bring someone into Brown's who would cause disruption to the staff or disturb our ladies with impertinence."

Fiona's eyes were very large and her countenance had faded to absolutely ashen.

Bailiwick sent her a glance of pure panic. "Yes sir. I mean, no sir, Mr. Wilberforce."

"No, I thought not." Wilberforce turned his glacial gaze back to Fiona. "Welcome to Brown's Club for Distinguished Gentlemen, Fiona. I am sure you will become a valued member of our little family."

He gave a tiny nod, to which Bailiwick bowed and Fiona curtsied deeply. As Wilberforce strode past them down the corridor and into the kitchens, they distinctly heard him murmur something.

"A veritable weapon of mass distraction!"

Bailiwick's knees weakened just a bit. He leaned a hand on the wall to support himself. "Oy," he breathed.

Fiona took a deep breath. "Well, I can see where flirtin' with Himself would come to no good."

Bailiwick glared at her blasphemy, but until his heart slowed its panicked beat he didn't risk a retort. He adored Fiona. He been able to think of nothing but her since his return to London weeks ago. It had been young Evan's idea to persuade Wilberforce to hire her, "so Billy-wick can stop his moonin'." Evan's sister, Pru, had admitted to Wilberforce that yes, she'd thought Fiona was a hard worker and would be popular among the staff. Pru also stated wistfully that it would be lovely to have another female in the house, for Brown's footmen hadn't truly mastered the art of ironing a lady's personal items.

Such imperfection in his staff had been the single necessary prod to Wilberforce's towering pride. A letter of hire had been sent to Fiona at once, forwarded by Mrs. Olive Rugg at Rugg's Inn just off the Great Northern Road. It had found Fiona willing to make a change from her life as actress in Pomme's Troupe of Traveling Players.

Now, however, Bailiwick found himself unaccountably tongue-tied and anxious in Fiona's presence.

How was he to fix her attention now, with other, more smooth-tongued suitors about? How was he to keep her focused on him with all of London at her feet, calling her to stroll the seductive streets?

Fiona, ever resilient, tossed her head as if her long, dark locks were not pinned up beneath her servant's cap and flashed him a wicked smile.

"Bein' that the interview is over . . ." She swayed close enough to walk her fingertips up the front buttons of his livery. "Why don't we find ourselves a bit o' privacy? Seems I recall we never did get to finish what we started that night you rescued me from them bandits." She inhaled deeply, and although her uniform was as demure as a nun's, Bailiwick imagined he heard the threads of her bodice protest against being expected to contain such a prodigious bosom with mere stitches alone.

Dry-mouthed and brain-fuzzed as she made him,

Bailiwick still managed to catch that playful hand before it walked itself down to the point of no return.

"I'll not be takin' you up on that offer, Fiona." His body groaned a protest, but his mind was made up.

She arched a dark brow at him. "No? You weren't too good to get hay in my hair last time we met."

"I be too good; I mean—" Oh, why couldn't he be the sort of bloke full of pretty words and handy blarney? "I'm due to go ridin' with Evan. Sir Colin bought Balthazar for me so I could—"

She spread her open palms over his chest. "Big man on a big horse. You could practically lie down on top of a horse that size. Think there's room for me up there on that big horse?"

His own much-flogged imagination made Bailiwick's eyes nearly cross with lust. He gulped. "No!" He stepped back, away from her tempting touch. "I don't want you that way—"

Her expression turned to chill alabaster as her hands dropped to her sides. "Well, no fear there, Mr. Bailiwick!" Her dark eyes flashed daggers. "There's plenty left who do!"

She stalked off, round hips swinging her skirts bewitchingly. Bailiwick could only watch her leave him and his stumbling tongue behind her.

"Don't want you that way," he muttered to no one. "Want you *always*."

In the chambers of Lady Madeleine and Lord Aidan, Evan scowled doubtfully at the cupboard set into the wall. "What d'you want to climb into that for?"

Melody tugged at his hand, pulling him closer. "Wanna ride in the box."

Evan sighed and opened the cupboard. Inside it looked like a large empty box, hung from cords and pulleys inside the wall.

Always intrigued by machinery, Evan felt his interest rise. "I get it! It goes up and down when you pull those. That's clever, that is."

"Wanna ride," Melody insisted. "Wanna ride up and see the lady."

Evan didn't pay much heed to the bit about the lady. He knew perfectly well that there was nothing above them but a sparsely filled attic, for he'd ventured up there many times when he'd first arrived at the club. In the end, however, it was only an attic and didn't compare with having his own horse!

"I don't have time to give you a ride," he told Melody impatiently. "I'm taking Ramses through the park with Bailiwick and Balthazar."

Melody frowned. "Rammees is a bad horse."

"Ramses is an excellent mount," Evan said, mimicking Lord Aidan's arch tones. Then Evan lapsed into his old street-rat speech: "He's right sparky at the jumps!"

Melody stuck out her lip mutinously. "Wanna ride." Her little round chin was set and her minute brows drew down in a scowl.

Oh, blast. Mellie was going to go and throw a fit and then he'd never get away for his ride. He slid a glance at the box in the wall. It looked sturdy enough to hold her feather weight and she certainly wasn't going to come to harm in the boring old attic. He'd tell Pru where she was, too. This time he'd remember to tell his sister, straightaway, not like last time.

He plunked his fists on his scrawny hips. "I'll ride

you up, but then you have to come down by the stairs. That's the deal."

Melody brightened, her sunny smile dimpling her round little cheeks. Evan couldn't help but smile back. When she looked at him like that he felt like a hero.

She held up her arms to be lifted into the box. "Up!"

Laurel's fury had dredged up words she hadn't even realized she knew.

Her throat was raw with shouting and her body ached from the tightness of her rage. Leaning her back against the implacable oak door, she wrapped her arms about herself, tucked her throbbing fists into her sides, and dropped her head in exhaustion.

The silence of the attic mocked her outburst. She was far, far above the street and no one could hear a thing over the rattle of carts over the cobbles anyway. The walls were of stone and the floor was so solid that the wide scrubbed planks gave up not a creak..

If it hadn't been so bright and clean, it would have made a marvelous dungeon.

The melodrama of her own thoughts twinged at her conscience. She wasn't locked in a prison. She was locked in a laundry room. That didn't invalidate the incredible truth of the locked door, but it did add an element of the absurd that made her unable to feel true fear.

Besides, this was Jack. *Jack.* Of all the people in the world, she could not think of anyone less likely to do physical harm to a woman.

Except he wasn't that Jack anymore, was he? War had changed him. Before the war, she would have sworn that a man like him could never lock her away. No, this wasn't her Jack. This was an entirely new man.

This was a man she could happily hate for the rest of her life.

With her own breathing harsh in her ears, it was a long moment before she realized that there was a sound in the room. She lifted her head and held her breath. The sound continued. It was an odd creaking noise, like a rusty hinge or a squeaking wheel.

And it was coming from the wall behind the wardrobe. Laurel crossed the room in a few strides and started pushing.

Melody sat curled up small in the dank little box, thinking that maybe she didn't want to go to the attic after all. Maybe the lady was gone now. Maybe Evan would go off riding with Billy-wick again and forget that she was up here in the stinky dark. Maybe she should yell down the shaft that she was scared and she wanted to come down.

Evan would roll his eyes. He wouldn't say a word, because he wasn't mean or anything, but he was a big boy and he never got scared. He would pat her on the shoulder and say, *That's all right, Mel.* Then he would stick his hands in his pockets and walk away whistling and go find someone braver and more interesting to play with.

So Melody clamped her jaw shut on that yell for help and shut her eyes against the darkness and covered her ears against the groaning of the wheel things that sounded like they were crying aloud.

The creaking stopped. Then the inside of her eyelids went pink instead of black. Through the muffling of her hands over her ears she heard someone say something that sounded like her name, only it was all choked and wet sounding.

She opened her eyes and blinked against the light now flooding into the little box through the open cupboard door. After a second she made out the shape of a lady, standing there, staring at her with both hands over her face. Only her eyes were showing. They were the eyes of the mean lady at the big, cold house.

Melody drew back into the box. She didn't want to talk to the mean lady. She'd thought it was a different lady. She'd thought it was a lady who wanted to talk to *her.*

Then the lady dropped her hands and Melody could see that it wasn't the mean lady after all. This lady was different. She had the same eyes and the same hair, but her face was pretty *nice,* not pretty *mean.*

She looked like the queen in the chess game.

Still, Melody decided that she didn't want to leave the box. The queen said something all choked sounding again and reached for her, but Melody pulled back from her hands.

The queen dropped her hands really fast. She looked sad, but Melody still didn't want to get out of the box.

Still, she hated to see people sad. "Are you going to cry?"

The queen blinked really fast. Then she shook her head. "No. No crying." Her voice was kind of scratchy, like Billy-wick when he had a head cold.

Melody wrapped her arms around herself. "That's good." She wanted to stare at the queen. She didn't know why. The queen made her feel funny. It wasn't scary, but it was new. She would stay in the box.

The queen wanted to stare at her, too. That was good. That meant that it wasn't rude to stare back. So Melody stared and stared. The queen stared and stared, too.

Nine

When Madeleine finished arranging the evidence on the table in the drawing room and stepped back, the four of them studied the entire sum of Melody's life before she'd come to them.

A small, tatty satchel, patched in three places. Two little muslin dresses, good enough at one time but faded now. An aged little pinafore, no longer quite white. Wee stockings, much darned. One pair of tiny, worn boots with broken laces.

" '*The mony stopped coming*,' " Aidan quoted softly. The note itself lay open next to the satchel, the carefully square writing misspelled in pencil.

Pru, who had never seen these particular items before, was wide-eyed. "The money had not come in a long while, I think." She reached out a finger and traced the minute heel of one stocking. "These are more darning than not. That's the way Evan's would get, when we had no coin to buy more. I'd keep darning and darning until they would shred in my hands."

Colin slid his palm up her back gently. "Those days are over, for Evan and for Melody."

"So tiny." Madeleine shook her head slowly. "She's grown so in just a few months."

"This Nanny Pruitt must have been beside herself

with desperation." Pru's face was set. "She loved Melody so dearly."

Madeleine lifted her chin. "We don't know that."

Pru traced a line of simple flower embroidery on the pinafore. "Melody says Nanny was old. She had trouble getting down the stairs, she told me. Yet she took the trouble to work Melody's favorite flowers into the pattern." Pru looked up at Madeleine sympathetically. "Accept it, Maddie. You weren't the first to love her."

Madeleine shrugged one shoulder. "Oh, all right. Nanny Pruitt was a kind old lady who didn't wish to give Melody up. That doesn't mean that she is in any better condition to take her now."

Aidan brushed a strand of hair away from his wife's brow, an uncharacteristically public show of affection. "I for one am glad Melody was loved. I would like to thank Nanny Pruitt for such careful care."

Colin leaned both hands on the table and gazed down at the items as if willing them to speak. "Is there anything special about these items? Anything rare?"

Pru shook her head. "Common as grass."

Aidan reached for the note and held it up to the light of the window. "So this is our only clue."

"Hold on." Colin squinted up at him. "What's that on the back?" He straightened and rounded the table. Taking the note from Aidan, he flipped it over.

"Lines," he announced flatly. "Scribbles. Faded old marks."

Pru held out her hand. "May I see?" Taking the note, she stepped over to the window and pressed it to the glass. The marks became very clear with the afternoon light behind them. "I need a pencil."

Madeleine reached for the bellpull, but Wilberforce

was at her side before she could so much as give it a tug.

"I have sent Bailiwick to fetch a pencil from the library, my lady."

Madeleine blinked. "How . . . prescient . . . of you, Wilberforce."

Wilberforce nodded a slight bow. "Thank you, my lady."

There came a great gallumphing of feet shod in giant boots as Bailiwick appeared in the doorway, a pencil clenched in his massive paw. "This is for you, my lady."

Pru waved a hand without turning around as she squinted at the note flattened to the glass. "Actually, Billy-wick, it is for me."

Bailiwick grinned, pleased at her absentminded use of the nickname. Wilberforce remained expressionless.

Pru took the pencil and carefully filled in the faint lines. Then she lifted the note down and laid it on the table.

Aidan scowled in disappointment. "It's nonsense."

Colin peered closer. "Is it one of Mellie's drawings? That shape there—that could be an axe." He straightened. "Her artwork does contain an unusually high body count."

Aidan snorted. "And whose fault is that? Pirates!"

The four of them regarded the squat axe-like shape and the long wavy line that trailed from it like a leash.

Pru sighed. "Is it just a scribble then?"

"No," came a voice just behind them. "It is a map."

They turned as one to see Jack standing there, rocking backward as if he'd been peering over their shoulders, which he had. Aidan quirked a brow. "Useful talent, that. I'd like to be able to sneak up on Maddie now and again."

"Reconnaissance training." Jack noted shortly. "Now, the map?"

"If it is a map." Colin handed it to Jack. "You've seen it before. It's the back of the note left with Melody."

Pru leaned close. "It just looks like scribble to me. How do you know it's a map?"

"Commanding illiterate soldiers. All they can do is draw, and badly." Jack held the note for a long moment, gazing down at it. "This shape is familiar. A bit like—"

"St. James Park! Where we take Melody to feed the ducks!" Madeleine exclaimed. "That's the axe handle— and the Green Park is the head of the axe."

Colin leaned forward and traced the line that arched away from the junction of the "axe head" and "handle." "Then that could be the Strand, following the edge of the Thames to the east."

"And look!" Madeleine tapped a mark with her finger, partway down the Strand, two lines bisecting. "I think that's for St. Paul's Cathedral."

Pru touched the strange daisy-like mark at the end of the Strand. "So what would that be?"

Madeleine laughed. "Why, Threadneedle Street, of course! Where all the streets cross!"

Colin frowned. "Everyone in London knows that crossing. Why would anyone need a map to Thread-needle Street?"

"Not to." Jack stared down at the map. "From."

Aidan breathed out. "From there to Brown's."

The game suddenly became real. "We found her," Pru murmured. "We found Nanny Pruitt."

"Jack found her," Colin pointed out. "I take no re-sponsibility."

No one saw Maddie kick Colin, but he took a sharp step away from her as an expression of pain crossed his face. "Sorry."

Jack turned to gaze at his friends. "Why look for Nanny Pruitt?"

Aidan blinked at Jack's question. "To discover Melody's family, of course. This Pruitt woman is our only link."

I'm Melody's family. It wasn't Amaryllis in my room on that one amazing, soul-stirring night. It was shy, young Laurel—a girl I'd scarcely spoken to.

And I'm keeping her in the attic.

Perhaps now was not the best time to bring that up, despite the fact that Aidan and Colin were wasting their time because of his lies.

His friends were happy. It glowed from their eyes and the faces of their brides. He would only soil that happiness with a confession of his misdeeds. He'd kid-napped and imprisoned a woman in the hope of mak-ing her love—er, *marry* him. Nefarious indeed.

No, it was better they remain in blissful ignorance. He couldn't ask them to make that choice between keep-ing loyal to him and retaining their honor by betraying him. He himself had no more honor to lose.

Furthermore, if they knew that Melody was indeed his child and that the proof of that was even now wak-ing up in her attic prison, they would have no need for Nanny Pruitt's help in tracking down Melody's "real" parentage.

And Jack wanted answers. He needed to give some-

thing back to Laurel. Perhaps if he discovered that
Melody's short little life had been happy so far, it would
help Laurel to forgive him. He wanted to understand
what had happened to Laurel three years ago. Obviously, she'd been somehow robbed of her child. The
need to know felt like a glowing coal in his gut.

Curiosity. That was new to him as well.

As for Colin and Aidan? Well, he likely couldn't de-
ter them from going. Gazing at his two friends, he found
that he was able to bear their company quite well.

"We'll go at once," Aidan said tightly.

"No." Despite her earlier briskness, Madeleine's
word was barely a sigh.

Pru looked away from her friend's pain. "By the
time you get there it will be rather late in the day."

Colin nodded thoughtfully. "Tomorrow is Market
Day. There will be many more people to question."

Jack gazed past them, through the window. "We'll
take Melody."

"To the market?" Colin frowned.

Aidan's brows rose. "Of course. Once having met
Melody, no one could ever forget her."

Jack nodded, then turned to leave the room.

As he left, he heard Madeleine whisper to Pru,
"How can he bear to simply let her go like this?"

I am her father. I will never let her go.

Not even to the woman who bore her.

It occurred to him that, as women themselves, Lady
Madeleine and Lady Lambert would never understand that—and if they objected strongly enough, his
decision might very well cost him the last friends he
had left.

Thinking of the blue of his daughter's eyes as they shimmered into his gray world, Jack closed his right hand into a fist.

It would be worth it.

She has my eyes.

In the attic, where the afternoon light streamed in slanting bars through the patches of grime on the windows, Laurel could not take her eyes off her daughter. Hungry for every detail, Laurel gazed until her eyes began to burn.

My eyes. My hair. My mother's nose.

Jack's chin, all tiny and female and adorable.

Melody's hands were clasped about her little knees now and her head was tilted as she gazed at Laurel with the same dark-lashed sky blue eyes Laurel saw every day in the mirror, every day when she looked at her sister.

Mine. My flesh, my blood, my heart.

Laurel realized that her open hands were pressed to her belly, as if protecting that empty, mourning womb. No more need to mourn. No more need to ache. Melody lived.

And she was beautiful.

"Hello." Was that her voice, all choked and damp? Laurel cleared her throat. "Would you like to come in?"

Melody shook her head quickly. "I don't like the attic."

Nodding, Laurel looked about the chamber. "Attics can be a little spooky, I suppose."

"It's not spooky." Melody leaned forward, her skirt rucked up as she sat tailor fashion. "There was a *Badman*." She said it quickly, as if it were one word. "The Badman made me climb out the window."

Laurel blinked. This must be a story. No sane person would make a child climb out of a window five stories up. "Where is the Badman now?"

Melody sat back in her little box. "Dead," she said, her tone quite matter-of-fact. "Maddie says I should say 'passed on,' but Papa just says 'dead.'" Melody smoothed the ribbon tied about the waist of her little dress, pooching her belly out in order to see it better.

Laurel wanted to scoop her up and squeeze her until she squeaked and never, ever release her. Instead, exerting iron control, she decided to mimic Melody's position and seated herself on the floor before the dumbwaiter, crossing her legs in tailor fashion as well. Melody's head was higher than her own.

"Who is Maddie?" Laurel asked casually.

Melody blinked dark-lashed blue eyes at her owlishly. "Maddie is Lady Blank'ship. She's one of my mamas."

Mamas. White-hot pain lanced through Laurel. She kept her expression pleasantly neutral. "You have more than one mama?"

Melody picked at a thread in her ribbon. "Maddie is a mama and Pru is a mama, but I don't have a *Mama*."

Her meaning was perfectly clear to Laurel. Melody had women in her life who mothered her, yet they had not claimed that sacred title as their own. Beneath her towering resentment, Laurel felt a flash of gratitude toward this "Maddie" and "Pru."

Although she was beyond tempted to tell Melody the truth, Laurel sensed that now was not the moment. In fact, it appeared she would be fortunate to lure her own child from a box in the wall!

"I have apples and cheese," Laurel announced offhandedly. "If you care for any."

"Do you have lemon seedcakes?"

Laurel cursed her lack of lemon seedcakes. "My apologies, Lady Melody. I do not. I shall speak to Cook sharply on that matter, rest assured."

Melody giggled and Laurel felt as though she'd been granted a gift.

"Still, won't you join me for a nibblement and a chat? I do get a bit lonely sometimes."

Laurel tilted her head and smiled calmly. Luring her child was like tempting a wary bird to her hand.

She very carefully refused to consider that enticing Melody was like the way Jack was trying to reach out to *her*. Those two matters were entirely and completely different!

Melody considered her for a long moment, eyes narrowed. As Melody pondered, she slowly brought a handful of rag up to her face and slipped a grimy corner of it into her mouth. She chewed it contemplatively.

Laurel watched in barely concealed maternal horror. Heavens, what *was* that thing? A balled-up knotted portion flopped to one side and Laurel spotted a pair of stitched-on eyes.

"Aren't you going to introduce your friend, Lady Melody?"

Melody held out the limp gray thing. "Gordy Ann."

Laurel leaned forward and reached up to gingerly accept it. Goodness, couldn't Jack afford to buy the child a proper doll? Laurel took the damp corner of fabric between her thumb and forefinger and shook it solemnly. "It is lovely to meet you, Lady Gordy Ann."

Melody giggled again. Then she dangled her little booted feet out of the dumbwaiter and primly smoothed her smeared and dusty pinafore before holding out her arms. "Pick me up."

Standing so quickly that her head swam a bit, Laurel placed her hands about her tiny daughter's ribs and hefted Melody into her arms.

Words like "solid" and "compact" and "warm" scuttled through her mind before being washed aside in the wave of emotion that swept her thoughts clean away.

Her heart fell with a thud. *I love her.*

It was as simple and as timeless and as effortless as that. *She is mine and I love her.*

I would die for her.

I would most definitely kill for her.

She'd had a child, but she'd never been a mother. She'd lost and longed and mourned, but this . . . this was an entirely different place in her heart. This burned fierce and hot and forever. This flowed soft and sweet and everlasting.

As she held Melody in her arms, it was all Laurel could do not to frighten her with the ferocity of her emotion. When Melody put tiny hands on Laurel's cheeks and peered into her eyes, Laurel blinked back the tears and smiled at her wary child.

"You cry a lot."

"You're right." Laurel breathed deeply and shook off her tremendous realization with a smile. "I'm an absolute watering pot sometimes. But I won't cry anymore today because I have a guest!"

Melody blinked in surprise, her wariness slipping. "Comp'ny?"

"Of course!" Laurel whirled them both in a waltz step. "You are my company!"

"Me?" Melody seemed slightly at a loss, not sure

what her role as guest might entail. "But this is *my* house."

"Perhaps, but this is *my* attic!" Laurel deposited Melody into a chair, although her hands lingered for a tiny moment, loathe to let her go so soon. Then she straightened in order to dip into her very best curtsy. "Lady Melody, how lovely of you to drop by. Might I ask after your husband's health?"

Melody giggled. "I don't have a husband. I just have Billy-wick. And Evan."

"Oh, heaven! Man-gossip!" Laurel flung herself into the other chair and leaned forward eagerly. "Now, tell me all about this Billy fellow."

As Melody launched into a long, involved description of Billy-wick, who apparently landed somewhere on the scale between ferocious giant and devoted lapdog, part of Laurel's mind filed away every detail, starved as she was for every moment of those missed years.

The rest of her burned with plans to steal her daughter away forever.

Ten

In his efforts to keep Brown's running as smoothly as ever despite the addition of ladies, maids, and two rather mishap-prone small people, head of staff Wilberforce was making his daily rounds through every floor of his domain. As usual, there was not a streak of dust or a wrinkle in the carpet. He slowed as he paced down the hallway of the highest floor.

There it was again. A sound, high and squeaking. A *mechanical* sound. As he listened carefully, head elegantly cocked, rather like an expensively groomed greyhound had he only realized it, Wilberforce heard the sound come from up, toward him, then stop.

Though he never ran, he did have a lively-paced stride when he wished to. He made it down the hall and into Lord Aidan's chambers just as little Melody opened the door of the dumbwaiter.

She greeted him with a wide baby grin. "Wibblyforce!"

As she tumbled out he caught her and set her onto her little feet. Straightening quickly, he gazed down at her with stern disapproval. It was the very same expression that had once caused a grown footman to leak tears. Melody only giggled up at him.

"Lady Melody, is there something wrong with the stairs?"

Melody pushed a lock of dusty hair from her face by wiping her chubby palm across her brow. It left a grimy smear behind. "I like riding in the box," she assured him. "But it's dirty." She wrinkled her tiny nose. "And it smells funny."

Wilberforce tried not to take the criticism of the dumbwaiter's condition personally, yet the long-unused appliance did fall under his purview, since it definitely was part of Brown's. He snapped a bow. "I shall have it attended to immediately, Lady Melody."

Melody waved a pudgy hand in a childish yet rather excellent mimicry of Lady Madeleine's graceful gesture. "All right." She walked away, dragging her rag doll by one "leg."

Wilberforce shut the dumbwaiter's cupboard and still had time to beat her short little legs to the chamber door. He blocked her exit with a bow. "My lady, forgive the impertinence, but I would prefer that you and young Master Evan do not play with the dumbwaiter. It can be very dangerous."

Melody blinked at him, one finger in her mouth, sucking contemplatively. He cleared his throat and went on. "Since I imagine that the only place where a young lady such as yourself might become quite so dusty would be . . . the attic . . . ?" He paused, waiting for confirmation.

Suck, suck. Blink.

Yes, most definitely the attic. He was actually quite surprised that she would go anywhere near the attic, considering the alarming situation she'd suffered a few months ago.

Lady Madeleine's rather regrettable husband had stolen Melody in an effort to punish his runaway wife. In fact, the madman had actually taken Melody out onto the roof and had dangled her far over the cobbles, threatening to dash the life out of her. Wilberforce found himself becoming rather overemotional at the memory.

It was the first and last time he'd ever fired a pistol. However, he held no regret for terminating the membership of that particular patron of Brown's. Some people simply were not cut from the appropriate cloth.

"The attic is perhaps not the best playground."

This blink was longer and, if possible, bluer. Perhaps a more direct approach was needed.

"What were you doing in the attic, Lady Melody?"

Melody removed her finger with a pop. "Playing with the queen in the tower."

Ah. An imaginary game. A version of Lady Madeleine's brief incarceration by that very former member.

Current wisdom had it that imagination was a good thing in a small person. Wilberforce had consulted a volume on the subject of small people, as he always wished to deliver the finest possible service to his charges, be they elderly lords or little girls with large blue eyes.

The attic itself was fairly harmless, now that he knew that she was likely to be found there on the occasions when she went missing, but the dumbwaiter was another matter.

"Might I caution you against further implementing the conveyance from which you have most recently disembarked?" He gestured regally at the dumbwaiter. "It is a highly suspect mode of transportation and likely to fail your expectations in ways both dangerous and tragic."

Blink.

"Do you take my meaning, my lady?"

She swung Gordy Ann dreamily back and forth. "No."

Wilberforce gazed at her for a long moment. "The dumbwaiter is bad. Do you understand?"

Melody brightened with comprehension. "No more rides?"

Wilberforce nodded briskly, satisfied. "Precisely." Then he withdrew the ring of keys from the inside tab of the coat of his livery. Detaching one with a snap of his wrist, he bowed, presenting the key to Melody across his palm. "This key will open any door you wish," he told her.

Melody clutched Gordy Ann beneath her chin and gazed at the key in awe. "It's magic?"

"Indeed." Since Melody could likely gain entrance to any room in Brown's using only her cherubic smile, Wilberforce didn't see much harm in giving her the run of the place. Better that she was able to come and go than to become locked in somewhere she couldn't be found. "Use it in good health, my lady. However, you must not play in the attic alone."

"All right." Melody picked up the key. She could wrap her fist about the shaft and not even touch the ornately curved bow or the businesslike bit on the other end. The hammered iron looked black and rough in her little pink hand.

She granted Wilberforce a glowing smile that made his own expression slip ever so slightly toward doting. Then she wrapped her arms around his knee in a quick hug. He felt Gordy Ann thump against his shin and then she and her mistress were both gone, Melody scampering down the hallway and out of sight.

Wilberforce passed a quick hand over his face to wipe away the smile that threatened to disturb the grave serenity of his demeanor. At least the little milady was getting over her fear of the attic. Life went on. After the disquieting events of the last few months, it was probable that life at Brown's might even become desirably dull once more.

Or, if not probable, at least it was something a devoted servant could secretly hope for.

Someday.

When Melody found Evan, he was too absorbed in the array of tiny metal soldiers he'd arranged on the floor of the room Wibbly-force called the smoking room even though it didn't even have a fireplace.

Evan lay on his belly with his chin on one crossed arm as his other hand rearranged the tiny soldiers once again. "Uh-huh," he grunted as Melody told him that there was a beautiful queen in the tower and that she was going to scold Cook for not having baked lemon seedcakes and that Gordy Ann thought that the queen was very nice even though she said she was a flowerpot.

Or was that "watering pot"?

Melody scowled at Evan's lack of attention. Finally, she flung Gordy Ann into the soldiers, knocking half of them down like bowling pins.

"Oy!" Evan scrambled up to his knees and began to pick the soldiers up. He shot Melody a furious look over his shoulder. "What'd you do that for?"

Melody scowled more blackly, feeling sorry but not

wanting to say so. She didn't like it when Evan was mad at her.

Still, mad was better than nothing.

Evan grumbled as he gathered his fallen men. "You knocked down Britain, you know," he told her. "You made us lose the battle."

"Don't care."

He made a disgusted noise. "I can't wait to go away to school!"

Melody's brow grew thunderous. "You don't want to go to school. You hate school!"

Evan snorted. "No, I don't. School is grand. They've got hundreds of boys there, and there's riding and sports and I get to bring Ramses with me."

"School has lessons." Melody didn't know where she'd heard that, but she was quite proud to remember it. "You hate lessons."

"No, I don't hate 'em. I just don't like doing 'em when I could be riding with Bailiwick instead."

"Uncle Colin won't be there. Pru won't be there." She'd held back her best and last ammunition. "*I* won't be there."

Turning to her, Evan grinned. "Hey, that's right. Even better." He poked her gently in the belly. "No more Mellie the Monster."

When her bottom lip began to emerge, he relented and hastened to reassure her, "Listen, Mel, I'll be home lots. I'll be home at Easter and Christmas."

Melody was distracted by the thought of Christmas. She'd heard a great deal about it since she'd come to Brown's. She didn't remember the last one, except she thought it might be that time Nanny had given her a plum tart and a hair ribbon. Nanny had told her a story about a baby, but she hadn't been listening because she really wanted to eat her plum tart. "I like Christmas."

Evan gave her a quick hug. "There, you see? You'll hardly miss me." He released her before anyone could catch him being nice to Melody. "Now, go on and play somewhere else. I'm busy."

Melody narrowed her eyes. "Playing with soldiers isn't busy."

Evan gave her a push and stretched out on the floor once more. "I'm not playing. I'm going to show Lord Bartles the Battle of Fontenoy." He happily began to arrange the soldiers once more.

Melody shuffled off, her head down. Then she stuck her hand in her pocket and remembered the key. Wilberforce said it was a magic key. Maybe it could open the attic door so that she didn't have to use the smelly box anymore. With a skip in her step, Melody scampered off to give it a try.

Maybe she would give it to the queen.

A present, like Christmas.

Laurel sat in one of the chairs at her table. The remains of Melody's little tea still sat untouched. A plate. A few crumbs. A little wedge of cheese with a wee precise bite taken out. It was all Laurel had to remind her of her daughter's presence.

That and the iron key in her hand.

A half hour ago she'd heard a little scratch at the door. The moment she had turned away from her contemplation of the street from her lofty window, she'd spotted the key being slid beneath the door.

She'd run to the door and knelt to take up the key,

just in time to hear the faintest echo of Melody's giggle on the other side of the thick oak.

With the breath stilled in her lungs, Laurel had inserted the key into the brass lock plate.

Turn.

It turned. The tumblers rolled over easily and the bolt slipped back into the door with a clear *click*.

I'm free.

The impulse to run flooded her. She opened the door to find that Melody was gone. Laurel dashed down the attic steps, intent only upon escape.

Yet she would be escaping alone. Although she might take everyone by surprise and be able to dart to freedom herself, they would never allow her to snatch Melody up and run out the front door!

As Laurel stood there on the attic stairs, one hand gripping the handrail so tightly that her knuckles went white, the war waged within.

Run. Get out. Flee the walls and the locks and, most of all, flee the evil captor!

Stay. Stay close to Melody, close to her tiny daughter, found at last.

Or . . . could she possibly do both?

If she stayed only until midnight she could flee this place with her child. It was simple enough. She had her own small bag already. She could sneak down, find Melody's room, pack another valise, and she and her daughter could be on the first ship leaving the London docks at dawn!

She would never have to see Jack again. Fury made her hands shake. Perhaps she could not blame him for the past, but she could most certainly blame him for the present! The worst of it was, it was as if he still didn't realize what he'd done to her with this locked door!

Should she steal from Jack? Blackmail him? All sorts of wild options ran through her mind.

No, it was best to make a clean escape. She had some resources, enough not to starve. When her parents had passed, she'd inherited a small portion from their estate. One day she might even thank them for that, if she could ever forgive them for their lies.

Yes, as plans went, hers was simple and elegant. The beauty of it was, no one would see it coming. All she had to do was take her plan back inside and lock herself away again.

So what was she waiting for?

Her feet moved slowly and reluctantly back into captivity. She closed her cell door and locked herself back into her attic prison. Even as the lock clicked back into place, a portion of her mind was screaming that this was madness.

So here she sat, gazing at the key that lay heavy in her palm, listening to the bells ring out the hours in some far church tower. London still bustled outside. The silent late-night hours were still far away.

At length, she thought to take a ribbon from her valise and tie the key around her neck. She dropped it deep inside the bodice of her dress, beneath her chemise.

Hours to wait until midnight. Then escape, fleeing into the night, braving the city on her own. She ought to rest.

She removed her gown and gave it a good brushing, hoping that the good black fabric would recover from her two days in the dust. It was unsurprising that Jack had not thought of providing her some way to keep clean.

The dress recovered well enough. Good. She wouldn't want to give a hack driver or a ship captain reason to think she couldn't pay her fare.

Then she hung the gown on a peg and placed her neatly packed valise beneath it on the floor.

She lay down in her nest of linens, but she knew she'd never be able to sleep.

Not a wink.

Eleven

Jack tapped hesitantly on the door. This time he heard nothing at all. Was she asleep? Ill? Had she flung herself from the window as enthusiastically as she had flung the cracked pots at him?

Opening the door slowly, he edged his view around it, prepared for incoming missiles. The room was silent and dark.

Well, it would be dark. You left her with not a stub of a candle.

Jack thrust his own candle through the door like a peace offering. Following it carefully, he waved it high to get the best view of the room. Where was she?

Lurking, probably. He ought to check behind the door itself.

No, not a sign of her. "Laurel?"

A small protesting murmur came from the corner of the room farthest away from the window. Jack stepped fully into the room and followed the noise until he found her, curled up on a pile of discarded linens. She'd made herself a sort of pallet, or perhaps "nest" might be a better word. All that Jack could see of her was her sleeping profile. Thick black lashes lay on her pale cheeks. The flickering candlelight gave away the bluish shadows beneath her eyes. Her nose was red. Had she been crying? Or merely screaming in rage?

She was so different now. When he'd known her she'd been a shy, serious girl, very unlike her sister. However, it was clear that the two women resembled each other more than he'd realized before. They had the same hair, the same eyes, even the same stubborn chin. It was more their personalities that had set them apart. Amaryllis had been a sprightly charmer, highly interested in lively entertainment. Young Laurel had been more interested in books than in parties and definitely not inclined to towering rages that involved quantities of porcelain shards.

That had been such a very long time ago. . . .

"Hello, Lord John."

Jack turned to grin at the slender girl hovering in the library doorway. "Well, if it isn't little Bramble Bush!"

That nickname always made her toss her head. She did it now. "My name is Laurel, Lord John."

He leaned his shoulder against the alcove wall and smiled down at her. "And my name is Jack. Lord John was my father."

She gazed up at him seriously. "All right . . . Jack."

Since he ought not to be noticing how her eyes were a softer, prettier blue than her sister's—especially since he intended to marry said sister!—he playfully slipped Laurel's book from her unresisting fingers and held it sideways to read the spine. "*Childe Harold*? Surely not?"

She bristled like a blue-eyed little hedgehog. It always made him smile.

"And what, pray tell, is wrong with Lord Byron's work?" She made a grab for the novel.

"Sentimental twaddle!" He waved the book out of her reach.

Her eyes narrowed. "Well, it's *my* sentimental twaddle. Give it to me."

He rolled his eyes. "You adore Byron, I'm sure. All silly little girls adore Byron."

She folded her arms, her lips pursed. Still, Jack knew he had not gone too far, for her eyes were sparkling. "What do I have to do to get my book back?"

Jack tugged on the dark braid that lay carelessly over her shoulder.

If he weren't already engaged to her sister, he might have asked for a kiss. Just in fun, simply to make Laurel blush, of course.

"Let's see. I could make you pick me an apple from the top of the highest tree in the orchard. . . ."

She raised a brow. "The apples are not yet ripe, my lord. Of course, since green apples will make you sick, I shall be happy to pick as many as you'd like."

"Vindictive wench," he accused fondly. "Perhaps . . . I could have you steal a bone from the cur that guards the gatehouse?"

She fluttered her eyelids. "Of course, my lord. Patches is a dear friend of mine and will gladly share a bone with you. I look forward to watching you gnaw the dirty thing."

His laughter made her smile, and for a single moment he saw a foreshadowing of a beauty that would make Amaryllis's touted splendor fade from any man's memory. Good lord, what a stunner!

Enough play.

He put the book back into her hands but kept his grip on it. "Please, tell me you only intend to read this poem steeped in the irony in which it was surely written?"

She released the book with a half smile. "Look at page twenty-nine."

Curious, he flipped the book open and paged to that passage. In the margins he saw a precise, penciled note. He squinted at the tiny writing as he read aloud. " 'Doesn't anyone else realize that Byron is chock-full of—?' " Jack blinked and raised a brow. "Nice young ladies don't use that word!"

Laurel slipped the book from his hands and clasped it innocently to her flat bosom. "Did I say I wrote that?" Then she strolled away to the sound of his admiring laughter echoing in the hall. She cast him one last flashing smile over her shoulder before she turned the corner.

Jack's own smile faded abruptly. "Damn." He rubbed his face with one hand. "When the lads catch on, it's going to be hip deep in suitors around here."

Lucky lads.

Now, standing in the dark attic, with the circle of candlelight showing him only a glimpse of delicate cheekbone and round, pale shoulder, Jack could scarcely remember the man he'd been—yet he could recall every word he'd ever spoken to Laurel.

How could he have pretended he didn't notice her? How could he have pursued empty-headed Amaryllis and let such a treasure lie unclaimed?

Yet he had claimed her, hadn't he? He'd known it was Laurel the moment he'd touched her, tasted her, enveloped himself within her—yet such was the power of willful self-delusion that he'd walked away from her thinking that his life was over because her sister didn't want him.

Laurel's hair was down, and the heavy curling length of it flowed over the piled bedding and trailed over one nearly bare shoulder.

Bare? Yes, but for a tiny muslin cap sleeve, her shoulder was bare. Where was her gown? Ah, hanging on a peg on the wall. Jack pulled the hideous thing down. Laurel should never wear black. Like Amaryllis, she was too alabaster. She needed color to warm her skin and set off her rich dark hair. Black was the color of death, of mourning.

I mourned my daughter! I shall never mourn my parents. Never!

Thoughtfully, Jack hefted the dull, black gown. No, there was no need for black. Laurel should wear all the colors of spring, for all the springs she'd missed in her despair.

For all the springs his actions had caused her to miss.

Laurel woke to the faint scent of beeswax in the room. Impossible. Jack had left her no candles. Her chamber was as dark as a tomb in the late night hour.

Crossing the distance to the wall with her hands held out before her, she felt for her gown. There was nothing there.

Frantically she swept her hands back and forth. Finding the peg and feeling it empty, she felt for the others and found them empty, too.

She kicked her bare foot into her valise. Had she packed it instead? Dropping into a crouch, she ran her hands over her valise. Open?

Open and very nearly empty.

Both of her gowns were gone.

She shivered as the walls of her prison seemed to

close about her in the darkness. How had he known? Had Melody innocently told him of the key?

The key! It still hung from its ribbon about her neck, warm from her body heat, clunking against her breastbone.

She wrapped her fingers about it, gripping fiercely. "To hell with you, Lord Jack Redgrave!" she muttered furiously. "I'll run naked if I must!"

The midnight silence was so complete that Laurel's own heartbeat throbbed in her ears. She'd crept from her attic room by feel, the remains of her belongings in the valise clasped tightly in her fist. Now at the bottom of the attic stairs, she waited with her ear pressed to the door, listening. After several minutes—and then a few more!—of not a sound heard, she pushed at the latch and let herself into the hallway. Two shielded sconces held low-burning candles, just enough to cast a dim light. It seemed bright to her eyes.

The room just to her left was the one she'd heard Melody calling from. Before approaching it, she took a moment to lift the glass chimney from the closest sconce and pilfer the candle stub. Armed with light, she swallowed and stepped closer to the door.

Jack would likely be inside. She couldn't allow herself to be distracted from her mission and she couldn't allow anyone, not even Jack, to stop her. She would steal enough of his clothing to get her outside; then she could buy a gown when the shops opened. She hated to part with a penny unnecessarily, but a gown could hardly be considered a luxury at this point.

Stop nattering to yourself and open the blasted door.

Taking a deep breath, she pushed the latch and slowly

swung the door open. Thankfully the hinges didn't make a squeak and she was able to cast the light of her candle slowly about the room to get her bearings.

It was a sitting room, cozy and overstuffed, although oddly cluttered, as if things were in there that didn't belong. An armoire stood pushed against a wall, and stacked about it were piles of hatboxes.

Lady's hatboxes. Curious, Laurel bent and held the candle low over the lid of one of them. An elaborately looping *L* adorned the lid like a maker's mark. Since Laurel was a female and resided in England, she knew precisely what that mark meant. Her brows rose, impressed in spite of herself.

Lementeur. Box after box of Lementeur's latest headwear.

Another time her fingers might have itched with acquisitive fancy. Now, however, she merely noted that either Jack had changed a great deal since she'd known him or he had a woman in these chambers. Brown's Club for Distinguished Gentlemen was getting more outré by the moment! At least she would not have to flee in trousers.

With one hand shielding the candle held in the other, Laurel pressed the latch of the far door and let it swing open of its own weight.

In the dim half-light, she could make out a large room that contained a large bed. Again, the furnishings seemed a bit haphazard, as if disarranged for some reason. She saw rolls of something lying on the floor near the door. Wallpaper?

Stepping closer, her breath held in her chest, she peered closer to see a man and a woman in the bed. The woman was small and lovely, with a long, thick dark braid down over her bare shoulder. The man was dark as well, but he was wider than Jack and not nearly so thin. In fact, he was rather pleasantly thick with muscle.

Jack's rooms were one floor below. He'd told her that but she had been too furious to listen.

This couple, whoever they were, had nothing to do with her daughter. She must have been mistaken about Melody's voice coming from these chambers. Stepping backward, she started to make her way back out of the room.

Then she noticed another door in a side wall. In the same moment, she stepped down on something soft. Bending down, she let her fingers part enough to make out a knotted wad of linen discarded on the floor.

Laurel's eyes filled and she clutched the rag doll close with one hand. Moving as swiftly as she could without making a sound, she crossed the carpet to the next door. Reaching a shaking hand that still dangled the rag doll, she pushed down on the latch.

In the next room, she found the nursery of her dreams. The spacious room was filled with color and joy and everything that could bring a child cozy pleasure. Forgetting her need for secrecy, she stood in frank awe as she raised her candle high to see more.

Then she spied the bed. The headboard was carved with two swans, swimming toward each other, their long arching necks forming a heart shape between them. Beneath the headboard, she spied a head of dark curls on the pillow, the tiny body curled into a ball beneath the thick coverlet.

My daughter.

And now she would be with her daughter forever, just the two of them.

Twelve

Having filled her gaze with Melody for several minutes, Laurel couldn't help gazing curiously about the room.

Everything in sight was either charming or cozy, every fabric soft and colorful, every toy special and imaginative.

This room was exquisitely complete in every detail. The others outside remained in a hectic state of disarrangement. Those people, whoever they were, had put Melody's happiness and comfort before their own.

Laurel set the candle down upon the dainty nightstand and lowered herself to sit upon the floor, her feet curled beneath her. Gazing at the round cheeks of her child, flushed with sleep, and the way her riotous curls were tamed into babyish braids for bed . . .

Melody was loved. This room, this absolute fantasy of a child's every possible desire, these toys made with love, the drawings done in a boyish, scribbling fashion, signed "Evan"—how could this be the same house where she herself was held prisoner by the man who had betrayed her so unbearably?

These people who loved Melody so—who were they? A boy named Evan, some chess aficionado who hoped to pass on the love of the game, that handsome man and that beautiful woman in the enormous bed, surrounded by luxury—what had they to do with Jack?

There was so much that Laurel didn't know.

However, there was one thing she was sure of. She would never be able to offer such a heavenly sanctuary to her daughter. All she could offer was a fugitive life, on the sparest of incomes, likely always fleeing the long arm of the Marquis of Strickland's power.

Not only was Melody loved, but she herself loved these people also. Laurel could see it in the way the gifts were grubbily treasured, lined up lovingly close to where Melody slept. Laurel could imagine her bidding each drawing and rag doll and carved creature a fond good night before climbing into her darling little bed and drifting off to sleep, safe and adored.

She, Laurel, was a stranger to this tiny girl. To be stolen away in the night would terrify and shock her. It would be the vilest of kidnappings, from her babyish perspective.

Laurel knew she must wait. She must make Melody want to come with her. She didn't truly want to live as a fugitive, didn't truly want that for Melody. Laurel wanted her child to have all the best, a good happy life, not one on the run.

I won't take her until she loves me. I won't take her until Jack agrees to let us go.

That would take time. And care, and ingenuity. She must turn her attention to Jack, discover what he wanted, and how to convince him.

Leaving the room, she turned back for a last lingering gaze at her beautiful, marvelous child. It would be worth anything, even putting herself back in prison, to be able to take her child far, far away from this world that she loathed so much.

In the stillness of the deepest night, Bailiwick woke from his usual stunned-ox variety of sleep to find small cool hands running over his naked chest.

Since he was not usually the swiftest thinker when first awakened, he was rather pleasantly surprised that he had no trouble snatching those hands from his body and rolling over on top of the intruder in one smooth motion.

She gasped, a small brush of minted breath against his stubbly cheek.

Fiona. Fiona pinned beneath him, her roving hands secured against the mattress on either side of her head by his hands. He lay full upon her and felt every marvelous feminine swell of soft flesh pressing into his harder form. Where he lay between her legs was very warm and even a bit . . . damp?

His body responded again, this time before his mind could recall that he was trying very hard to prove to Fiona that he wanted more than simply a taste of her ample physical charms. When she felt his sudden and ferocious erection rise and press into her plump thigh, skillful Fiona twisted herself adroitly into a more exact position and wrapped the aforementioned thighs about Bailiwick's hips before he could pull away.

"There's a lad," she murmured in husky approval. "Time to give poor lonely Fiona something to write home about."

He dared not release her and roll off, for he would wager she'd be on him again faster than Balthazar on a sugar lump. He hadn't the slightest idea why Fiona wanted his particular . . . er, sugar lump, but he did know that his Fiona was a woman of considerable determination.

She swiveled beneath him. There was nothing but the thin knit of his drawers between her damp center and his throbbing . . . er, sugar lump.

"Fiona . . ." He was mad to push himself away. Completely barkers.

Yet somehow he did just that. Rolling away from her clinging hands and determined thighs, he flung himself off the narrow cot and stood there in the chill room in nothing but his third-best drawers and the embarrassing evidence of just how very much he did want what she offered so freely.

Too freely.

He'd sworn he wouldn't take until he could give. He'd vowed to himself that he would prove to her that she was worth more than a bit of a thrill between the sheets. No one saw what he saw—not even her.

"You're not turning me away again." She said it flatly, as if it had never happened before. Looking at her, sitting up in the bed with the sheets pressed to— but not quite concealing!—her full breasts, with that hair like shining midnight flowing down over sweet milky flesh, Bailiwick realized that quite probably she'd never been refused much in her life.

He ran a hand over his flushed face, willing his poor sheets to crumple just a little higher, please, just enough to cover that perfect pink nipple; oh damn, now he could see them both—

"No."

She licked her lips. His drawers protested that they were never meant to stretch thus.

"I thought that were just because Himself put the fear of God into you. Samuel told me there's rooms in that attic where you can howl like a banshee and no-one'll hear—"

Bloody Samuel. Bailiwick promised himself that Samuel wouldn't be visiting any secret attic love nests for a very long time. "I'm telling you . . . *no.* I won't have you climbing into my bed."

Arched black brows drew together and anger flashed in those beautiful eyes. "Why? You sent for me! You wanted me here bad enough then!"

"I want you here." God, this wasn't going to go well; he could already tell. But he couldn't tell her what he wanted. She wasn't ready to hear it—and he couldn't ask it. Not yet. She'd only laugh at him. He was nothing but a gawp, a looming, lowly underfootman. Not enough brains to rise far in the staff. He might never be enough for a beauty like her. Still, it would kill him if he didn't at least try. "I just don't want you *here.*"

She lifted her chin. "I'll not be askin' again, Mr. High-and-Mighty Johnny Bailiwick. You can count on that."

She slithered out from beneath the covers and had her nightdress over her head in a flash. Bailiwick watched mournfully as her perfectly lush heart-shaped buttocks disappeared from his sight. If he mucked this up, he'd never see that magnificent arse again!

She tossed him one last scornful look over her shoulder as she stalked from his room. "You'll be sorry, you great lummox!"

He already was.

Not all of Jack's dreams were nightmares.

He sprawled across his bed, his naked body too hot

for the covers. His breath came quick through his parted lips. His mind might slumber, but his body lived every moment of the dream. His cock lay thick and rigid against his flat belly and his skin gleamed with sweat.

Jack wrapped his arms about her, clasping her close as he rolled between her virgin thighs. Still lost in her panting, pounding heartbeat state, she seemed barely aware as he pressed his thick erection to her wet, swollen core. He replaced his hand with his mouth, kissing her deeply as he held her head in his two large hands.

She wrapped her arms about him and kissed him back.

Jack thrust, hard, a single forceful motion.

Her wail of surprise was lost in his mouth. He held her as she clung to him, shaking from the shock.

He'd never taken a virgin before. Regret stung a part of him, but he shut it off. He would wed her soon, so it scarcely mattered. Tonight or their wedding night? He would choose tonight. He would choose this blinding, spontaneous explosion of passion, this abrupt and welcome gift of ecstasy.

With his cock deep inside her—she was so tight around him it was nearly painful—he kissed her mouth, her face, her hot tears from her cheeks. Her hands were small and fierce as she clung to him. He was grateful for that. She could have pushed him away.

Would he have stopped if she had? His mind was blurred with lust and echoing need and the last, agonizing shreds of his nightmare. He closed his eyes and kissed her again. The lust and need won, driving out the nightmare like an exorcist.

He clung to that, clung to her. She had the power of a goddess to save him from his own demons. Inside her body, inside her mouth, the hot, wet, tight feel of her, the warm, sweet taste of her, he was whole. He held them before him like a sword and shield, holding back the darkness.

For now. For this time out of time.

She began to kiss him back once more. He could feel that her body was easing. He thrust carefully at first, for he wanted her to feel pleasure, but she soon became wet and slippery and so damned snug around him and he could not stop.

Lost in her, lost in the aching, perfect grip of her body, of the grace of her clinging arms and stroking hands upon his back, lost in the perfect sweetness of her kiss, he drove himself to the brink of ejaculation.

No. Make it last. Take it all.

He rolled from her and onto his back. Taking her head in his hands, he kissed her long and tenderly, holding his breath and allowing his arousal to bank instead of burn.

Her mouth was so sweet, so giving, so dizzying in its power to make him forget—

He wanted that mouth. She would not do it. Only practiced lovers would. Yet his need for her to use her mouth on him overcame his hesitance. He pulled her lips from his and pushed her head gently down.

She went, so beautifully willing in his hands. Taking his still-swollen erection in one hand and tangling the other fist in the silken cloud of her hair, he put the tip of his cock to her lips.

She kissed him, her lips moving over his erection curiously. A gentleman would bathe away the remnants of their sex, but he could not wait another moment. He pushed his cock into her parted lips. Startled, she went still, but she did not pull back.

Using her hair to guide her, he pressed her down, entering her mouth, closing his eyes as the hot wetness of her mouth enveloped him.

She learned quickly, his bride. It was not long before she caught on to the sucking pressure that he needed. The delicious agony of her mouth drawing on him, just as he had drawn on her perfect, pointed nipples, made him throw his head back on the pillow and moan.

He pressed her, pushing his erection deeper and deeper into her until he felt the head of his cock in her throat. He wanted her to suck faster and faster, until he spilled down her throat, until she could taste him on her tongue, until he dripped from her lips like cream.

She obeyed every motion, every suggestion of his hand in her hair. She bent over him, sucking as she withdrew, rolling her tongue around him as she came back down, taking him so deep into her throat she sometimes shuddered in reaction.

His eyes closed. The world and its pain and its black, horrifying truth receded. Everything shrank around them until there was only this room. This bed. This woman.

Until there was only her sweet, giving, enthusiastic mouth.

Never had a woman been so generous with him. There was no bargaining, no demand for gifts or money or even praise. She simply gave him what he needed, as if she wished for nothing more in the world than to ease his pain.

His body went rigid. He felt his testicles begin to tighten. She would be tasting him now as the drops of precome spilled out onto her tongue.

*The thought excited him beyond measure. He tight-
ened his fist in her hair and pushed her head down for
one last deep entry—*

*And then he pulled her away from his rigid, quiver-
ing cock.*

*It was too soon. There was so much more he wanted
to share with this amazing creature. The things he
wanted to do to her played across his fevered mind,
driving out any other images, any other thoughts.*

*As he rolled her beneath him and kissed the taste of
himself from her lips gone swollen and soft with sucking, he knew that only the rising of the sun would end
this night of passion.*

*She wrapped her arms about his neck and kissed
him back fervently, her body warm and responsive beneath his. He slid his hands down her sides and cupped
her shapely buttocks in his large hands.*

Now there was a fine idea. . . .

In her attic chamber, Laurel moaned huskily in her
sleep. The covers were too heavy, pressing down and
rubbing her sensitive nipples to points. Awkwardly, she
kicked them off her. Her body was hot and damp. Moist
tendrils of her dark hair clung to her temples. Lost in
her dream, she pressed her thighs together, rubbing
restlessly.

*Laurel wrapped her arms about Jack's neck and kissed
him back fervently, her body warm and responsive beneath his. He slid his hands down her sides and cupped
her shapely buttocks in his large hands.*

*She felt his fingers sliding over her bottom and simply
lifted her hips to ease his access. She'd taken him into
her body and into her mouth and taken great pleasure*

from both. The way it had felt to pleasure him, the weight of his heavy hand in her hair, compelling her to swallow more and more of him, the way he'd tightened and moaned for her, only convinced her to give him everything he asked for, no matter how surprising.

He wrapped his big hands around her thighs, lifting them to enclose his hips. It brought his large erection to lie in the valley of her wet center. As he kissed her, he moved forward and back, the thick length of him pressing and massaging her clitoris. She could feel every rippling vein, every bump. The blunt, swollen head of him rubbed her perfectly with every stroke. As her pleasure grew, so did the wetness that eased his way and he began to move faster against her.

She dug her hands into his hair and kissed him hard, moaning into his mouth. She was going to come again for him, just as he seemed to wish. She began to buck slightly, matching his thrusting movements to increase her pleasure. On and on, wetter and hotter, more breathless and more restless beneath him, she rode the thick rod of his erection, rocking into him again and again.

Just as she was about to reach the pinnacle once more, he pulled away abruptly. She whimpered in surprise, but he only wrapped his big hands about her waist and flipped her onto her belly. He tugged her bottom high, but when she tried to go onto her hands as well, he pushed her shoulders gently back down to the bed.

Her nipples, sore and tender, rubbed against the coverlet. She squirmed, feeling strange lying with her bottom thrust high into the air. Pushing herself up onto her hands once more, she tried to turn to face him and kiss him once more.

With perfect ease, as if she were no more than a large doll, he flipped her onto her belly again and lifted her bottom. This time he slid his great hands down her arms and wrapped them around her wrists.

He lifted her hands gently and placed them in the small of her back. Then he wrapped one huge hand around them both, pinning her thus, facedown and powerless.

Alarm and tingling dark eagerness rushed through her, mingling with her still-high arousal. When he moved between her feet, forcing her knees apart, she gasped into the bed linens, already nearly fully excited.

When she felt the thick head of his erection pressing into her, she jumped and whimpered in anticipation.

He meant to take her like a mare! And she was once more pinned and helpless, unable to protest, unable to defy his superior strength.

How wicked that she liked this feeling! How shameful that she wanted him to take possession, to take control! How incredibly arousing that his dark wildness took this form, that it was her he chose to make his accomplice in this wicked, shameful, arousing game!

She gave herself over completely. She would do anything for Jack. Anything.

She would even come repeatedly and loudly, her cries lost in the bed linens, as he thrust his thick erection into her helpless wet, quivering hole again and again, deeper and deeper, using his other hand to reach around her and rub urgent circles around her clitoris, stealing orgasm after orgasm from her pinioned, trapped, entirely willing body!

At last he drove a single deep thrust into her, growling out his satisfaction, shooting his fluids deep into her, his erection throbbing inside her, driving her to gasp yet another breathless, weary, helpless orgasm into the mattress.

He released her hands and moved out from between her legs. She fell to the bed, weak and quivering, her breathing broken by the tiny, shimmering aftershocks of ecstasy. She was sore and sweating and could scarcely think, her mind was so dazzled by the wicked dark pleasure he'd given her.

He rolled down to lie beside her. With one large hand, he pushed her hair back from her face and kissed her long, until both their hearts eased their frantic pounding.

She was glad it was so dark, for she was sure a flush of helpless shame covered her entire body. She'd so enjoyed his dominant play. It satisfied something deep and shadowy inside her to be his helpless plaything. She was a wicked, shameless creature.

However, she was his *wicked, shameless creature, and as he pulled her into the curve of his body, her back to his front, and wrapped a large, heavy arm about her, she went willingly, sinking into him as if she might never come up for air. Her trust in him was absolute. Jack was hers now and she was his.*

Forever.

Just as she drifted off into the seductive sea of sleep, his big hand opened on her belly. The heat of his large palm sank into her, starting small tingles of anticipation to radiate outward from it.

Protesting, she shifted restlessly. Her buttocks pressed and ground into his lap as she fought to go to sleep.

Then, when she felt his massive erection rise once

more behind her, she could not help the hot, wet rush of excitement that swept her.

He wanted more.

A breathless little laugh escaped her lips. Heaven help her, so did she!

If one observed the fusty old brick building from the street outside, one would never realize that inside Brown's Club for Distinguished Gentlemen, that creaky bastion of elder statesmen and geriatric lords, such risqué tom-foolery graced the sleep and dreams of some of its patrons.

St. James Street would never be the same.

Thirteen

Morning routine at Brown's Club for Distinguished Gentlemen was decidedly unlike that of the surrounding clubs. Oh, the staff rose early, as was quite usual. The members rose late.

Wilberforce inspected. The servants served. All was quite as it should be in a gentleman's establishment.

It was when one counted the children that the routine departed from the norm.

Melody rose revoltingly early, usually to amble cheerfully up and down the halls until someone cobbled together food. This process usually attracted Evan, for he was never one to miss a meal. Or a snack. Or a crumb.

After the children breakfasted, Evan went to his lessons, and Melody?

Melody made the ritual daily round of all her dearest grampapas.

"I say, old man, do you hear something?" Lord Bartles paused as he adjusted his cravat in the mirror over his dressing table.

Sir James looked around the room as he smoothed the front of his waistcoat and tucked his watch fob into place. "Not a thing, no, not a single thing."

Melody giggled as Lord Bartles continued to pretend to see his reflection in the mirror, only inches from her face. She sat tailor fashion on the top of the dressing table, playing with the silver combs and snuffboxes arranged there.

Lord Bartles straightened. "I could have sworn I heard something high and squeaky."

Sir James rubbed his chin thoughtfully. "High and squeaky, you say?"

Lord Bartles casually rested his elbow on the top of Melody's head while he thought it over. "Yes, it was quite high and it was indisputably squeaky."

"Did it sound like a creature, do you think?"

Melody chortled as Sir James came over to the mirror. When he lifted her hand to use as a comb through the sparse silver strands on his head, all the while intently gazing into her face with a self-absorbed expression on his wrinkled face, she bubbled over with glee, bouncing on her bottom on the dressing table.

Lord Bartles considered the question seriously. "Yes, it did sound a bit like a creature. In fact, it sounded quite a bit like a . . ."

Sir James paused in his Melody-assisted arrangement of his hair. "Like a . . . ?"

Lord Bartles narrowed his rheumy eyes and peered closer at his dressing table. "I think, it's possible—" He straightened as abruptly as his arthritis would allow and pointed indignantly at Melody. "It is! Look!"

Sir James squinted at Melody. "Oh, heavens! It's a—"

Lord Bartles huffed indignantly. "I'm going to have a word with Wilberforce. There's a Mousie in our rooms!"

Sir James gave a girlish if somewhat creaky "eek" and stepped back. "A Mousie!" He wiggled his fingers in alarm. "Quick, fetch the cat!"

Lord Bartles hobbled forward once more, this time with his hands full of downy gray and white fur. "Go on, mighty hunter! Catch that Mousie!"

When the tiny kitten plopped into Melody's skirted little lap, she gasped and pressed pudgy little hands to her cheeks. *"Kitty!"*

Lord Bartles and Sir James stood back to enjoy the fruits of their labors. It hadn't been easy keeping the tabby kitten a secret for three days. However, it had been worth the questionable toiletry habits and faint lingering odor of sour milk to see Melody's rapturous little face as she clutched the big-eyed, bat-eared, rat-tailed little monster to her little chest.

"Go on, then," Lord Bartles said gruffly. "Take the flea-bitten beastie and show it to young Evan."

Sir James lifted Melody down from the dressing table and set her free to run from the room clutching the kitten.

Lord Bartles sniffed. Sir James looked at him sharply. "Sentimental old fool."

Lord Bartles: "Blasted dander. Can't bear cats."

Sir James looked wistfully after the vanished kitten. "Nor I. Hideous creatures."

"Too right. Fur everywhere." Lord Bartles brushed disconsolately at his sleeves.

Sir James gazed at him for a long moment. Then Sir James patted Lord Bartles gently on the shoulder. "Poor old dear. This time we'll get a black one, shall we?"

It was a credit to Jack's reputation—and perhaps his title had a bit to do with it—that the esteemed dressmaker Lementeur made himself available to His Lordship at such an ungodly early hour of the morning.

Jack sat with the man he knew as Button, drinking coffee and chatting. Well, it almost resembled social chat. Button would ask a casual question about some of his favorite inhabitants of Brown's and Jack would answer willingly, if monosyllabically. Button offered his condolences on Jack's uncle's demise. News traveled fast, which was to be expected. Jack nodded shortly, grateful that the man didn't congratulate him on his subsequent advancement.

It was very nearly a conversation. Jack felt oddly comfortable with Lementeur. Comfortable enough that he eventually allowed himself to reveal his reason for banging down the door of the House of Lementeur just before dawn.

"I don't sleep," he offered, all by himself without prompting.

"Really?" Button's response was casual. "Some of us find it refreshing."

Jack tried again. "I need a dress."

Lementeur nodded. "One assumed, me being, after all, *me*."

Jack reached into the potato sack he'd scrounged from the dark kitchens of Brown's in the middle of the night and pulled out a handful of black gabardine. He thrust it at Button, who took it gingerly, delicately shaking away the threads of burlap until he could unfold the gown.

"Ah." He nodded. "Very svelte. And such an elegant height. Perhaps a bit . . . somber."

"Mourning." Jack took a sip of coffee. "But that's done."

"Hmm." Lementeur tapped a fingernail on his china saucer. It rang bell-like through the quiet establishment.

"So the lady in question is done with her mourning. Perhaps a subtle lavender, for the half mourning?"

"Color." Jack handed Lementeur the other gown. "Mourning is finished. Never should have been in the first place."

Button kept the pile of fabric in his lap with difficulty. "Goodness. Did you leave the lady entirely without?" It was a gentle jest, said with a twinkle, until Jack gazed at him with arrested horror in his expression.

"Ah." Button deftly changed the subject. "Perhaps a hint of the lady's coloration? Is she fair-haired?"

Jack grunted. "Dark."

"Darker than, say, Lady Madeleine?"

At Jack's nod, Button contemplated the extremely modest neckline of one of the gowns. "Is the lady perhaps interested in a somewhat bolder décolletage?"

Jack went still, thinking of Laurel's breasts, high and full, and how they would look bursting from a fashionably low neckline. . . .

"My lord?"

Jack snapped back to attention and swallowed hard. Button allowed himself a tiny smile. "I shall take that as an affirmative, shall I?" He poked at an unexciting satin bow and made a disapproving moue. "Will the lady be visiting us for a fitting?"

Jack shook his head. "It's a surprise."

Button's eyes flashed amusement. "A generous one, my lord. I am filled with impish delight at the very notion! You say you wish four gowns?"

Jack nodded. "Three for day. And one . . ." He waved a hand at a fitting mannequin that stood nearby. It was draped in cloth of gold and shimmering scarlet silk, in preparation for a new work of art worthy of a queen. "One of those."

Lementeur's brows rose. "More coffee, my lord?" He sat back with his own cup, a gleam of satisfaction in his eyes. "Three gowns for day and one for evening. Does Your Lordship have any particular color in mind? Something to match the lady's eyes, perhaps?"

"Blue."

Button stirred his coffee with a finely wrought silver spoon, though he'd added no cream or sugar. The spoon rang sweetly against the fine china, making Jack think of tiny distant bells.

"So many shades of blue to choose from," Button mused. "There is the gray-blue that simply begs for a silver gown. There is that particular shade of blue-violet, though that is quite rare. There is the blue of the sky—"

"Yes," Jack said. "The sky."

"Dark hair. Eyes of sky. Goodness, that sounds just like little Lady Melody, doesn't it?"

Jack shot Button a sharp glance, but Button only stirred his coffee contemplatively, a pleasantly blank expression upon his puckish features. "A bit, I suppose."

Button tapped his spoon lightly on the rim of his cup, then laid it on the saucer. Putting his coffee down on the table untasted, he stood.

"I believe I have something that might come in useful, since we cannot leave the young lady in the altogether. . . ."

"You knew!" Melody poked her beloved Button in the arm. "You did know, didn't you? How?"

Button pursed his lips. "I fear I cannot reveal my sources."

Melody folded her arms and sat back on the sofa with a scowl on her face. "It was Uncle Wibbly, I suppose. Men! Always banding together!"

Button returned the poke, albeit more gently. "Actually, little Milady, it was you who told me. You'd come in with Lady Madeleine the afternoon before and you were full of news, like a little seedpod just waiting to burst. Your queen in the tower."

Her jaw dropped. "Then you knew she was locked in the attic! And you did nothing to help her?" She narrowed her eyes at Button. "You, sir, are nothing but a *man*."

Button blinked. "How . . . odd. I am quite sure I've never been classified thus before. However, if you are too upset with me to hear the rest of the tale . . ."

Melody shot him a grumpy glance. "Oh, you might as well carry on."

Button bowed gracefully in counterpoint to her rudeness. "As you wish, my lady."

When Button rushed away to find something to cover the lady's alleged "altogether," Jack opened his mouth to protest that assumption, but Button had already disappeared into the back of the shop. He stayed gone, which left Jack with nothing to do but contemplate the headless mannequin and wonder if the gowns were going to help his case with Laurel at all.

He realized as he sat there that he wasn't buying the gowns so that Laurel would forgive him. It would be a desirable side effect, but the fact was that he couldn't bear for Laurel to don a single black garment ever again. Laurel deserved so much finer a life than that. Laurel deserved silks and satins in every color.

Laurel deserved cloth of gold.

So here he was, buying gifts like any other suitor, discussing the lady's eye color as if he had any right to. It was nice, though, behaving like an ordinary man in the midst of an ordinary courtship.

"Ordinary" wasn't a word that often referred to his life.

That's because you do mad things like lock a lady in the attic and hide her existence from your friends, and let's not forget that bit about your hands and where they most certainly shouldn't be roaming!

Ordinary seemed further away by the moment.

"Ah." Lementeur emerged from the curtained area behind a sort of raised dais with a large box across his arms. He was followed by a young man of startling beauty carrying an assortment of smaller boxes. "Cabot, put the rest of those things in his lordship's carriage."

Lementeur placed his own box on the table and lifted the lid for Jack's inspection. "This should fit the lady quite well."

Jack gazed down at the folded gown and shrugged. It looked like a pile of pale blue silk to him. "It's a bit plain," he said.

Lementeur shrugged one shoulder elegantly. "But of course. It is just the thing for a stylish summer's day."

Jack could only nod. As his carriage began to fill up with items he didn't quite remember ordering but that Lementeur assured him were absolutely necessary, Jack began to worry about Laurel's response to the gift.

It wasn't a bribe. It was simply a gift. Because he . . .

And that's where his mind halted every time. Laurel herself was like a dangerous pit into which he might fall if he wasn't careful. He was feeling again, and this time he was feeling things he'd never felt before.

God only knew into what dangerous waters that might lead him.

Button came to stand before Jack, dusting his hands as if quite proud of himself. "Well, my lord," Button said, beaming, "your carriage is packed. I shall have the other new day gowns done up by tomorrow."

Jack blinked. "This sort of thing . . . doesn't it take time?"

Button smiled angelically. "Isn't it wondrous what happens when cost is no object?"

Jack was being robbed, openly, gleefully, and with great amusement. He nodded, resigned. At least the bloke's coffee was bloody good.

Button spread his hands wide. "And what use is gold without someone to spend it on?" He shook a playful finger at Jack. "You should marry this lady with the sky blue eyes, my lord. Then you would be free to spoil her forever."

As Jack took his leave, using as few words as possible, of course, that idea would not leave his mind.

Spoil her forever.

He might rather enjoy that, actually.

As the Marquis of Strickland left, Button, who was now a richer man, shook his head with a sigh. "The mess people make of love."

Cabot, always nearby, nodded. "Indeed."

Button smiled up at his beautiful assistant. "Fortunately for all the lovers of London, I am as talented at mending as I am at making."

Fourteen

Laurel stretched luxuriantly, murmuring in satisfaction as she woke fully. She was marvelously comfortable, warm as toast and snuggled into a fine mattress—

Her eyes popped open as her hands gripped the sheets. Yes, sheets. Sheets on a mattress. The mattress was on the floor, but . . . She rolled over and hung her head off the mattress. There was a small carpet on the floor. Several of them, actually, arranged and overlapped until hardly an inch of the sanded wooden planks remained visible.

The carpets gleamed with the rich jewel tones of costly weave, the colors bright in the morning sunlight that streamed in through the window—

Her head snapped up. The formerly grimy window was clean. Well, it was cleaner, at any rate. Each pane had been carefully wiped on the inside, and the outside glass in reach of the opening was industriously smeared about.

He'd done it in the darkness, leaning out the window over the cobbles, likely unable to see what the hell he was doing. He'd done it all in the dark, toting carpets and the mattress and the coal bucket that now stood before the glowing hearth.

In total silence.

He'd lifted her into the bed without her knowing. Her eyes widened and she took a peek beneath the covers. Her chemise was still on, though the hem was rucked up to the tops of her thighs. The key still hung around her neck, dropped on the ribbon down between her breasts. If he'd peeked, he certainly would have found the key.

Yet he'd not disturbed her in the slightest.

Granted, she was a rather sound sleeper, but she wasn't *unconscious*.

"Bloody hell," she whispered, impressed. Then she scowled and flopped back onto the mattress, pulling the covers over her face.

She would not find it endearing. Fine, her jailer tried to keep a nice cell. Well, bully for him!

Then she smelled bacon. Whimpering with resignation, she peeked over the edge of her covers, tracing the smell to the small table that held a covered tray. Sniffing deeply, she also detected her very favorite smell in the world.

Buttered toast.

Her stomach growled ferociously. She'd eaten very little the day before, for once Melody had given her the key, she'd begun to stow her bread and cheese and apples into her valise in preparation for their escape.

Her belly had not been in favor of that notion at all, and now it paid her back with a cramp of hunger. She swallowed hard. Such ravenous hunger was unfamiliar to her. For so long she'd scarcely cared to pick at her food. It all tasted of sawdust to her. Now, everything smelled astonishingly good. Just as the bright threads of the carpets in the sunlight glowed in her sight. It was as though her senses had awakened the day she'd learned her daughter lived.

Despite the circumstances, she could not deny that the world was brighter, her heart beat faster, the gray grief had been banished. She felt alive—but that was because of Melody, not him. It had nothing to do with the . . . er, *stimulating* marquis.

Nothing at all.

Breakfast, on the other hand, was of vital concern. Grinning, Laurel scrambled out of bed and trotted across the room in her chemise. Lifting the lid, she inhaled in ecstasy. Yes, bacon and buttered toast. A boiled egg in a silver eggcup. However, there was no utensil with which to tap the shell from the top of the egg.

Men.

Still, there was a kettle steaming next to the coals and an elegant china teapot ready with fragrant tea leaves waiting inside. Small containers of sugar and milk accompanied it.

Laurel folded her arms and exhaled in frustration.

No teacup in sight.

"Oh, Jack," she sighed. "Really."

She was going to have to pour the tea directly down her throat!

It wasn't the least bit adorable, this masculine inability to prepare a proper tray. Not even a smidgen.

Lifting a slice of toast to her mouth, she took a bite, then froze.

Across the room, on the other side of her new mattress, there hung a dress on the hook.

She choked down the bite of toast, blinking in

astonishment. It was blue silk, a sweet, happy blue, like a summer sky.

Her favorite color.

Her feet crossed the room before she realized she was in motion. Her hand reached for the beautiful silk—

She jerked it back just before she could dirty the shimmering stuff with her buttery fingers. Dashing back to the tray, she glared down at the distinct lack of napkin.

Men!

Then she spotted a pottery pitcher sitting in a washbowl on the hearth, near enough to the coals to warm the water a bit. Perfect. There was no soap, but she scrubbed at her hands in a frenzy, then dried them hurriedly on the rear of her chemise. Scuttling eagerly back across the room, she raised her hands and lifted the dress reverently from the hook. Holding it out before her, she marveled at the elegant simplicity of it.

She'd never been one for bows or ruffles. That was Amaryllis's territory. Laurel admired the Grecian purist styles of Lementeur. . . .

L on the parcels belonging to the lady downstairs. No, that woman's luxuries had nothing to do with Laurel, hidden in the attic. This gown was a very nice gown, but it would be impossible for Jack to simply wave a hand and summon an artist of Lementeur's exalted abilities to whip up a gown . . . overnight?

She held the gown up to her shoulders and looked down. It looked like a perfect fit, even to the length. She laughed in delight, whirling in a circle. Her foot hit a stack of boxes that had remained previously out of sight next to the bed. They tumbled to the carpet, spilling out shimmering ribbons and delicate muslin and slippers and gloves and—

On the lid of each and every box there was printed a single symbol.

L.

Laurel's mouth went dry. She froze, standing there surrounded by the spilled treasure that amounted to a single complete outfit by the famous and entirely unreachable Lementeur.

And she'd almost touched it with her buttery fingers.

Carefully, as if she might ruin it simply by breathing on it, Laurel laid the lovely gown onto the bed and stepped back, her hands behind her back.

Knotting her fingers together, she gazed at the luxurious, exquisite, and entirely unacceptable gift.

She couldn't accept it. Ever. To do so would be to give in, to surrender, to *lose*.

"Damn it."

It was enough to make any woman cry, to turn away such a beautiful thing. She'd never owned anything like it, for she'd gone straight from girlish muslins to black mourning. This was a woman's dress, not a girl's. This was a celebration of femininity and bosom and buttocks and shapely ankles and elegant arms.

In this dress she would be a match for Amaryllis.

Rocking meditatively back and forth, Laurel pursed her lips and pondered the fact that if she didn't wear the dress, then the next time Jack came to the room he would find her in nothing but her brief chemise.

In no manner was that a good idea!

So she really had no choice. After all, he'd stolen her other gowns. It was this or near nudity!

In addition, when she made her escape with Melody

she would be able to sell this gown and all its accompanying bits for a sizable sum.

A slow smile crossed her face. In fact, this wasn't a gift at all! This was simply a small partial payment on Jack's infinite debt! A hundred such gowns wouldn't give her back what she'd been robbed of.

He *owed* her this dress.

Grinning like an idiot, Laurel lifted the gown from the bed and continued her giddy spin, her beautiful new gown shimmering in the sunlight like the rarest jewel.

Of course, there was no mirror to see what she looked like when she put it on.

Men!

At breakfast, Melody was full of her adventures in the garden. Someone, most likely Bailiwick, had told her that seeing a toad would bring good luck. Someone else, most likely Evan, had told her that touching a toad would give her warts. Therefore, in Melody's mind, warts had become a symbol of luck.

"Do you have any warts, Papa?"

Jack paused in the act of lifting a forkful of rather excellent eggs—he couldn't remember the last time he'd had an appetite for breakfast!—to his mouth to ponder the question. "I don't suppose that I do."

Melody shook her head sadly. "That's too bad."

Jack felt it only polite to inquire in return, "How is your own wart situation this fine morning, Cap'n Mellie?"

Melody brightened. "I touched a toad, so I'm going to get one!" She held her index finger high. "Can you see it yet?"

Jack gazed at her finger intently for a long moment.

Then he regretfully shook his head. "No developments as of yet, I fear."

Melody scowled. "I hope it comes soon. I don't want to poke the toad again. It felt nasty."

"One might imagine the toad feels similarly about the encounter."

Melody slid down off her chair and made her way to Jack's side by the expedient of walking under the table. She scarcely even needed to duck. Jack leaned back and politely lifted the tablecloth high for her exit. Madeleine entered at that moment.

"Melody! Pray, go *around* the table."

Melody clambered into Jack's lap without a single sign of remorse. "Papa needed a cuddle, Maddie." She curled her short arms about his neck and laid her head on his shoulder. "He hasn't a single wart."

Madeleine blinked at Jack. "Congratulations." She hesitated at her usual place, then moved closer to Jack and Melody's end of the table. Wilberforce materialized with his usual impeccable timing to seat Madeleine in her new chair. In mere seconds, a steaming plate of breakfast was centered precisely before her and her milk and tea poured to exactly her preferred consistency.

Madeleine smiled at Wilberforce. "Exquisite, as usual."

Wilberforce bowed. "I shall inform Cook. He will be delighted."

As Wilberforce moved smoothly on to refresh Jack's coffee and switch Melody's breakfast to the new side of the table, Jack uncomfortably realized that he had never once complimented Brown's most excellent cook.

Jack cleared his throat. Everyone froze, their gazes locked on him. Feeling decidedly odd at that point, he gave Wilberforce a stiff nod. "Please add my compliments to Lady Madeleine's."

Wilberforce blinked, which practically qualified as a startled step backward for him. "It will be my pleasure, my lord."

When Wilberforce left the room, Jack flexed his shoulders in embarrassment.

Maddie sent him a small smile of chagrin. "I apologize for the stunned face, Jack. It's only that you so rarely speak to anyone but Melody."

Melody nodded emphatically. "She's right, Papa. You mostly only talk to me." She laid her head back on his shoulder. "And Gordy Ann."

"Gordy Ann is an excellent listener."

Lady Madeleine hid a smile behind her napkin.

Melody snuggled more deeply into his hold. "That's what Uncle Colin says, too."

Laurel had been a good listener, once. If Jack spoke, really spoke, to her, would she care to hear anything he had to say? It seemed an insurmountable task, cracking himself open like an egg before her furious glare. He'd done so many unforgivable things. If it might make any sense to ask penance of himself, he could try to fight free of the silence and the gray.

He willed himself to be different, to come out of himself, to reach for her, to touch her hair, bury his face in her neck, run his hands over her body, so much more bountiful now after motherhood, so rich and hot and wet to his touch—

"Uh, Jack?"

Jack yanked himself out of his heart-thumping fantasy to see the breakfast room empty but for Colin, who stood by the table munching a piece of toast and frowning at him quizzically.

Jack swallowed, feeling heat in his face. "Good morning. Where did Melody go?"

Colin worked his breakfast into the side of his face to answer. "I saw her going upstairs a quarter of an hour past." He snorted. "Where did you go?"

Oh, I was upstairs as well. Inside the attic. Inside Laurel.

"Lost in thought," he replied gruffly.

Colin chewed and swallowed. Then he grinned. "You were lost all right. I was just about to fetch you a map."

Jack stood, tossing his napkin to the table. His plate sat before him, his breakfast now ice-cold.

He didn't need a map. He needed Laurel. No, wait. It was Melody who was the important one. It was Melody who brought him out of the bleak place into the light.

Perhaps it was all three of them that he needed. Melody, Laurel . . . and himself.

What he needed was his family.

Fifteen

In the attic, Laurel sat genteelly at the table, clad in her lovely new gown, feeling like a goddess from the skin out after a breakfast, a quick washbowl bath, and donning the most luxurious underthings on earth.

With her beautiful daughter cuddled on her lap, showing off her new kitten, life could not be better at this moment. Laurel let the balm of Melody's childish chatter soothe every missed moment, every lost hour, every empty day of the past, and wash it away in the brightness of their future.

"I want to name the kitty."

Laurel smiled. "That's an excellent notion. Names are very important."

Melody nodded. "Billy-wick nameded me little Milady, and Maddie and Pru nameded me Mousie, and Wibbly-force nameded me Lady Melody."

"That's a great many names for such a small person." Laurel's tone was mild, but inside she ached to belong to this childish world. Lady Madeleine and Lady Lambert and even the staff of this madhouse all had given her child nicknames and gifts and time and affection, while Laurel had been off alone mourning something that wasn't lost. Years wasted in grief.

Melody lifted her head and gazed up at Laurel with

those blue eyes so like her own. "You can name me Mousie if you want to. Maddie won't mind."

Laurel's eyes misted at Melody's sweetness. Then she shook off the wistfulness. "Oh, that's all right. I already named you. I named you first." She tentatively ran her fingertips through those dark curls, encouraged when Melody didn't seem inclined to pull away. "I named you Melody, the moment you were born."

"Oh." Chubby hands continued to tease the kitten with the string but after a moment stilled. Melody turned wide eyes up to meet Laurel's gaze. "Nanny told me that my mama nameded me."

Laurel's heart thudded, but she managed to smile calmly at her daughter. "Nanny was quite correct."

Melody's tiny brows nearly met as she pondered this development. "Are you my mama? Really, really?"

Laurel couldn't help a small, damp laugh. "I am really, really your mama. I always have been."

Melody blinked, then turned back to playing with her kitten. After a few moments of giggling at the mad little creature's antics, she caught him up in her arms and squeezed fervently. The kitten went quite happily limp and soon a thunderous purr filled the room. Laurel laughed out loud. The world had begun to shimmer with joy in the last moments and she refused to question the lightness bubbling up through her soul.

Melody would come around. It would take time for her to adjust to this new situation, time for her to believe, time for her to—

"Mama, I nameded the kitty!"

Laurel's breath caught. *Mama.* The name was a healing balm to her scars. Passing a quick hand over her eyes before Melody could see, Laurel took the kitten in her hands and held him up ceremoniously. "Young sir, you have been named! From this point onward, thou shalt be called—" She looked down at Melody.

"Nanny!"

Laurel bit her lip, for by the look of his giant ears and paws, Nanny was destined to be a large, rangy tomcat. Then she lifted him high. "Thou shalt be called Nanny," she intoned. "A name to be reckoned with, in the annals of feline history!"

Melody giggled. "You're funny, Mama."

She would never tire of hearing it. Laurel deposited the kitten back into Melody's chubby little arms. "And you are most beloved, Daughter." She kept her voice soft and Melody didn't seem to hear her.

"I'm gonna tell Evan." Melody scrambled off Laurel's lap and trotted to the door. "And Billy-wick and Wibbly-force and Papa . . ." The list rambled on until Melody was down the attic stairs.

So many people to tell.

Melody might very well tell someone about Laurel, locked upstairs. Let her tell. Let the world know what sort of man Jack truly was.

Laurel was so bloody tired of secrets.

I have no one to tell my great news.

I found my baby.

Hugging her arms about herself, she leaned back in her chair and contemplated the whitewashed beams of the ceiling. The attic didn't seem like a prison today. Consecrated by the return of her child, the room felt filled with light.

And air. Laurel felt her chest expand, as if she'd been living with too little air for too long. Breathing deeply, *living* deeply, had hurt too much before. Now it felt as if she'd broken her way out of a dark and stifling pit, gasping and filling her lungs for the first time in years.

Reaching into her bodice, she pulled out the key and contemplated the pebbly iron thing. She could leave anytime she liked.

She should leave. She would be right to leave.

Dropping the key back down in her bodice, she turned her unseeing gaze out the large window.

The fact that she didn't really want to anymore disturbed her more than any lock on any door.

Colin tapped on the door to Melody's nursery. Aidan was waiting out front with the carriage and Jack was . . . well, Colin wasn't quite sure where Jack was. He did have a tendency to disappear lately. When Colin had thought Melody was really Jack's daughter, he would have made a joke about the apple dumpling not falling far from the tree. . . .

Pain twinged through him. He heard Pru call out to enter and he pasted a grin on his face as he opened the door, even though he didn't feel much like smiling.

Pru was just finishing up setting Melody's braids to rights. Her eyes were only a little red, but her nose nearly matched her flaming hair. Still, she managed to put a bright smile on her face when she turned Melody around to inspect her.

"There. You look good enough to eat, Mousie-love."

Colin leaned a shoulder against the door frame. "She looks like a doll. Do you think lace is a good idea for an outing?"

Pru shot him a reproving look as she straightened the bow on the back of Melody's tiny frock. "I simply don't want anyone to think we haven't been taking proper care of her," she said carefully. "If you find . . . this *N-a-n-n-y* person, and she tells us where to find her *m-o-t-h-e-r,* then you'll be grateful that she looks so nice."

"Goodness," Colin murmured. "I only meant that with three men looking out for her this afternoon, there's no telling what she might spill on the dress. I suspect that our hindsight is always better than our foresight in these matters."

Pru stood and dusted her hands briskly. "Nothing sticky or wet. Or brown."

Colin grimaced. "Not a problem. I've no taste for anything like that."

Pru gave a damp little laugh. "Caramels. Chocolates. Pork pies." Her laughter grew much damper all of a sudden. She dropped her face into her hands and turned her back.

Colin shooed Melody out of the chamber. "Go find Cap'n Jack, Mellie. He'll take you down to the carriage." Then Colin took his wife into his arms and held her while she shed the tears she'd been fighting all day.

"I don't . . . want her . . . to goooo!"

"Of course not. None of us want that."

She sniffled. "Your bloody Jack does. He's not upset at all!"

Colin blinked. "My bloody Jack is practically the walking dead, remember? It will hit him later, and then he'll get a jolly good brood out of it. Years, probably."

She sniffled again. "You think so?"

Colin pressed her away to gaze down into her lovely, blotchy face. "Are you saying that you'll be glad that he'll be devastated later?"

"Am I?" Her face crumpled slightly. "I think so. I'm a terrible person."

"Yes, you are." He pulled her close again. "An absolute harpy." He dropped a kiss onto her crown of fiery hair. "I married a monster."

When she punched him in the ribs, he laughed, but the sound that came from him was a little damp as well.

Once Laurel had sent Melody on her way, she had little to do but tidy her cell and ponder her predicament. Her key gave her power over her own destiny, and she ought to exercise it by running far and fast from captivity. Yet her heart wished to stay.

However, once she'd arranged and rearranged every item in her increasingly comfortable chamber, once she'd stacked Lementeur's boxes of treasures—the ones she wasn't yet wearing—in the wardrobe and even smoothed every possible wrinkle from the packing tissue and nibbled away every scrap of food on her bountiful tray, the memories began to eat away at her nerves.

Four walls. A window far above anyone's notice.

A locked door.

Even the sound of her own pacing footsteps was so familiar as to send shivers of terror down her spine.

Ten paces by twelve. That was the precise size of her bedchamber in her parents' house. She'd thought of it as her house until the day it became her prison. Then it was the house of Mr. and Mrs. Clarke, those terrifying beings who looked precisely the same as her own fondly indifferent Papa and Mama.

If Laurel was one to believe in possession by evil

forces, she would have thought her parents had been replaced by demons.

Instead, she was left with the simple, sane, and irrefutable conviction that her parents simply didn't give a fig about her. Nothing was to delay or interfere with Amaryllis's triumphant marriage. No scandal would be allowed to touch their family and the wealth and connections that they would soon achieve. No one would stand in their way!

Especially not Laurel.

Odd Laurel, whom no one in Society seemed to understand. Strange, serious, all-seeing Laurel, who held up a mirror to their own ridiculousness. The girl who never gossiped or giggled or flirted with her fan. The girl who always asked the questions they were least willing to answer.

She was the girl who saw Lord John Redgrave come home from the war and didn't turn away from the loss and darkness emanating from him.

And she was the girl who became with child and never, ever named the father, not even when her meals consisted of bread and milk and her candles burned down and weren't replaced and her chamber was emptied of anything but a bed and a dressing gown.

This time her attic cell was luxuriously appointed compared to the monastic starkness in which she'd spent those long months of her life.

She put her hand in her pocket and squeezed the iron shank of the key. This time she was the gatekeeper.

This time she was the one who decided her own fate.

It seemed like hours that she stood by the window and gazed unseeing at St. James Street below. She didn't leave the dark room of her memories until she saw a tiny figure clad in petal pink lace hop down the steps of the club, hand in hand with a tall, lean man clad in black.

Jack.

Laurel forced her gaze away from him, concentrating on her daughter instead. Melody was walked to a carriage, a majestic black-lacquered vehicle with a crest on the door.

Was he taking her away? Had he learned of Melody's illicit visits and decided to remove her from Laurel's vicinity?

Surely not. Surely if anyone would be removed it would be Laurel. This was Melody's home, strange situation though it was. That lovely nursery, all those devoted strangers—no, there was no sign of luggage or belongings. Her panic was unjustified. It was simply an excursion.

Laurel watched the pantomime below, imagining Melody's bright chatter, imagining that the servant bowing low as he opened the carriage door was saying, "Enjoy your outing, my lord," or some such politesse.

Jack would only nod, she knew. If he responded even that much.

She watched in astonishment as Jack turned to the servant and spoke to him. The man's face brightened and he smiled at receiving such attention from the marquis himself. Then her eye was caught by the little figure in pink, ambling around the back of the carriage while Jack was busy in conversation.

Melody skipped along the safer edge of the street for a moment. Then she seemed to spot something across the way. She held still for a long moment, gazing at whatever it was with a finger in her mouth.

Watching from above, Laurel felt a chill of warning. Jack didn't see it. He turned to glance toward Melody but seemed to see nothing wrong and turned back. How could he not see that Melody was poised to move, like a kitten waggling its back end before it pounced?

Laurel's fingers scrabbled at the catch of the window. It creaked stubbornly and for a long moment refused to open. The breath stilled in her lungs as Melody took a tiny step out into the street, intent on some strange attractant on the other side. Then she took another step. And another. Laurel broke a nail and then another until finally the catch turned and she pushed frantically on the glass.

Melody went up on her toes in excitement and then she took another quick step—

Right into the path of an oncoming horse pulling a gentleman's gig smartly down the street. The window gave beneath Laurel's panic at last and she filled her lungs.

"Melody!"

Sixteen

"Melody!"

Laurel's cry was lost in the shrieking neigh of the startled horse. The high-strung creature reared in its traces, hooves pawing the air above Melody's head.

Then Jack was there, scooping Melody into his arms, taking an iron-shod hoof to the shoulder as he rolled both of them out of the street. The blow spun him about, yet he kept Melody safe in the curve of his body, pressed to his heart.

Two men scrambled out of the carriage and ran to help. The fair-haired one helped Jack to his feet while the dark one swept Melody into his arms for a brief hug before he set her down and began checking every inch of her for harm. Laurel waited, fingers tight on the edge of the window, unable to draw a full breath until she saw the dark man drop his shoulders in relief and send a reassuring wave toward the other two.

Then Laurel looked down at Jack. He had one hand on his other shoulder, absently massaging it. An inch or two to the left and the blow would have come down on his skull.

He hadn't hesitated. He'd thrown himself between their child and the deadly hooves and taken a blow that might have killed him.

Laurel stepped back from her strained pose half out of the window and pressed her palms to her midriff. She felt sick and a bit dizzy from the fear that had flooded her veins. She watched as Jack went to Melody and went down on one knee before her. There went the knees of his trousers, too. He took Melody's little chin between his fingers and gazed into her face, speaking to her.

Laurel frowned, but he wasn't being overly stern. Melody didn't cry or cringe away. She simply nodded solemnly, with her thinking finger in her mouth. Then Jack pulled her close, tucking her tiny head under his chin and holding her that way for a long moment. Laurel stared, unable to deny the catch in her throat at the sight. He was a good father, not at all like her selfish, uninterested parents.

Then Laurel saw him swipe a quick, secretive hand over his eyes. In her heart, tenderness warred with anxiety.

He loves her.

And then . . .

He'll never let her go.

Inside the luxurious carriage of the Marquis of Strickland, Melody had her pick of laps to ride on. A wealth of papas, all for one bighearted little girl. As usual, she chose Jack's lap. Snuggled into his warmth with his arm loosely crooked about her plump little tummy, Melody explained her venture into the street.

"There was a boy," she said. Then she stuck her finger in her mouth.

Jack gently extracted it. "You ran into the street to talk to a strange boy?"

"He's not a strange boy. He's a nice boy. Like Evan."

Colin hooted. "Better not let Evan hear you call him a nice boy, Mousie. He'll be sure to do something not so nice to prove you wrong."

Aidan raised a brow. "That's rather harsh, Colin. He is your brother now."

Jack gazed down at the top of Melody's shining head. "What is the nice boy's name?"

Melody twisted her ankles to better admire the new little white boots that Pru had put on her feet. "I don't know. He's the running boy."

Jack frowned. "Where does he run?"

"Where are we going?" Melody bounced in Jack's lap. "I want to go to the park! The park!"

Aidan leaned back in his seat. "I didn't see a boy, but there are a number of messengers trotting up and down St. James. She's likely seen him before from the window."

Jack let the bouncing Melody leave his lap to stand on the black velvet seat with her head sticking out of the carriage window, her carefully arranged curls tangling in the breeze. He kept a grip on her sash, just in case. Though his shoulder burned like fire, he wasn't about to let go of her anytime soon.

Colin watched him with narrowed eyes. "It wasn't your fault, Jack."

Jack said nothing. Aidan sat up straighter, his gaze sharpening on his friend. "Oh no. Don't you even think it! Jack, you saved her!"

Jack kept his gaze on Melody. She was laughing in delight at the speed of the horses' trot. "I almost killed her," he whispered.

"No," Colin said firmly. "You're brilliant with her. Children wander off. It's practically written in their maniacal little rule book! Chapter one, page one: 'Must wander off at every opportunity.'"

Memory made the bruise on Jack's shoulder twinge sharply. Imagination only made it worse. A blow like that could have killed his tiny daughter. He could see it now, her little body broken and still on the cobbles. Jack shook his head. "I should have watched her."

Aidan leaned forward. "You were watching," he said softly. "You saw her start to cross."

"No." Jack met his friends' eyes for the first time since the rescue. "I didn't see it. I heard—" He looked away. "Never mind." He let out a breath. "So, we are off to the market near Threadneedle Street."

Colin nodded. "Loads of people about today. If that's where *N-a-n-n-y* originated, then there's bound to be someone who recognizes Melody."

Aidan turned his gaze out the small square window. "Perhaps."

Colin glanced at Aidan but, with unusual sensitivity, did not tease him about his gravity. "Today is simply information gathering. No need to do more than that. These things take time, after all."

Jack said nothing. Information was precisely what he was after. The need to know what had happened to Laurel burned within him. What chaos had he caused? How could he start to make amends until he fully understood his crimes?

Nanny Pruitt had the answers that Jack desperately needed. Of course, when the truth came out, he was going to have a great deal of explaining to do.

Gazing across the spacious carriage at Colin and Aidan, Jack knew that moment was going to be hard. He'd never been much good at explaining.

He wasn't even sure he could explain his actions lately to himself!

The Threadneedle Street market was organized chaos, heavy on the chaos, a little light on the organization. This was a varied market, where one could buy a melon, a parakeet, and a book on social revolution in the space of a few stalls. Melody bounced on her toes, thrilled by the spectacle.

"I want to see the birdie! Papa, can I have a birdie? Ooh, spoons!"

Colin grunted. "No need to take her to see the Royal Menagerie. We can just bring her here and buy sausages while we're at it."

Aidan rolled his eyes. "You and your blasted sausages."

Colin blinked, hurt. "What's wrong with sausages?"

As they ventured farther into the market and the way became more crowded, Colin swept Melody up to sit on his shoulders. She held on to his ears and kicked her little white boots, most content with her vantage point. "Look, Papa! I see chickens!"

Aidan glanced at Jack. "What are you going to do about that?"

Jack looked away. "Not fond of chickens."

Aidan put a hand on his arm. "You know what I mean," he said, keeping his voice too low for Melody to hear. "When are you going to tell her that you are not her papa?"

Sometime on the far side of never. Jack slid his arm out of Aidan's grasp. "One thing at a time."

Aidan eyed him for a long moment. Jack didn't meet his gaze. "I suppose," Aidan said slowly.

Colin turned around and walked backward. "Are you two going to make me do all the—"

He walked directly into a cart full of apples, jostling it hard. Apples began to tumble down from their carefully stacked pyramid. It was a rain of red and green, thudding down around Colin's feet. Melody clapped her hands with joy.

The hawker wasn't so pleased. "Oy! Them's me livelihood, ye blighter!" A stout, red-faced woman rose up from behind the cart, wielding an apple in each hand. "Ye'll be payin' top price for—" She stopped and blinked when she saw three well-dressed gentlemen.

Colin held out both hands in apology. "I cannot express my regret, my good woman."

Aidan simply reached into his pocket and withdrew a gold coin. "This ought to even matters out." He tossed it to the apple seller, who snatched it out of the air with the ease of long practice and then gave it a good bite.

Mollified by her profits, which were more than she usually made in a fortnight, her ruddy face became wreathed in smiles. "Let me fill ye a bushel, kind sir. I've the finest apples in London, I do!" Then she squinted up at Melody atop Colin's shoulders. "Well, hello, pet! I ain't seen ye for ages!"

Melody grinned and waved both hands. "Hello-hello, apple lady!"

Aidan stepped forward, frowning. "You know this child?"

The apple seller sobered, intimidated by such a tall,

grand gentleman's fierce attention. Her eyes wide, she looked from Melody to Aidan but said not a word.

Colin swore and pushed Aidan away with one hand in the middle of his chest. "Step off, you great oaf! You're intimidating the witness."

Aidan took a single step back and clamped his jaw shut, but the look he shot Colin was thunderous. Colin ignored him and swung Melody down to stand on her feet among the fallen apples. She immediately squatted and began to fill her arms with them.

Smiling genially, Colin oozed charm at the worried hawker. "Ignore my dour friend, madam. He's just hungry." Colin cast an apple over his shoulder at Aidan without looking. Aidan caught it with a sharp snap of his hand. "Now, my good woman, as you can see, we've brought this child to the market to find out where she came from. Do you know Melody?"

The woman stared at them. "Everyone knows the little poppet. She's a right favorite in the market. Ain't seen her for a while, though."

Colin gazed at the woman mournfully and shook his head, but he waved a hushing hand over Melody's bent head. "Do you remember who she was with last time you saw her?"

The woman nodded. "Aye. She came every week with the old woman. Bought seven apples every time. Got so regular I'd pick out the best and save 'em back for 'er, though I let her pay for bruised." She thrust her chin at Melody. "Seven days. Seven apples. All for the little one, none for herself."

Melody stood with her skirt held wide, the expensive lace full of street-grimy apples. "I founded them for you!"

The apple seller bent low and took the apples back one by one, putting them carefully into a bushel basket, though they were only fit for pigs now. When she was done, she tsked at Melody's skirts. "What would your old Nan say 'bout that if she were here, eh?"

Melody ignored the dirt and held out her arms to be picked up. With a glance for permission from Colin, the hawker lifted Melody and put her on one vast hip. "Wipe yer hands, then, missy, and I'll give ye a fresh one."

While Melody bit into an apple so crisp that it made Jack's throat feel parched in envy, the woman continued. "It's been months, it has. Where's the miss been all this time?"

Colin leaned an elbow on the strut holding up the awning over the cart. "Oh, we've been looking after her. But now we can't find . . . er, *N-a-n-n-y.*"

The woman gazed at him without comprehension. Aidan leaned forward. "We're looking for her old Nan."

"Oh." Light dawned. "Why didn't ye just say so?" The woman wrinkled her brow and gazed into midair for a moment. Melody was happily mangling the apple, which was too large and round to fit into her little mouth. Jack took it from her and cut it into neat slices with the penknife from his watch fob.

"I think she lived that way." The woman tilted her head to illustrate direction. "I never knew 'er name or house, but I don't think it were far, 'cause the miss walked it well enough on her own little feet. The old bird wasn't up to carryin' 'er them last weeks."

Jack spoke for the first time. "Was the lady ill?"

The hawker scrunched her weathered face. "I'll say

she were. Went from spry to frail in the span of a single spring, she did."

Jack looked at the other two men. "The apothecary."

Colin nodded. "Yes. He'd know her address if he delivered to her."

The hawker nodded. "Aye, there's a shop not two streets over. Likely she'd have used that one. Might have seen her with a parcel from there once."

Aidan tossed the woman another coin. She grinned at him, flashing tangled teeth. "I'd have told ye for free, handsome, but I thank ye kindly anyway."

Colin snorted. "Stop your flirting and come along, Aidan."

They left with Melody hefted to Aidan's hip. She waved farewell to the woman over Aidan's shoulder, opening and closing her pudgy hand. "Bye! Bye! Sell lots of apples!"

The woman laughed. "Bless ye, pet!"

The apothecary was precisely where the hawker had directed them. Outside the shop, Aidan and Colin hesitated, a reluctant glance passing between them. Jack entered without pause. Colin took a deep breath. "We're about to find out, aren't we?"

Aidan worked his jaw. "Whether we like it or not."

Side by side with Melody between, they entered the shop, each holding one tiny hand.

Whether they liked it or not.

Seventeen

Wilberforce was not one to intrude into his charges' rooms, but the chief of staff of Brown's Club for Distinguished Gentlemen now stood in the center of the chambers used by the Marquis of Strickland and gazed about him in mystification.

It was most unsettling. The carpets were missing. Simply vanished, as if by magic. Where could they have gone?

If his lordship had asked to have them cleaned, Wilberforce would surely have been informed. His staff was in far too much terror of him to forget that little detail. Even then, the floor would have simply been covered by clean carpets from storage, not left bare and dusty.

Dust again! In his club!

It wasn't the girl's fault precisely, he supposed, but ever since the eye-catching Fiona had arrived, the male staff—which was to say all of them!—had been as inattentive as restless schoolboys in springtime!

All except for Bailiwick. Wilberforce's youngest, and largest, underfootman did everything that was required of him, but he did it with such a stoic expression of grim determination that Wilberforce would almost rather the lad did a bit of mooning once in a while instead.

Fiona was indeed a hard worker and the ladies had already expressed their appreciation of her way with hairdressing, so Wilberforce could not fault the girl herself.

But for a guest to have his room stripped of carpets and left bare! What was this club coming to?

However, when Wilberforce checked the other, empty rooms on the floor, he realized that it was more than simply a new distraction in the staff.

Stalking from the room with a hint of a scowl on his patrician features, Wilberforce determined to check every single room on every single floor.

Something had gone seriously amiss in his domain.

And nothing *ever* went amiss at Brown's!

In the attic, Laurel bit her lip as she put the key into the lock. Once out of her cell and into the main room of the attic, she quickly ran down the stairs and pressed her ear to the door that led to the top-story hall. She held her breath until her head started to hum but heard not a sound from the club.

Slowly she turned the latch and peeked through the crack in the door. Nothing to see but the long stretch of patterned carpet and some sort of vase on a small, gleaming table halfway down.

She let herself out of the attic stairwell and tiptoed to the top of the staircase. Gazing down, she saw not a sign of life.

It wasn't this floor she wanted to visit this time. No, this time she was after bigger game than viewing Melody's nursery.

Laurel was on her way to Jack's rooms.

He'd told her that he lived in the rooms just below

Melody's. Lifting her skirts a little with one hand, Laurel placed the other hand on the railing and trotted lightly down the stairs. When she found that the floor below was every bit as deserted as above, she finally allowed herself to breathe normally. Apparently mid-afternoon was nearly as good a time to go adventuring as the middle of the night! It almost seemed as though the customers of Brown's took naps, silly thought though that was!

There were a few doors to choose from on this floor, but the first was clearly deserted. Dust cloths covered the furniture, and there seemed to be a distinct lack of carpet. The next room was much the same except that it oddly seemed to be missing the mattress on the large carved bed frame.

"Jack, you thief," Laurel murmured.

She knew the third room was his the moment she stepped through the door. It wasn't that it was full of possessions, for it was nearly as stripped as the other rooms, including the lack of carpets. It was the way the air felt, as though charged with him, like the air before a storm.

She walked slowly around the perimeter of the room, keeping her gaze away from the big bed in the center, letting her fingertips trail lightly over his few possessions. He still liked to read, for books were the most numerous things. There were odd exotic bits—shells and strangely heavy foreign coins and carvings of animals she'd only seen in drawings. A giant triangular tooth mystified her, as did a globe of blown glass wound in what looked like fishing net. Rectangular ivory things, smooth to the touch, were carved and inked in odd, foreign symbols. Were they some form of money? Game pieces?

The things that he must have seen! All those far-away lands, all those fascinatingly different peoples! She was at once envious and curious.

Had he realized the gift of such freedom? Did he understand how much richer his existence was than hers, trapped in one house and then another?

Or was he too lost in the night to appreciate the privileges of his days?

Her fingers slipped lightly over several books on a shelf. Then one caught her eye. *Childe Harold.*

She'd given him a copy once, just for a joke. He'd laughed and told her he'd keep it forever. She hadn't believed a word of it.

Taking the book down, she flipped the cover open. There was an inscription there.

To Jack, from Bramble. If you'll stop moving your lips, you'll soon be reading much faster.

She'd thought herself so clever then. How dismaying it had been to realize that she was just an ignorant child after all.

Yet Jack had laughed aloud and tugged her braid and said, "I'll call on you if I need help with the big words, shall I?"

When she'd conceived of the notion of snooping into Jack's room, she'd had the idea of discovering his secrets, learning his motives, so that she could better manipulate him into letting her take Melody. The thought of some sort of blackmail had even flitted through her mind.

Yet now that she was here, breathing him in with every inhalation, all her thoughts seemed to be centered on remembering him the way he used to be.

He was so beautiful then. Laughing, teasing Jack with the warm dark eyes and smile that made her knees weak. She'd worn herself out with restless, girlish lust over him then. Her nights had lasted interminably as she'd tossed and turned, unable to sleep for thinking about his eyes, his smile, his large hands, and the way it felt when his fingertips had brushed her neck when he'd tugged at her braids.

She'd worn braids long after she'd meant to change to a more mature hairstyle, simply in the hopes that when she saw him next he would reach out to touch her again.

Inside, she'd been aware on some level that if Jack ever realized the maturity of her feelings for him—heavens, the way she imagined him naked and sweating!—or if he even became truly conscious of the fact that she was no longer a schoolgirl at all, he would cease his attentions at once.

He saw her as his future sister. They were friends, nothing more. She dared not tamper with that, either. She needed his friendship so desperately. With him, she could say every little thing that crossed her mind, no matter how odd. The strangest things could leave her lips and she would know that Jack would understand, though no one else would.

In addition, as long as she kept Amaryllis assured of her plain, serious nature, then her sister would have no reason to turn her vindictive gaze upon her. As it was, Amaryllis only mildly noted Jack's interest in her, making the occasional acid comment that it simply proved that he'd make an excellent father one day, he was that fond of silly children.

A small laugh broke from Laurel's lips at that memory. If Amaryllis had only known how prophetic her words would be!

When Jack came back from the war, however, he was no longer the teasing young man Laurel had adored so fervently. He was much more, although her sister didn't seem to see it.

Amaryllis had loved the uniform, not the man. She'd loved the idea of a secret engagement to a soldier. She loved the *idea* of Jack, although she had originally tried to attract Blakely, who was, of course, the better heir, only a breath away from becoming the marquis.

Jack had genially shoved his cousin aside in order to pay homage to Amaryllis, and she'd preened under his attention.

However, when Jack had returned without Blakely, his soul dark and broken, Amaryllis had already decided upon another matrimonial target. Jack wouldn't be able to marry for another year due to mourning, and Amaryllis wanted her perfect, privileged future *now*.

Furthermore, miserable Jack wasn't properly attentive. He was silent and brooding and prone to leave the room just when Amaryllis was waxing her most scathingly entertaining.

Laurel, however, had loved him more than ever. His pain had made her ache, her heart breaking for him. She'd followed him everywhere those weeks, unwilling to abandon him to his grief, unable to breach her own restraint. On the few occasions when they'd spoken, he'd been as kind as ever, but it was as if the light had gone out behind his eyes. She wanted to wrap her arms about him and hold him until his pain faded and he realized how much she loved him.

And for one night, she had.

Laurel wrapped her hands around one of the carved bedposts and leaned her forehead against the cool wood. That night—oh, sweet heaven, that night! Inhaling deeply with her eyes closed, Laurel breathed Jack into her.

The scent of him was a little sandalwood, a little horse and leather, a little freshly washed linen, and a deeper, more seductive note that was all man. All *Jack*.

She bent over his pillow and breathed. As if drawn down by magnetic force, she found herself lying on his bed, her face buried in the pillow, nearly weeping for the growing ache inside her.

Memories assaulted her, turning her limbs to liquid, wreaking chaos on her mind, seducing her body with memories of his big hands on her, of his hot mouth, of the way he moved inside her, the way he'd swallowed her cries with his mouth even as he'd taken her higher every time.

He'd taken her over and over again that night, until she'd scarcely been able to walk or sit the next day. They'd simply not been able to get enough of each other. She would roll off him or out from under him and begin to drift off in exhaustion, her limbs tangled with his, skin still slick with sweat and juices, her heart still pounding from yet another mind-scrambling orgasm. . . .

His hand would be resting on her belly, or her thigh. She could feel the heat of it searing her damp skin, awakening senses only just satiated.

She rolled onto her back and closed her eyes against

the draperies shirred above her, letting that night play again in her mind.

His hand, lax at first, would shift ever so slightly. Down, toward her pubic mound, or up, toward her sensitized breasts. She would roll into him, unable to resist that roving hand. . . .

Laurel's hand slid down her throat and into her bodice. She rolled her nipple gently, feeling it harden the way it had stiffened again and again at Jack's merest touch. She did the same to the other one, enjoying the sensation of her rigid nipples grazing the silk of the gown.

She was naked beneath Jack's bribe. She'd told herself that it was because she meant to sell the lovely underthings, so she'd removed them and packed them safely away in the wardrobe.

Now, as she tugged the priceless skirts high with her other hand, she wondered faintly if she'd meant to do this all along.

There were no accidents with her and Jack. They moved toward each other like orbiting planets, unable to resist the laws of nature.

The merest touch of his hand left her submissive to his every desire. His big, hot hands . . .

Her fingers stroked her labia, petting it soothingly. If Jack were here he would cup it with his wide palm, warming it with the heat of his own body until she swelled and dampened in his hand.

Dampness tickled her fingertips and she slid them gently between, stroking herself softly. How could one night have changed her so? How could one man's passion have awakened this side of her so easily?

She'd been shameless that night. He'd not even needed to speak to persuade her. He'd penetrated her body, her mouth—he'd even pressed her small breasts together and stroked himself between them until his juices had splashed hot on her neck. Anything he'd wanted to do to her, or have her do to him, she'd been his willing, eager partner, moving at a touch, responding to a sigh.

It had been more than lust. It had been trust, deep and abiding. She'd had no shame because she'd had no fear, not of Jack. Even now, even after he'd locked her away and stolen her clothing—even after he'd pinned her arms above her head and stolen an orgasm as easily as another man might have stolen a kiss!—she had no fear of him.

Her fear was of herself.

Turning her burning face into the Jack-scented pillow, kneading her rigid nipples with one hand, she rubbed her slippery fingertips over her clitoris until her knees spread wide of their own volition and her pelvis rocked uncontrollably and she rubbed faster and faster until she called out his name as she pulsated and came at her own hand.

When her shuddering and gasping had eased somewhat, she rolled facedown onto his pillow, her trembling legs sprawled wide. Loathing herself for needing such a release, furious at her body's wicked, slippery betrayal, she wept her broken heart into the feather-stuffed thing that was a poor replacement for the man she'd once thought she'd loved.

She wanted him still, as she always had.

No.

Bloody hell. She wanted him *more*.

Eighteen

In the shop just a brief stroll away from the bustling market, the three men stood silently as the apothecary, who recognized Melody immediately, confirmed that Mrs. Pruitt lived mere steps away in a block of shabby terraced houses that were no more than a single room wide.

As they turned the corner onto that block, Melody began to stare about her, eyes wide, finger placed for thinking. "I like this street!" As they neared the address, she pulled at Jack's hand, towing him down the walk.

At a set of grimy stone steps, long unscrubbed, she let go and ran happily up the steps to the old, stained door. "Nanny!" She patted the door with both palms. "Nanny!"

"This doesn't look good." Colin shot a worried glance at Jack. "The shutters are closed and the knocker has been removed."

Aidan ascended the steps and knocked briskly on the door. "Mrs. Pruitt?"

Melody tugged on the door handle, pushing and pulling with all her might. "Open the door, Uncle Aidan! I want to see Nanny!"

Colin edged closer to Jack. "The apothecary said she was quite ill. What if she's passed on?"

Jack gazed at the dark, shuttered house. The truth was trapped inside it, as locked away as if someone had written it into stone and flung it into the sea. The question of what had been done to Laurel and Melody would not be answered today.

Colin strode to the house next door and tapped the knocker briskly. After a moment, a maid came to the door. She was a poorly little thing, with barely the energy to peer up at him from under her oversized mobcap.

She had nothing to offer about the old woman. "She were there until a few weeks ago," the maid said with a shrug, picking at her teeth with a grimy fingernail. "Ain't seen her since."

"Is your mistress at home? She might be able to help us."

The girl wrinkled her nose and scratched her head. "Missus ain't here," she told him wearily. "She and the mister went to Covent Garden what for to see the play." Then her gaze narrowed, belated suspicion creeping in. "I ain't goin' to tell ye more than that, so be off w' ye!"

She shut the door in Colin's face. He grimaced at Aidan. "I ought to have let you flirt with her. You have a way with women with poor oral hygiene."

Aidan wasn't amused. "Shut it. Melody's going to fall apart when she learns that she won't see her Nanny after all."

He was quite correct. Melody could wail like a banshee when she felt it was necessary, and she clung to the door handle, even as Jack lifted her into his arms.

"Nanneeee! I want Nanneeee!"

Jack held her close and patted her soothingly, but

Melody had had a long, stimulating day and this disappointment wasn't going to go away anytime soon.

"Nanneeee!"

Despite the fact that his eardrums must have been aching, Jack held her close all the long walk back to where the carriage awaited on the other side of the market. By the time they climbed inside, she'd worn herself out with wailing and was reduced to quick, broken breathing punctuated by whimpers.

Jack kept her in his lap while Colin helped her blow her nose and wipe her tears. Aidan fidgeted helplessly.

"What are we going to do?" he burst out finally. "We don't know any more than we did yesterday!"

Jack tucked Melody's vastly cleaner face into his neck and began to whisper a story into her hair. It was a recounting of the time he'd found the conch shell he kept in his room. He'd found several while diving in a reef and supped on the creatures inside, roasting them on sticks over a fire he'd built on the beach. She went particularly quiet as he described digging the wiggling things out with his knife. Melody always did love a gory tale.

When he glanced up, Colin was giving him a mystified look and Aidan was frankly green.

"And I thought my stories were lurid," Colin said with a shudder.

"Must we discuss it?" Aidan clamped his jaw shut.

Jack shrugged his uninjured shoulder. "It succeeded."

It had indeed worked miraculously. Melody lay limp but mostly calm across his lap, her booted feet dangling and only the occasional hitch in her breath. Large blue eyes blinked slowly at them, her lashes still spiky with tears. Her finger wearily worked its way into her mouth as they watched. This time Jack let it be.

Aidan frowned. "One day she's going to pull that out and there won't be anything left of it."

Colin shrugged. "It could be worse. Pru told me that Evan used to keep his in his nose."

Jack looked at his friends. "Tomorrow. By ourselves."

"Indeed. We don't want to put her through that again." Colin let out a slow breath. "One more day then. Pru will be happy." Then he looked askance at the once pristine pink lace dress. It was filthy from the fallen apples, and somehow during their adventures a vast rip had appeared down one side of the overskirt. "Who do you think is going to kill me most thoroughly, Pru or Button?"

Aidan leaned back in his seat and closed his eyes. "I'll buy her another dress. I'll buy her ten. Button does love it when we overdo."

Button had already made a fortune from Jack earlier that day, but he said nothing. Patting Melody's back rhythmically, he gazed unseeing out the square little window at the passing city.

He hadn't visited Laurel yet today.

He wondered if she liked the gown.

After depositing a weary and overstimulated Melody into Pru's capable hands, the three men had made their way down to the kitchens in the hopes of cadging something tasty to make up for their missed dinner. Cook gazed at them all expressionlessly, then interrupted his evening routine to whip up three plates of roast with gravy and parsnips.

Colin, Aidan, and Jack tucked in right there at the

servants' table, unwilling to wait for someone to set the dining room.

Colin nudged Aidan. "The new girl is something spectacular, isn't she?"

Aidan only grunted. Colin laughed and shook his head. "Sorry, old man. I forgot you were most thoroughly saddled and bridled."

"As are you." Aidan turned his gaze on Colin sourly. "I am deeply in love with my stunningly beautiful wife. That being said, the new girl is most definitely something spectacular."

Jack, however, wasn't watching the darkly delicious Fiona flirt shamelessly with Samuel. His gaze was on the large underfootman lurking nearby. Bailiwick had a lovesick expression on his face and a single rosebud in his hand.

Colin and Aidan caught sight of Bailiwick as well. "Oh no," Colin breathed. "Don't do it, son."

Aidan folded his arms. "He's going to do it."

Colin winced. "I can't watch."

Jack, however, watched carefully. He might not yet be much of a human being, but he'd never lost his soldier's powers of observation. Bailiwick loved Fiona. Anyone with eyes could see that, except, apparently, Fiona herself.

Was everyone so? Was everyone blind when it came to their own hearts?

He'd been blind to Laurel's feelings for so long.

Could Laurel now be blind to his?

Could he?

Bailiwick walked slowly up behind Samuel and loomed silently. Fiona flicked him a single scornful glance, her dark eyes flashing, and then ignored him.

She even upped the level of her flirtation, leaning forward to murmur something and reaching out to run a fingertip down the front buttons of Samuel's livery waistcoat. Samuel flushed hotly and moved closer, saying something most likely entirely indecent and mutually pleasurable, by the glazed look in his eye.

Samuel was the only one startled when he was lifted bodily away from Fiona. With a yelp, the smaller man—who wasn't a small man at all, in any other company!—was flung away to stumble down the hall and make himself scarce for a few days.

Bailiwick then stood dumbly before Fiona, who was glaring at him with her fists on her mind-numbing hips and her black eyes flashing fury. Preparing to blast Bailiwick, she inhaled deeply. Every man in the room noticed her doing so.

"Damn." Colin gulped. "I think I'd better find Pru."

Aidan nodded. "She's probably with Madeleine. I'll go with you."

They pushed back from the table and hurried away from the combined threat of female fury and female wiles. It was a potent brew, but it left Jack cold. Oh, he could appreciate Fiona's tempestuous attractions, but they stirred him not at all. Why then did the merest thought of Laurel's dark hair tumbling over her lovely ivory skin make his knees weaken with need?

It was clear that Fiona had a similar effect on Bailiwick. He simply bowed his head when Fiona's fury overflowed. Her scathing words would have driven any sane man scuttling down the hall with his tail between his legs, but Bailiwick only stood there, openly offering himself as target.

When she slowed down enough for another impressive inhalation, Bailiwick spoke.

"I ain't like Samuel."

Then he thrust the single perfect rosebud into her hand and turned and walked away, his wide shoulders slumped.

As he passed Jack, Bailiwick turned his agonized gaze to meet Jack's.

"Them blokes only want one thing. She'll suss it out when I don't budge." The giant underfootman walked on, stoic determination evident in every step.

It was really too bad that Bailiwick didn't glance back over his shoulder, or he would have seen Fiona stamp her foot, swipe at her eyes, and then raise the rosebud tenderly to her lips.

Perhaps not so blind after all.

Buoyed by Bailiwick's stout, if wretched, resolve, Jack mounted the stairs into the attic. It was time to face Laurel, to face down his past, to make the confession of his sins. Secrets had caused this mess. It was time for all the secrets to be brought out into the daylight. If the price was too high, at least Jack would suffer in a state of honesty.

It was the best he had to offer her right now. His secret owed her. It had cost her her bright future. It had consumed every day and night that he should have spent at her side for the past few years. She should know why he had ruined her life.

When he entered, Laurel was sitting in a chair by the little table, smoothing tissue paper with her hands. It was an odd practice. Jack couldn't understand why she bothered.

When he asked her, she gazed up at him with such a glare of frustration that he nearly took a step backward.

"I," she said slowly, as if to an idiot, "have nothing better to do."

Ah. Right.

Then he saw that she wore his gift. The color was quite nice on her, very nearly the color of her eyes. The bodice was a bit tight, but like most men, Jack rather thought all gowns should be made thus. "You look . . ."

Lovely. Stunning. Desirable. His throat went dry. He had the most dishonorable thought that he might just keep her locked up here forever, his to do with as he wished.

And oh, the things I wish!

She lifted a brow and waited.

He choked. "Clean."

Her blue eyes widened. "Thank you. So kind of you to notice." She turned back to her paper smoothing, the implication being that even that tedious activity was more diverting than his conversation.

He had no argument there. Turning abruptly in frustration with himself, he paced the room for a moment. It didn't take long. Soon he was back, gazing over her shoulder at her smoothing, soothing hands.

It was a charming view, actually. She'd pinned her long hair up so nothing foiled his view down her neck and into her bodice. She went still. "Do you see anything you fancy?"

"Yes." He answered truthfully, his mouth not quite connected properly to his thoughts. Her breasts were full and soft—rounder than they'd been years ago, heavy and mature. The shadow between them seemed like the entrance to heaven.

I held them in my hands, in my mouth. I—

Then he heard the echo of his own reply. "I mean . . . no."

"How devastating for me," she said flatly.

Her sarcasm did not sting him, for he realized that she was at last speaking *to* him. Furthermore, her bottomless fury was quite . . . relaxing. Much preferable to the constant worried gazes and careful, coaxing tones of his friends, who treated him rather like the family idiot. An idiot who possibly carried knives. And explosives.

Laurel didn't treat him as if she worried he was simply trying to decide how to die. She treated him as if she rather wished he would make up his mind and get it over with.

How refreshing.

"I have to tell you . . . something."

She flicked him an indifferent glance. "Right now? I'm terribly busy, you know."

If she'd been wearing her braids and if he'd been the same man he once was, he would have given her braid a tug for such cheek. Blinking, he was surprised that he could even remember being that man. It was rather encouraging.

The man he was now opened his mouth and began. "I never told you . . . about what happened to Blakely."

She kept on smoothing. "I know about Blakely. He died in battle."

"No," Jack said simply. "He didn't."

Her hands stilled. He rather thought she was listening quite hard, but she only said, "Oh?" as if she didn't much care if he continued.

How simple it was to confess before her loathing.

After all, she could scarcely think worse of him than she did now, could she?

He sat upon the bed, his hands loose in his lap, and he told her everything.

Nineteen

The words came slowly, piecing together in Jack's mind as if trying to reassemble a note torn to shreds. Yet they did come, in the end, for she made no response, asked no questions. Her hands continued to smooth paper, slowly passing over and over it, the sound like the sea on a beach, rhythmic and soothing.

"My cousin was not . . . suited to war. It was not so bad when we were merely foot soldiers. We gambled and drank and marched and passed the time with the other men. Blakely enjoyed being an ordinary man. Inevitably, however, whispers of his rank and wealth leaked out to the officers. Perhaps it was Blakely himself. He was ever loose tongued when imbibing. What better way to curry favor with the future Marquis of Strickland than to promote him quickly? For motives of political power, Blakely was put in command of the troops before he was ready."

Jack was still for a long moment. "Blakely would never have been ready."

The room was so quiet, so still but for the soothing sound of waves. Jack wanted to lie back on the bed and rest in this den of peace, but he would only bring his nightmares with him into sleep.

He did not think Laurel would be inclined to save

him from himself this time. Remembering his mission, he went on. "He was not a coward, my cousin, but he was of a foolish temperament. He was . . . inclined to rush in without thinking. There is no place for a man like that in command."

He raised his hands to his face, pressing against his eyes, though he'd long ago shed the last of his tears. His eyes were hot and dry. He pulled his hands away from his face and looked at them, as ever surprised to find them clean of blood.

"His men were loyal. I should know. I was one of them. We followed him, believed in him, advised him as well as we might. Blakely did not mean to lead us all into the valley of death. He simply couldn't see the gaping maw of our fate before us, though others of us plainly did."

He let out a sigh, a long breath, like releasing a dark spirit. Then he said the words: "So we mutinied."

He closed his eyes and listened to the slide of her palm across the paper. He followed it, clung to it, let his breathing match it. He fancied it might go on forever, like the sea itself, unchanging and eternal. For the rest of his life, he could come to this room and hear the peaceful, rhythmic sound of Laurel's hands.

"Because of his orders, we were cut off. The French were all around us. We hid like animals in the rocks of the mountains and waited for our commander to save us. He would not, or could not. I still do not know.

"I took the lead. I hoped to somehow salvage Blakely's honor, to declare him ill and unable to command due to circumstances beyond his control. He would have none of it. He said I betrayed him. I could have saved him, just as I saved all the others, but Blakely would not retreat. He had some notion that it would be cowardly. Better to die in error than to live to fight another day."

The waves went on. Jack wanted to close his eyes and sail away on those waves, to be stroked by those relentless hands, to sleep cradled on that beautiful bosom.

To wake next to that beautiful figure and roll her beneath him, sleepy and soft, willing and damp.

The willing part might be a problem, once she knew the truth.

"In the end, I left Blakely in order to lead the others back through the bloody field of battle to the main column of the British Army. We crept like rats in the dark, without pride or bravery. It was the only way to bring them back alive."

The room remained quiet. The ceiling did not crash down upon his head. The deepest secret in his life was being revealed, and not only was the world not ending, but also Laurel had not even ceased in her task.

Perhaps things could go on as before. Perhaps if he told the truth, just once, then the tangle of his thoughts would ease and the words in his mind would line up neatly and obediently behind his lips.

"I left him behind." He inhaled, then let out a slow breath. "I killed him."

The sound of the paper waves ceased. He opened his eyes to see that Laurel had turned to gaze at him. "The French killed him," she said softly. "He went to war. He did not have to go. You did not cause his death."

He gazed into the clarity of her sky blue eyes. At sea, a sky like that meant that a man could sail forever.

"I read once that despair . . . is when you are no longer able to sustain, even for the briefest moment, the notion that all will be well in the end."

She rested her hands in the skirt of her gown and blinked at him solemnly. "Yes. That is precisely the definition."

Sweet, serious Laurel, seeker of words. How he wished she would give him the right ones.

"The reason I despaired, the secret that has turned me into . . . ," he waved a hand over himself, "this, is . . . I killed my cousin with my own hands."

He saw the denial in her eyes and went on before she could interrupt him again. "It was after the retreat, you see. Once I had the men, at least, most of the men, safely back with the Army, the next morning I broke ranks to go back into the battle, to find Blakely and persuade him to retreat."

The next part—that would be the hardest. That would be the moment when her clean blue gaze would flinch from his, when she would turn her face away, when she would no longer listen, no longer speak.

She would turn away from him. The entire world would, if they knew.

So why was he telling her? Why was he cracking himself open like an egg to let her gaze at his foul and rotten center?

Because perhaps if she understood how many pieces he'd been in, she might realize . . . what, that he'd not been responsible for his actions toward her? *Coward.*

No, what he truly wanted her to know was that it had all been his fault. He ought not to have taken the comfort she so innocently offered him. He ought not to have sheltered in her arms and her body. He was a murderer, not a gentleman. He'd been a scoundrel to involve her, an irresponsible fool.

And she . . . she'd been an angel.

Now the angel would finally see the devil in him.

He kept his gaze locked on hers. He must see her response. He owed it to Blakely to pay for his crime with her repugnance.

"I found Blakely. And when I found him, I killed him."

Laurel sat with her hands dropped serenely in her lap, showing no sign of the alarm that shot through her. *Not killed, surely. Did not save, perhaps.*

He gazed at her with all tension washed from his expression. "You are thinking that I take the blame where it is not due. You are thinking that Blakely died from a French bullet, or a battleground disease, or a fall from a horse—but I tell you he did not."

He held out his hands again as if to show her. They were large hands, finely shaped and a little callused from his life on board ship.

"I see no blood on your hands," she said evenly, though fear chilled her belly. He seemed to truly believe it.

He made fists, then relaxed them, letting his hands drop to his knees. "There is no blood when you wrap your hands about someone's throat and strangle the life out of them."

Shock echoed through her, bouncing around as if she were naught but an empty shell. It could not be. He could never, ever—

"Strangle?" She could scarcely choke out the word. It was like a stone in her throat.

"It was surprisingly easy." Jack's gaze went far away for a moment. "His legs were gone. There was nothing to save, they were so shattered by cannon fire. He would have spent his life as a helpless invalid, being carried from room to room by servants like an infant, never to ride or hunt or even stride around his estate on a fine day."

Laurel drew back. "Men live without their legs. A rich man could afford the help." It was too awful to contemplate, what Jack claimed to have done. Such an awful, wicked waste. "There is so much to offer even a man who cannot walk. What of music, and books, and—?"

Jack shook his head slowly. "You speak of a life of the mind, a life such as you might make for yourself. You have the imagination to see a different future. Blakely was not that sort of man. To him, his life was over. Even should he have survived surgery and infection, he had already lost everything he loved most." Jack's gaze focused on hers, as if remembering that she was there. "I've never told anyone that I'm a murderer before."

Laurel didn't move, didn't react, didn't even blink, but inside she was raging against the calm self-loathing she saw in his eyes.

Mutiny and murder. She'd wanted a way to blackmail him. Now she had one. Of course, the fact that her heart ached for him, that she nearly had to press her two hands to her bosom to keep it from breaking in half at what he'd been forced to do, well, that had nothing to do with anything. That was simply the sort of thing that happened in captivity. After a time, one stopped knowing where one ended and one's captor began.

Still, the fury that always seemed to live just beneath her skin now had a target. "Blakely was an idiot."

"Oh yes." Jack almost smiled. "Everyone thought so, even before he decided to go to war."

"A selfish idiot to boot." She gazed at Jack, seeing it as if it were enacted before her eyes. "He forced you to do it, didn't he?"

Jack's brows lifted. "It was my decision."

"Ha!" she barked rudely. "Selfish, silly man, too concerned with himself to realize what it would do to you if you respected his wishes. He begged, no doubt. Told you that if you hadn't defied him, it never would have happened. Made you feel responsible, and then took the coward's way out!"

"He did not suicide. I killed him."

"No, he was too cowardly even to die at his own hand. I imagine there were weapons lying all around him, like leaves in the fall. Did he take one up to use on himself?"

Jack blinked. "It was my responsibility. He was like my brother. When he chose to disobey his orders and advance, I should have stopped him."

"I knew it!" She sprang to her feet and began to pace. "It was his responsibility to refuse command if he was too stupid to do it well! It was his responsibility to listen to wiser heads in battle! It was his responsibility to get his men to safety. Instead, you had to do it all for him, even down to his own suicide." She folded her arms. "Bloody weakling!"

Jack gazed at her, startled. "I—" Then he shook his head. "It does not change the fact that I took his life. It does not wash away the memory of the way it felt when the life left his body under my choking hold."

She could not bear it. In an instant she was across the room, kneeling at his feet. *"No."* She took his hands in hers. "I *know* these hands. These are not the hands of a killer."

He went very still at her touch. "You should stay away from me. My hands have already done things to you they should not have done." He swallowed. "I don't think I am quite . . . civilized anymore," he said hoarsely.

She saw a vein throb in his neck. Her own heart sped. His hands . . . his large, skilled, uncivilized hands. Suddenly she realized how small she was at his feet. Even sitting, he towered over her, his wide shoulders blocking the slanting late-afternoon light. So powerful a man, yet his hands shook slightly in hers.

Too close. Too dangerous. Hot, wet wanting flared between her thighs. Yet she dared not move, dared not stir him one way or the other—or herself.

The breathless moment hung like a Chinese rocket in the sky. The explosion was imminent.

Nervously she licked her lips, a quick dart of her tongue.

In that fraction of an instant he was upon her.

Twenty

Jack pushed Laurel down to the carpet and rolled onto her. He never released her hands, only kept them trapped in his. He spread them wide on the floor, pinning her. His mouth came down onto hers, desperate, starving, and most delightfully uncivilized.

Laurel fought him, writhing and bucking beneath his heavy weight. She wasn't sure why, for she wanted it as badly as he did, except that he frightened her a little.

Or perhaps you frighten yourself?

Oh yes. She terrified herself. All that fury, all that dark loss and pain she carried within her, became something else when this man touched her. Rage turned to passion in a blink, fury into lust. She wanted to take out her pain and her betrayal upon his body with her mouth and her hands and the heavy, damp, aching need between her legs.

I don't think I am quite civilized anymore, either.

He moved against her, though they lay fully clothed. She could feel him, thick and rigid, pressing between her thighs, into the wet, aching core of her. Layers of cloth did nothing to stop the heat of him from radiating into her as he ground his erection into her. He matched the rhythm of his thrusts with the rhythm of his tongue deep into her mouth.

Taste, heat, and the bondage of her hands drove her mad. She kissed him back, moaning into his mouth, panting, whimpering as the swell of his erection rubbed her throbbing clitoris into fully engorged excitement.

Every time he touched her, it was like that night all over again. The world as she knew it went away and they were lost in a maelstrom of violent lust and aching need and, threading through it all, the most tender caring. How could something be part healing, part giving, and part wild, grief-stricken retaliation?

Unless it wasn't him whom she retaliated against. Could it be the two of them, together, taking vengeance on the world itself, refusing to lie down and die beneath its cruelty? With their bodies and their mouths and their hot, roaming hands, did they cry out, *We live!*?

Then came the voice in her mind: *If you lie with him he might let you take Melody.*

If I lie with him, I might never come up for air again.

The hell of it was, she couldn't at that moment decide if that was good or bad.

She felt herself sliding away, falling into him, forgetting why she'd come here, why she'd stayed. Pulling her mouth from his with a gasp, she turned her face away. "No! Stop!"

He went very still on her. After a breath, she looked back to see that he gazed down at her with eyes nearly black with lust and need. She swallowed. "Let me go?" Her voice was a husky whisper. She tried again, this time remembering to add some conviction: "Let me go!"

"You want this." There was a hardness in his face and she saw a glimpse of the soldier. She could almost see the smoke of the battlefield wreathing within his eyes. "I can feel you, hot and wet against me." He pressed into her again. "You want me inside you."

She let out a breath that was almost a moan as another rush of damp lust proved him quite right.

No. That was the word she struggled to recall. "No."

He went still once more, but he did not release her. "I can feel how wet you are. I can feel you throb against me. I could be thrusting inside you right now. You could be screaming your orgasm into my mouth like you did yesterday and no one would hear a thing."

Because she was in a cell. Because she was his prisoner, pinned to the floor, overpowered and vulnerable. Heaven save her, but the thought excited her further.

He wanted her. She was his prisoner and he wanted her *nonetheless*. That was the darkness inside him, the wild lawlessness given him by battle. That wildness drew her, excited her, made her want to hike her skirts and let him take her on the floor like a Viking prize. That damaged edge of him was what had drawn her to his room in the middle of the night once. It was what made her climb into his bed to soothe him. She'd known where it would lead from the moment she'd touched the latch on his door. She'd known that the spark that had always lain between them would flare into a bonfire in the dark.

She'd taken *him* that night.

And she could take him now. She was no prisoner in this house. She was a spy.

He doesn't know that. He thinks you are his captive. Now his blood is hot and he wants you nonetheless. Afterward, when his head is clear, he will think he has committed a crime, another crime, and he will loathe himself to destruction once again.

Because she couldn't allow that, because she was no Blakely, she fought down the thudding runaway horse of her desire and shook her head. "Let me go, Jack."

Black need flashed rebellious in his eyes for an instant, setting off an answering wicked rush of depraved hope within her hungry body. Then his hands loosened about hers and he rolled off her.

She sat up, rubbing at her hands and pushing her skirts down, tucking her feet modestly to one side. When she looked at him, he was sitting half turned away, one hand over his face.

"My apologies," he said tightly.

She could feel the battle raging within him still. His need was so much more than lust, so much more than simple loneliness and loss. He was a strange, complicated man, full of odd strength and not a few flaws. Iron turned to steel upon the anvil of battle, gleaming brightly beneath the soot and blood, he was a beautiful lean sword of a man.

The right woman could wield such a man and keep him by her side forever, all the stronger for him.

That would not be me. I am too cracked and badly glued. I could never hold all of him.

Recalling the impulse to fall into him and never emerge, she shuddered. *I am not strong enough. He would take me over. He would own me.*

She could not allow that. She'd fought so hard to keep herself before and she'd lost. Another such loss as that would end her.

Taking a deep breath, she stood. There was a mark of dampness soaking the front of her skirt, ruining the fine silk, proof of her lust for him. She slipped Lementeur's beautiful shawl quickly over her shoulders, letting the length fall down the front of her gown to hide the stain. Only then did she turn back to see that Jack was also standing, fastening his surcoat. The cut of it did not completely hide where he'd pressed into her. Nor did it conceal the thick bulge of his persistent erection.

After the first glance, she carefully kept her gaze on his. He met her eyes, but his were hooded and unreadable in the early-evening gloom.

Laurel lifted her chin. "I need candles."

He said nothing for a long moment. The gloom increased, turning him into a silhouette against the bluish windowpanes.

When he spoke, his voice was a growl. "Will you agree to abandon your plan to flee London with Melody?"

"Would you believe me if I said yes?"

"I would."

"I could say yes and then run with her when you let me go."

She saw him nod.

"You could. I would find you." Then his head tilted a little. She wished she could see his face. "But you do not lie, Laurel."

She folded her arms. She sometimes forgot that he saw into her as easily as she saw into him. "The truth, then? No, I do not agree. I will have my daughter, Jack."

His fingers slipped into his waistcoat pocket and withdrew the key. With a start, Laurel recalled her own key, still tied about her neck, entirely forgotten within the bodice that she'd nearly allowed him to rip from her body. It was all she could do not to clutch at it protectively.

"I regret this, but I must leave you to think on it

another night." He turned to leave, but just before he stepped through the door he turned back, his face slightly averted.

"Thank you," he said quietly. "You were ever a good listener."

Then he was gone, the *clunk* of the lock tumblers the last sound in her silent cell.

When Jack returned down the main club level—by way of his room to change his trousers, of course—he hesitated outside the old club room, which had transformed from a masculine den of peace to a great scrambling, toy-filled, occasionally pet-infested family parlor.

They would want to know where he'd disappeared to. Oh, they wouldn't ask out loud, but Colin and Aidan would give that slow assessing gaze they always did, as if they were gauging his current tendency toward madness.

And who could blame them? You almost assaulted Laurel against her will.

Yet he hadn't. He was not quite the scoundrel he'd thought himself, it seemed. The civilized man had won out. It was a small victory, but he would take it.

He only wished he didn't have to endure their questioning gazes every time he walked into a room. Taking a breath, he put his hand on the latch and pushed the great oak doors open—

To find that no one so much as noticed his entry. They were all, Colin, Pru, Aidan, Madeleine, Evan, and all the old goats of the club, clustered around something at the far end of the room.

"How about a lemon seedcake, love?" Jack heard Colin plead. "Would you like a nice lemon seedcake?"

Jack raised his eyebrows when he saw Pru punch her husband in the arm. "Cook didn't bake any today," she hissed at him.

Colin shrugged. "Sorry," he muttered back. "I panicked."

Now Jack heard it, the rapid hitching breath of a child who had cried herself into a frenzy. "I-I-I-want Nanneee!"

Urgently he pushed his way into the crowd. It required picking up Lord Aldrich by the elbows to set him aside and frankly unwrapping Madeleine's shielding arms with gentle but implacable force, but at last Jack found his daughter at the eye of the storm.

He knelt before her. Melody, whose face was blotchy and tearstained and not a little snotty, wailed and threw her arms about his neck. "I—I want Nanneee!"

Enfolding Melody to his heart, he stood. Without a word he turned and walked away from the milling crowd of concern. They allowed it, for Melody had gone instantly quiet in his arms.

Pru, as always, was not as tentative as the others around him. "Where is he taking her?"

Jack heard Colin reassure her as he strode from the room with his daughter.

"Don't worry, my love. Jack has always been decisive in a crisis."

That, at the very least, was true.

Blakely had known that. *You had to do it all for him, even down to his own suicide.*

Astonishing, how those fierce words had pierced Jack's gray world with a single shimmering beam of insight. They cast new shading on everything he'd thought about himself in the last four years.

As usual, Laurel saw it all.

Now his daughter was in need. He'd been selfish. He'd kept Laurel to himself long enough.

Carrying his tiny child cradled to his chest, he climbed flight after flight of stairs at a trot. He knew what Melody needed. There was only one person who could fill the hole that Melody had been reminded of today.

What Melody needed wasn't her old Nanny or even a mob of loving semi-relatives. What Melody needed was her mother.

Twenty-one

Since she had no candles in her attic cell and no reason to remain awake anyway, Laurel had used the last blue moments of twilight to prepare for bed. After a quick wash in the washbowl, she cleaned her teeth with the corner of a handkerchief—an old one, of course, not one of the luxurious wispy ones from Lementeur!—and donned the fine lawn chemise. She was just feeling her way through her dark room to her bed when she heard the lock turn in her cell door.

Turning, she was momentarily blinded by the light of a candle held high. Then, holding her hand up to shield her enlarged pupils, she peered past it. "Jack?" Had she finally caught him improving her room? He carried something. . . .

"Yes." He stepped into the room and closed the door behind him. "I have someone you should meet."

That's when Laurel's eyes adjusted and she realized that small parcel in Jack's arms was not a thing but a small and sniffling person. Laurel's heart thumped to see them together, here, right before her. She'd known Melody resembled her, but it surprised her to see that her daughter also resembled Jack. It was less obvious, but she had her papa's stubborn chin and slant of cheekbone tucked beneath her chubby baby face.

Look what we made, Jack. Isn't she beautiful?

Laurel said nothing, however, waiting. Did Jack know of Melody's visits?

He knelt and put Melody on her little booted feet. "Lady Melody, I would like to introduce you to your mama."

No, he didn't know. This was simply Jack, bringing her what she'd come here for, bringing her and her daughter together at last. Laurel bit back a damp laugh. Timing had never been Jack's strong point. "Hello, Melody."

Melody let out a great, hitching breath. "Mama?"

Laurel melted and held out her arms. Melody ran into them and wound her sticky little arms about Laurel's neck. "Hello, my Melody," Laurel whispered. "Did you have a rough day?"

Melody puddled into exhausted tears into Laurel's neck. Pulling her daughter close, Laurel stood and carried her to the nearest chair. Laurel cradled her baby in her lap, rocking Melody's body slowly back and forth as though she'd done it all her life. Jack followed and put the candlestick on the table next to them. Laurel looked up at him. "Are you wondering why she came directly to me?"

"No. She ran right to me the first time she met me."

Laurel smiled and closed her eyes. "Don't we all?" she murmured, too low for him to hear. The feeling of her baby in her arms, needing her, clinging to her, rang a bell so far down inside Laurel that she feared she might turn inside out from the eruption of love in her heart. Her own eyes dampened as she opened them to gaze up at Jack. "Thank you," she whispered.

He shook his head. "Don't thank me. I ought to have

let you see her the first moment you came to the door."
He rubbed a hand across his face. "Just . . . don't . . .
Please try not to hate me when I lock your door again."

Laurel's arms tightened about Melody. "No, don't
take her, not yet!"

Jack let out a breath. "No. She needs you tonight. I
thought she might sleep here, with you."

Joy bloomed in Laurel. "All night?" She looked down
at Melody and pushed her hair back from her damp
little forehead. "Do you hear that, my Melody? Would
you like to sleep here with me tonight?"

Melody removed her finger from her mouth and
looked at Jack, her brow scrunched with worry. "What
about the Badman?"

Jack knelt down to look into Melody's face. "The
Badman is dead. Wilberforce killed him."

Melody blinked. "Promise?"

Jack took her chubby little hand in his huge one.
Laurel's heart melted to see that their thumbs were exactly the same shape, large next to tiny.

"Melody, I vow to you upon my honor that the Badman is dead. He was shot, dropped off the roof, and
then they buried him in the ground. No one has ever
been as dead as the Badman is dead."

Laurel blinked. This was all very . . . graphic. Perhaps the Badman was not the unreal character she'd
imagined. She frowned at Jack and mouthed a question. *Who?*

Jack gave his head a quick shake. *Later.*

"I am very fond of information," she said aloud in a
conversational tone. "I dearly love to know things. Especially things about people. Especially people I'm
fond of."

Jack slid her a warning glance. "There's a book I shall lend you. A story about a lady and the wolf who shadowed her."

Melody nodded. "*My Lady's Shadow,*" she chimed in with scarcely a hiccup of remaining hysterics. "Uncle Colin wrote it for me."

"Oh, that helps," Laurel replied with only the tiniest caustic hint in her tone. "Since I know precisely who Uncle Colin is." Her pointed glance at Jack underlined her irony.

Then she looked back down at Melody. "So will you stay with me, my Melody?"

Melody gave one last massive sniffle, then snuggled into Laurel's body happily. "Can Gordy Ann stay, too?"

"Of course."

"Gordy Ann is her doll. Sort of a doll." Jack rubbed his chin as he gazed down at the frankly nasty wad of knotted linen currently residing in Melody's armpit. "Gordy Ann is a cravat. It's a long story."

"Another story!" Laurel squeezed Melody. "I have so much catching up to do!" Then she turned to Jack, her lips forming a question. She halted as she gazed at him, kneeling so close, his handsome face somber. He was looking at the two of them together. Laurel knew what he was thinking, for she'd just been thinking it a few moments ago. *How can I keep them apart?*

This man had abandoned her, and when she'd found him again he'd locked her up. And yet he'd given her back her daughter tonight. Love and hate fought a tangled battle within her, and she wasn't sure sometimes which was which.

Then she remembered what she'd wanted to ask him. "Won't—" *Careful.* She'd almost said *Maddie and Pru!*

"Won't people wonder where she's gotten to?"

He blinked at her in bland surprise. "I will not be questioned."

She frowned. "Really?"

Something wry tweaked a corner of his mouth. "It does little good to question someone who never speaks."

She raised a brow. "You? I cannot shut you up."

Melody nodded. "Papa talks to me, too." She played with the thick braid of Laurel's hair that hung over one shoulder. "Just me and Mama," she said sleepily.

Jack stood. "I'll leave you and Mama to your bed," he told Melody. "Good night, Lady Melody. Good night, Laurel."

He turned and left so silently that Laurel began to understand how it was that he could rearrange her room every night without her knowing. She smiled down at Melody, whose sleepy eyes had turned to gleaming little slits in the candlelight. Her bottom lip pooched out and there was a single teardrop still glistening on one round little cheek. Laurel kissed it off.

Tonight Jack had made her chamber most beautiful of all!

Laurel opened her eyes in the dark room and blinked, wondering why she'd woken. There was even more moonlight tonight. Perhaps it was too bright to sleep?

Then soft childish snores came from the pillow beside her. Oh yes. She was not alone. Smiling, she reached out to stroke the mussed curls of her tiny daughter.

Melody slept in a ball, her chubby cheeks softly puffy with sleep, her thick dark lashes peaceful on those cheeks. So quiet and sweet after the bright chatter and tearstained outburst of the day. She was such a beautiful child.

My child. My Melody.

Joy coursed through Laurel yet again. She rather thought it would strike her like for this for the rest of her life, this stunned and blissful recollection that all she'd thought was lost was hers at last.

Melody snuffled, then stuck a filthy corner of her decrepit doll into her mouth. Laurel withdrew it gently. Pooching her lower lip out, stubborn even in sleep, Melody stuck the doll back in.

"Good luck with that."

Laurel lifted her head quickly, looking past Melody's sleeping form to find the source of that deep murmur.

A large upholstered wingback chair had appeared in her chamber. It was turned to face out the large window. She could now see long legs clad in snug fawn breeches extending from the chair, and a dark-sleeved arm draped over the armrest. She stared at the broad, shapely hand that dangled open and relaxed from that armrest. It fascinated her, for it was the first time she'd seen any part of Jack at rest.

At least, it was the first time since that unforgettable night.

Images flashed across her reluctant mind, as dazzling and fresh as ever. Some memories burned too hot to ever fade.

Jack, lost and confused in the darkness, gasping out the details of his nightmare that wasn't a nightmare but his own tortured reality. Jack, gentle and giving, reaching for her in the dark. That hand, doing things—wicked, wonderful things!—to her body that her innocent imagination could have never conceived of. Jack, above her, inside her, thrusting gently, naked and gleaming with sweat, straining to control his passion in order not to hurt her.

He would never harm her. Ever.

So finding him sitting in the dark wasn't so much alarming as it was anomalous. Why was he here? With his view restricted to the window by the wingback chair, he clearly wasn't doing anything eerie like watching her sleep.

Her pride bridled slightly. Why wasn't he watching her sleep?

She sat up. "Why are you here?" she whispered sharply. "Do you not even trust me to watch over her for one night?"

The hand tightened slowly over the end of the armrest and he slowly, wearily gained his feet. As he stood, she drew back, pulling the covers protectively over her bosom. Silly, since he'd seen her bosom before—but she was *not* going to think about that! Still, it made her feel less vulnerable.

Then he turned toward her and her breath caught at the hollowed grief caught in the moonlight glinting off the planes of his handsome face. A sharp ache bloomed in her heart to see it.

"What is it?" she whispered, forgetting her wariness for a moment. "Tell me."

"I . . ." He passed a hand over his face. "I cannot . . . I do not dare sleep."

The nightmares. The dreams that were not dreams but memories. On impulse, her hand lifted, reaching out to him. She gazed at that hand in alarm. What was she doing?

He doesn't deserve to suffer alone in those horrible memories.

His gaze locked onto her hand. He stared uncomprehendingly, as if he didn't dare believe it was real. He didn't make a move toward her, which only made her open her hand and gesture him closer.

I don't want him closer.

I cannot bear to see him so terribly alone.

He took a single step, halting when a board creaked beneath his weight. He was like a wary wild thing, a strong but gentle creature, unsure of his welcome.

She kept her hand out, confidently now. She had nothing to lose by comforting him. A new gratitude had grown in her this evening. He'd given her Melody tonight. He'd kept Melody safe and he'd sought Melody's mother in good faith. It still stung that he'd thought himself in bed with Amaryllis, yet Laurel had to admit that the burn had become more of a twinge over the last days.

Jack gazed down at that slim white hand, glowing almost ghostly in the moonlit room. It was a small, frail thing, a weak and useless weapon in his darkened, bloodied world.

It was a lifeline. It was his last and best hope.

His hand was moving.

Astonished, he watched his own flesh reaching across the space, across the void, across years of emptiness and black despair, reaching out—

Her gentle fingers wrapped around his, warmth to his chilled skin, softly at first, only touching, only holding.

Then she began to pull.

She towed him in, step by halting step, until his knees

touched the bed. Then she released his hand and patted the mattress on his side of Melody's sleeping form. Like a sleepwalker himself, he lowered his body onto the mattress, lying atop the covers, and slowly let his head rest upon the unused half of Melody's pillow.

Laurel gazed solemnly at him and then tucked her own dark hair behind her ear as she considered him. "You don't have to sleep," she said softly. "But you should rest."

Then she lay back down, curling herself around Melody and closing her eyes.

To Jack, the attic had swiftly become a secret little world where time and history did not seem to weigh so heavily upon him. With Laurel, he was as alive as he was with Melody. He could speak and think and feel as he had not been capable of for years. When he was with her, he could breathe.

When I'm with her, I am real.

If he could only, somehow, win back Laurel's trust. He hardly dared think it, but the idea would not leave him. It shimmered on his horizon like a sunrise long awaited. Dangling just out of his grasp was a future of such warm and sweet possibility, a future where he could actually have everything he'd ever dreamed of.

Jack lay quietly for a long time, listening to Laurel's breathing go from awake and careful to sleeping. He would not sleep. He wouldn't want to subject Laurel and Melody to his nightmares. That was fine, however. He didn't need to sleep.

And yet he did. Deeply, effortlessly, and without a single dream.

Twenty-two

"Jack? Jack, slow down! I want to walk with you!"

Laurel picked up her skirts and ran down the lane to where Jack had halted to wait for her. She was panting by the time she came even with him, but she brushed her hair back out of her face and smiled up at him. Had he noticed that she wore her hair loose, not braided? Did he realize that her bust had grown considerably and her new gowns showed it off admirably? Was he even aware that while he'd been away at war her seventeenth birthday had come and gone and that she was more than ready to be courted, but only by him?

"Do you not wish to go shooting with Papa and the others?"

Jack didn't meet her gaze. "I don't care to hear the rifles."

"Oh. I'm not fond of the sound myself." Laurel fell into step with him, taking a little skip now and then to match his long-legged stride. Occasionally she would sneak a glance up into his narrow face. He was so drawn and thin now. He'd only recently come back to England, and although Mama had been a bit too boisterous in her urgings to "eat up, my lord; you're wasting away," Laurel thought he looked like a sad angel.

They'd walked together before, but those moments had been full of laughter and teasing. Jack had been fond of threatening her with insects of various types, while she had discovered that he truly had no desire to ever be within a mile of a spider. They had spoken of books and plays and music. Laurel confessed her desire to attend the opera in Covent Garden. Jack confessed that he'd found it most relaxing and sure to help one catch up on one's sleep.

Now they walked in silence, as if they each walked alone, although Jack did eventually shorten his stride for her benefit.

When they came to the footbridge that crossed the river, they saw that a recent storm flood had washed out several of the center planks. Jack instantly turned back, but Laurel had tried for several days to gain his notice and wasn't about to let their walk end so soon.

"Oh, do come on, Jack. It isn't all that bad. We can just jump across the missing ones."

She started without him, knowing that he would follow rather than leave her in a risky situation. When she gained the center of the footbridge, she realized that it was indeed worse than she'd thought. A good six feet of planks were missing, leaving a gap crossed only by the narrow long beams. Those were no more than a few inches across and green with moss and decay.

"Well, that explains why the nails didn't hold," Laurel said cheerfully. "I'll cross first, shall I?"

Danger seemed to be the secret for rousing Jack from his benumbed state, for he grabbed her hand urgently. "It isn't safe, Bramble! Don't try it."

Laurel nearly closed her eyes in the pleasure of his hand on hers and of hearing her beloved nickname from his lips. He hadn't called her that once since he'd come back. Encouraged by her progress, she flashed him a mischievous smile. "Catch me if you can!"

The first few steps of her crossing went surprisingly well. Then she began to teeter slightly, but she stepped boldly on. Nearly there. It wasn't until she turned to flash a victorious smile at Jack that she lost her balance, only two steps from the other side. With a squeak of alarm, she slipped between the crossbeams and plummeted into the storm-swollen river.

How foolish. What a terrible idea. Now I'm going to die and I didn't even have the chance to tell him I love him.

The river agreed with her summation. It tossed her so violently that she had no idea which direction the surface was. The fabric of her skirts and spencer took on so much water that she could scarcely move her limbs to swim.

Then a powerful arm wrapped about her waist and pulled her upward. Her head broke the surface just as she was about to lose her breath forever. Jack towed her toward the bank, making perfectly good progress with a single arm stroke. He pulled her up onto the grass and held her there tightly against him while he caught his breath.

Laurel choked and gasped and furiously tried to fight her way free of her tangled hair. A large, warm hand came to gently smooth it away from her brow.

"Those braids would have come in handy today," said a low voice in her ear.

With a gasp, Laurel realized that she lay in Jack's arms. When she turned to face him, his lips were a mere inch from hers. Her body pressed front to front down the length of his. She swallowed and blushed, even as she vowed to herself that she would not redden.

"H-hello." What a moronic thing to say.

"Hello, Bramble."

"You saved my life," she said huskily.

"Not that you deserve it." He picked a blade of grass from her wet cheek. "You might have died, you idiot brat."

She'd been incredibly stupid and she knew it. Feeling like an idiot, she bit her lower lip in embarrassment.

"Don't do that." His voice turned odd, sort of deep and rough. Was it the choking in the water?

Laurel released her lip instantly. "I'm sorry," she whispered. "I won't do it again."

His grip on her tightened for a long moment. He couldn't seem to take his gaze from her mouth.

Laurel wanted him to kiss her, which would be entirely appropriate and romantic, since he'd just saved her life. It was a well-known rule and even Amaryllis would have to abide by it. There wasn't anything Laurel could do to make it happen, however, for her knowledge of such matters was extremely limited.

Then Jack abruptly rolled away from her and stalked away, leaving her soaked and muddy and bewildered on the bank of the river. For a long moment, she simply lay in the wet grass and cherished the memory of his big, warm body pressed to hers and his hands as he'd touched her face. It was by far the most romantic moment of her life.

After a few minutes of this, she became uncomfortably aware of her soaked gown and petticoats and her nastily muddied hair. Sitting up, she sighed at the state of her new clothing.

*Jack was leaving tomorrow. If she'd learned any-
thing from this experience, it was that she ought not to
put things off for one more moment. Amaryllis wasn't
interested in Jack any longer anyway. Laurel had heard
Amaryllis complaining to her friends that he'd grown
so boring she could barely stand him.*

*She should tell him. Tonight. He usually avoided the
evening entertainments. She would find him in his
room and she would confess her love.*

*Renewed by her decision, Laurel stood and brushed
the mud and grass from her skirts as best she could.
Then she straightened, looked about her, and frowned.
Wait a moment—*

She was on the wrong bloody bank of the river!

It isn't enough to simply remember past feelings.

Laurel went from dream to wakefulness with the ef-
fortlessness of simply continuing a thought.

Her once-upon-a-time love for Jack had been genuine but wildly ardent, built of hopes and fantasy.

Now, it was more complicated. She was a different
person, hammered into a different shape by the events
that had followed his disappearance from her life.

He was different now as well. Not as lost. Not as
empty.

She could admit that she was happy to see him coming back to life. It didn't mean she loved him still.

Laurel opened her eyes. Someone was kicking her in
the ribs.

She reached her hand down to find a chubby pink foot
poking into her side. "How extraordinary," she com-
mented sleepily, and tickled it.

She'd never known that a child could giggle in her

sleep. Laurel closed her eyes again, savoring this knowledge. There was so much to learn. She was like a desiccated sponge, interested in soaking up every drop of knowledge about children in general and this sleepy, pink little person in particular.

Laurel pulled the tiny foot closer and kissed it. Then she blew a rude sound on the sole of it. Melody giggled again, no longer asleep. "Mama, y'silly." She stretched like a kitten.

Laurel realized that she was not at all comfortable and reached beneath her back to discover the grubby ball of Gordy Ann. "Good morning," she greeted the doll politely. "If it's all the same to you, milady, I think you're going into the washbowl."

Melody rolled onto her belly and kicked her little feet into the air. "That's what Pru says. She makes Gordy Ann go swimming every time I take a bath."

"Well done, Pru," Laurel murmured. She sat up and stretched herself, feeling tired and a bit stiff from sleeping with what felt like a dozen monkeys. She rubbed the back of her neck.

A dozen very busy monkeys.

Who were members of a marching band.

She wouldn't have traded a second of her night for her weight in gold. She smiled at Melody. "I think I smell bacon!"

She looked up and froze. If she hadn't been so distracted by waking up with her baby, she would have realized at once that things were very different.

Her attic cell had transformed into a luxurious chamber.

"Luxurious" wasn't adequate.

It was bloody posh! There were books stacked upon

a finely detailed rosewood bedside table that hadn't been there before. A matching writing desk stood across the room.

Jack's large wingback chair now sat throne-like next to the hearth. Richly worked hangings, almost like tapestries, hung from the laundry hooks, nearly covering the two longest walls. She and Melody lay under a thick layer of velvet coverlets.

And there, by the window, was something that made Laurel's heart melt with the thoughtfulness behind it. Her fingertips traced the smile on her lips as she gazed at it. Somewhere in this madhouse of a gentlemen's club, he'd managed to find a Windsor rocking chair. Or had he filched it from some woman's garden in the middle of the night?

Laurel could scarcely wait to try it out, but her stomach growled. It sounded as though someone had let a bear into the room. She gave the doll a mock glare. "Gordy Ann! I'm surprised at you!" Melody collapsed into giggles.

Breakfast for two lay beneath the silver cover on a tray. With the usual eggs and bacon there was a bowl of porridge. Laurel peered at it. "Oh, dear. It has lumps in it."

Melody climbed into the chair like a monkey. "I like lumps!" She wiggled her bottom until she was right up to the edge of the table. Her chin barely cleared the tabletop. The stack of books came in handy at once.

They broke their fast sitting in the bright, warm, luxurious room in their chemises, giggling and sipping tea with their pinkies ridiculously raised.

Afterward, Laurel rocked her daughter on her lap and sang every song she could think of. Melody sang one as well, about riding a little pony. Then came a very imaginative tale about bandits and rolling pins and barrels of ale.

Laurel smiled. Her daughter was so creative.

With a start, Jack opened his eyes in the dimness of his closed bed curtains. For an instant, the rich brocade pattern jumbled in his vision without meaning, then resolved itself into draped fabric and silk fringe. He forced himself to truly look at it, to note the tiniest of details, hoping to distract himself long enough to allow the dream to fade far away. The fringe was becoming a bit tatty in one spot. He looked closer. The stitches that held it on the curtain had popped. The longest one swayed slightly in his vision. He blinked slowly, just so he'd have to seek the thread out once more. Concentrate on the thread.

After several minutes, he tentatively checked his memory for the details of his dream. Faded, blurred, without terror, the merest memory of a memory that slipped away even as he focused on it.

Gratefully he sat up and rubbed his face with both hands. Another close escape.

Last night he'd slept alongside his lover and his child. Those few hours had been the purest and most restful sleep of the last few years. He'd awoken rejuvenated in the middle of the night. He'd tried to express his gratitude with a few more gifts for the room. Then he'd found his own bed, hoping for yet more of that refreshing rest.

Not quite, but one had to be grateful for small graces. At least he hadn't woken up screaming.

When he rose from the bed, the air chilled his naked

skin. He'd learned to sleep in nothing. Otherwise, his dreaming mind might turn the collar of his nightshirt into a noose, or the twisted nightshirt into piled bodies that he lay beneath.

Now, stretching, he treasured the freedom of his nudity. He only wished he had Laurel naked with him.

Outside, he could hear the noises of a spring dawn in the back garden as he tied his dressing gown about his waist. Birdcalls tempted him closer to his window, and he thrust back the draperies to reveal the restoration of the once fine garden in full progress. The graceful figure in the hat, leaning over a flower bed, was either Madeleine or Prudence. A flash of red hair braided down the woman's back. *Ah, that would be Pru.* She poked enthusiastically, if a little amateurishly, at the young green plants in the bed. Jack saw Madeleine hurry forward. He could imagine the gentle way Maddie would explain the proper handling of seedlings. She was inherently kind.

Following the flight of a bird she disturbed with her dancing steps, she looked up then and waved to him, grinning. Pru straightened and waved as well, smiles on their lovely faces.

Abruptly Jack felt a wash of strange and unusual welcome. How odd. Brown's was his house, in effect. He was one of the few living descendents of the original charter members. Redgrave men had occupied these very rooms since the building itself was completed.

Yet standing here basking in the glowing smiles of the Ladies of Brown's Club for Distinguished Gentlemen, he'd never felt so at home.

*   *   *

Down in the garden, Pru waved and smiled back at Jack standing in his window.

"There's something strange going on with him," she muttered without altering her smile.

"Oh yes," Maddie replied cheerfully, waving. "I've never seen him so warm . . . so . . ."

"So human?" Pru asked dryly.

Maddie turned to her in surprise. "Precisely!"

Pru sighed. "Colin is thrilled. He thinks we should delay searching for Nanny. He wants Jack to keep coming back to life."

Maddie frowned. "That's dangerous, don't you think? If . . . if we lose Melody, we'll all be devastated, but Colin and Aidan have us to turn to. What will Jack do?"

Pru contemplated the club with a tiny frown line between her auburn brows. "I don't know what it is, precisely, but there's something about that man. . . ."

Maddie nodded. "It's as if he keeps forgetting that Melody might be leaving us. Do you know I actually heard him laugh yesterday?"

"Really?"

Maddie shrugged. "Well, nearly."

Pru rubbed the back of her arm across her brow, for her gloved hands were too dirty to use. "Forgetting or . . . have you ever noticed how he simply gets up and leaves the room lately? As if he cannot bear to sit still."

"Or as if he has somewhere important that he needs to be."

"And he disappears for hours."

Maddie leaned close, though they were alone. "I saw him carrying a Lementeur box to the rubbish bin," she whispered. "A big one."

Pru's eyes widened. "It must have been one of ours, an old one." Her expression was comical in its doubt. "Mustn't it?"

Maddie shook her head. "It was an awfully big box. And he's an awfully big man."

Pru looked at her in horror for a long moment. Then a snicker broke from Pru's lips. Maddie cracked up as well, hooting with laughter.

If Jack had looked out his window at the garden at that moment, it would have mystified him greatly to see the lovely Ladies of Brown's Club for Distinguished Gentlemen cackling like geese in the garden.

Twenty-three

Jack trotted down the stairs to the main club room to join Aidan and Colin for the day's Nanny hunt.

He'd just gone up to the attic to release Melody and to thank Laurel for letting him stay last night. He'd not slept long, but it had been deep and refreshing.

He'd found Laurel stretched out on the bed, napping, and Melody playing tea party with Gordy Ann and the breakfast dishes.

"Mama says I sleep like a monkey band."

Jack didn't know what a monkey band was, but he'd spent a night or two with Melody in the past and knew that it was both enjoyable and exhausting.

He'd ushered Melody out and surreptitiously locked the door behind them. "Leave Mama be for now, Melody. If you want to see her, come talk to me. And . . ."

Melody wasn't very good at secrets. He hated to ask her to lie.

Melody danced down the attic stairs ahead of him. "I have a secret mama," she sang. "She's the queen in the tower."

Jack paused, considering, and decided that that would do nicely.

Now he was running late to meet Aidan and Colin,

and he preferred not to draw attention to his frequent "absences."

As he turned the corner of the stairs at the second floor, he was forced to back into the corner. Bailiwick, even as large as he was, was overwhelmed by the giant stack of parcels in his arms.

"Have you been shopping, John?"

Bailiwick peered around the pile in his arms. "Oh, sorry, milord. Didn't see you there. Couldn't fit meself into the servants' stair. It's Fiona what's been shoppin' for the ladies. She said there's naught feminine in the place. Don't know what all, but creams and mirrors and whatnot."

Jack nodded, since he could do little else, still pinned into the corner as he was. "Tools of the trade, I suppose?"

Bailiwick brightened. "Oy, that's what it is! I didn't think o' that, milord. Every craftsman has to have his tools!"

Jack cleared his throat, but the hint was lost. With a scowl of concentration on his broad face, it appeared that Bailiwick was taking a small vacation in order to think.

"What d'y think a lady's maid might need in the way o' tools, then?"

Jack gazed at the ceiling. "Well, gowns of course, but those would be for the lady, really."

"Them would be the costumes, right enough."

Costumes? Ah, the lovely Fiona had a background in the theater, didn't she?

"And props, I suppose. Fans and . . . things." Jack frowned. Ladies were complicated creatures, weren't they?

Bailiwick pondered that. "And the stage, that would be the ballroom, eh? Nothing a lady likes better than a ball."

Yes, that was true enough. At least, all the ladies of Jack's acquaintance seemed to like them.

Bailiwick frowned. "Seems like there ought to be somethin' I can give her for her new position, like. I want her to like it here. I want her to stay."

Jack gazed up the stairs thoughtfully. "If I had the answer to that one, my friend, I'd be a very happy man."

Bailiwick continued up the stairs at last, muttering to himself, "Costumes, props, stage . . ."

Jack went on down the stairs, freed at last.

Nothing a lady likes better than a ball.

Another thing he'd stolen from Laurel.

As the horses pulled the carriage away from Brown's, Jack gazed back at the brownstone façade of the club, realizing that he didn't want to go looking for Nanny.

He wanted to stay with Laurel.

Actually, he wanted to climb into her bed in the luxurious attic and wake her with his mouth.

Nevertheless, this search was meant to help that cause. He hoped to bring back some answers for her. She ought not to have to live with her questions unanswered, with her truth shadowed by others more concerned for their reputations than for her heart.

Eventually the carriage rolled into the neighborhood of Mrs. Pruitt's abandoned house.

Aidan thought they were wasting their time. "The woman is long gone, I'll wager. She dumped Melody and left the city to avoid just this sort of confrontation."

"I know that the trail leads here," Colin insisted. "Someone must know what happened to Mrs. Pruitt."

Aidan looked around them as they left the carriage to go on foot. "This is an awfully long way from the club. She's old. How could she have walked there with Melody?"

Just then a cart full of casks trundled past them. As the cart headed away, they could see a couple of girls, dressed in gray work gowns and wearing the sort of scarf that factory workers donned, riding facing backward on the back of the cart with their feet dangling. Though their faces were gray with fatigue, one of them noticed Colin watching and sent him a saucy wink.

Aidan grunted. "I suppose that answers my question."

Colin blinked. "Did you see that little vixen? I'm married! Couldn't she tell I'm married? I look married, don't I?"

"You dress like a bloody grampapa."

Jack glanced at Colin. "Or a white-haired accountant."

Aidan and Colin snapped their gazes to him, startled. Their expressions said it all. *The stone speaks!*

Colin's eyes widened. "Did Jack just make a jest?"

Aidan nodded. "I heard a jest."

Colin patted down his weskit with both hands. "I need ink and paper. I must mark the day."

Aidan smirked. "I'll help you remember."

Jack let out a breath. "Arse," he muttered.

Aidan laughed. "Colin, someone just called you a name."

Jack slid a black glance to Aidan. "Arse squared."

Colin guffawed and punched Jack in the shoulder. Then the two of them had the sense to let it go as they continued to walk into the bustling market. Jack was glad of that, but he was also aware that such a brief moment of their old camaraderie was more than he'd given his friends in years. It wasn't much of a moment, for his wit was buried too deep to be actually sharp, but it left him feeling just a bit lighter as he walked with his friends beside him.

Unfortunately, that lightness did not last for long.

A crash from one of the shops drew their attention. Aidan and Colin turned to see a baker standing over a stout woman who was down on her knees in the shop doorway, frantically gathering up the buns that had rolled out onto the cobbles from a dropped tray. The baker was red faced with fury.

"Ye stupid cow! Now ye done cost me a fat penny, ye great clumsy—" The baker's fist rose high.

Colin and Aidan stepped forward, but Jack was already there. When iron fingers wrapped around the baker's thick wrist, the furious man tried to turn.

"I don't think so." Jack's voice was distant and cool. "I think you're going to help her pick them up."

"What ye think yer doin', interferin' in a man's business! Bloody toff!"

Jack's gaze was strange and withdrawn, but his fingers tightened on the man's wrist. "I think," he said again, more quietly, "you're going to help her pick them up."

Colin cleared his throat. "Er, Jack?"

Aidan put a hand on Colin's arm. "Let him be."

Colin turned aside to whisper urgently, "He's lost again; can't you see that? He might just kill the bastard!"

Aidan shook his head. "He's all right."

In fact, Jack was not all right, not quite. The feeling of the man's bones and flesh beneath his fingers, the blow still tense in the man's arm, ready to fall on the woman the moment Jack was gone—

His heart was pounding a great noise in his head, like the drums of battle. Any moment he expected to smell the bite of gunpowder, the strange metallic tang of blood. With great effort he focused his gaze on the baker's. "You. Will. Pick. Them. Up." It was the merest of whispers.

The man truly looked at Jack for the first time, finally seeing past his own rage to his imminent danger. His meaty cheeks paled and his bulbous eyes blinked rapidly. "Ah, right, ah, sorry, guv'nor." He winced and his knees started to buckle. "I'll just be pickin' up those buns now," he wheezed.

Then Aidan was at his side. "Let go," he told Jack quietly. "Open your hand."

From a distance, Jack saw his fingers open and the man's thick wrist, banded in white pressure marks, slip from his grasp.

Jack then looked at the woman, still kneeling on the cobbles, her eyes wide as she gazed up at him. "I am the Marquis of Strickland. You may find me at Brown's Club, should you require further assistance, madam. Anytime."

A calculating gleam entered the woman's eyes. "Aye, milord. I thank ye for that." She watched as her husband picked up the remaining buns with shaking hands. "Eh, Buxby? Did ye hear his lovely lordship? Pick up the bloody buns!"

Jack found himself walking down the sidewalk, away from the shop, Aidan and Colin on either side.

"That was, ahem, rather chilling." Colin rubbed at the back of his neck. "Do warn us next time you're feeling homicidal, won't you?"

"I wasn't homicidal," Jack replied. It was true. The man might have seen the war in Jack's eyes, but Jack had not been about to bring the war into the market-place. Not even close. "I wasn't even violent. Haven't started a brawl in years."

Colin blinked. "Well, that's an improvement."

Jack sent his friend a wry glance. "Kind of you to notice."

Aidan's lips quirked. "Another jest. Is that some sort of record, Colin?"

"I'm keeping tally. So far it's a personal best."

Jack kept walking, feeling a bit like he'd passed some sort of test. A humanity test? *I was a good lad today. I didn't kill anyone and I told a joke.*

Welcome back to the human race.

In the end, it was the local washerwoman who told them where to find Nanny Pruitt.

"Always ask those in service," Colin gloated, for it had been his idea.

Nanny was indeed dying. She'd closed up her house and gone to a women's sanatorium run by the Sisters of Mercy. After some whispered discussion, the nuns in charge decided to allow three men into the inner sanctum.

"She was once a midwife," the nun leading them informed them. "She would come to deliver our . . . unfortunate girls."

They found Nanny Pruitt lying in a bed in a great open ward. Every bed was in use. Old women, young women, from seamstresses, to prostitutes, to beggars. The dividing lines of Society seemed to blur here.

Jack looked around him. No one wanted these women. They had no children willing to care for them, no husbands to support them. In this male-controlled world, any woman could end up penniless and alone in her old age.

It would not happen to Laurel. He would make sure of that. A marchioness would never wind up in a pitiable place like this.

In one of the beds lay a white-haired woman whose body was wasted but whose eyes were bright. She watched them walk down the ward, her gaze knowing.

The nun stopped at the foot of the woman's cot. "Mrs. Pruitt, these men have come to speak with you."

Nanny Pruitt examined each of them from head to toe with her sharp eyes. "Do you have my Mellie?"

Colin knelt next to the woman and took her hand. "We do. Thank you for bringing her to us."

Her bright eyes counted them off slowly. "Three men for one little girl." Her wrinkled lips pursed. "She does that, doesn't she?"

Aidan snorted. "She does indeed."

"She's past three now. You should be teaching her the numbers and letters. She's a smart one. She'll pick it right up."

Jack nodded solemnly. "I shall see to it."

She peered at him for a long moment. "It's you, isn't it?"

Jack glanced at Aidan and Colin. "If you two would do us the courtesy?"

Colin scowled. "What is this?"

Aidan took his arm. "Let's walk out for a moment."

Colin turned with Aidan, not having much choice without putting up a struggle, but he cast a questioning glance back over his shoulder at Jack. Jack lifted a hand to wave them on, then turned back to Mrs. Pruitt once they were gone.

"Yes. I am Melody's father."

Twenty-four

Nanny Pruitt regarded Jack for a long moment. She shook her head. "You don't look like a monster."

Jack only nodded again. "I know I don't."

"But you are."

"I think perhaps I have been. I don't know about now. I'm trying to be better."

She tilted her silver head and gazed at him for a long moment. "See that you do. No girl deserves what that one got."

Jack bowed his head.

"Her parents were devils, they were. Before I went in to the girl, that man offered to pay me extra if I could make sure the child 'failed to survive.' "

Jack flexed his jaw. "He's dead now." It was probably a good thing, since it meant Jack needn't bother to kill him.

"Good riddance. And that woman! Evil creature, shoutin' at her daughter that she deserved the pain of labor for being a 'sinful whore.' " Nanny snorted. "She was a mother herself. I wonder how she explained her own labor pain."

"She is gone as well."

Nanny folded her twisted arthritic hands over her sunken belly. "I know it. Ain't that fine? I outlived 'em both."

Jack liked her. "You kept Melody and told them she was dead, didn't you?"

"I did. She was such a sweet, easy baby. She didn't start being a handful until she could walk. Then she plain wore me out." She smiled. "I love that little demon, that's what."

"So do I."

Nanny's mind snapped out of her memories and back into focus. "You sailed off. That's what the girl said when she was deliverin'."

How to explain the past? "It was a mistake. I never knew about Melody." He frowned. "If Mr. and Mrs. Clarke thought Melody was dead, why did they pay for her support?"

Nanny smiled until her wrinkles had wrinkles. "That weren't support. That were *blackmail*." She grunted. "Go ahead and tell the magistrate if you want. I'll not live out the month anyway."

Jack wanted to know one more thing. "Why didn't you go to Miss Clarke when you ran out of money? She was devastated when she lost her child. She would have been so grateful."

Nanny frowned at him in surprise. "That one? Cold as an icicle and twice as sharp? She sent for me, she did, tryin' to find out why her parents had been payin' me. I told her and she laughed, straight to my face, and said she didn't know what I was talkin' about and if I spread such lies about her she'd have me cast into the irons."

Jack rocked back on his heels. *Oh, Amaryllis, you have so much to answer for.* "That wasn't Melody's mother. That was not the girl you tended. You met her sister."

Nanny looked doubtful. "Be you sure? Looked just like her, but older and meaner. Well, I suppose you'd know the difference, of all people."

"One would think," Jack muttered under his breath.

"So I thought I'd best find the father, bein' as I were failin' quick. 'Brown's,' she said, over and over again. She got a bit delirious there near the end o' the birth. Lots of 'em do, you know. 'He's at Brown's.' I asked her for more, but she wouldn't look at me. Just kept sayin' that." Nanny smoothed the fold of blanket over her midriff. "Made me cry, that girl did. Saddest girl in the world when I told her the baby died." She rubbed at her wrinkled cheek, suddenly impatient. "I should have known it weren't her at that great house, all sneering and haughty-like! Birdbrained old fool!" She faded a bit, mumbling. "Didn't even know there was a sister. . . ."

Jack took a step back. He didn't think there was much more Nanny could tell him. When he started to move away, Nanny sharpened on him again.

"I know my Mellie's happy. I know you take great care of her."

"I can assure you we do."

"No need assurin'." Nanny smiled. "I keep my eye on you lot. I send that boy over to watch every week, I do. Melody used to set a great store by him. She called him 'the running boy,' because he liked to never hold still."

The running boy. Melody had recognized him, had nearly run into the street to see him. They should have listened more closely. Of course the boy was someone Melody knew well.

Nanny faded out again, plucking restlessly at her

blanket with her bent and twisted fingers. Jack eased away and found the sister in charge. Colin and Aidan found him there, counting coins into the nun's hand.

"If she needs anything at all, just bill it to my account at Brown's. I'll tell our man there to take care of any expenses, as long as . . ."

The sister closed her hand over the coins and made them quickly disappear beneath her habit. "It won't be long, poor dear."

Jack nodded and took his leave. As he strode from the sanatorium, Aidan and Colin were on his heels.

"What was that about?" Colin demanded. "Why did you want us to leave?"

Jack simply kept walking. Even the most minor explanations would lead to major complications. Aidan put a hand on his arm.

"Jack, I think you need to let us in on . . . on whatever this is. We can help."

Jack stopped and turned, gazing at his friends.

Help? Help me persuade a woman whose life I've ruined ten times over that I'm the answer to her every prayer? Help me keep her locked away until I can figure out a way to make her love me again?

Or help me betray her one last and final time by taking her daughter from her forever?

He rubbed a hand across his face. "I—" It was no good. They would never understand. "Soon. Everything will be made clear soon."

As soon as I decipher how to seize what I want without letting go of what I have.

Wilberforce stood just inside the main club room, apparently staring into space. In fact, he was mentally sorting where everyone and everything *ought* to be in his domain.

Lord Bartles and Sir James were at the chessboard by the fire as usual. Young Master Evan was there, learning yet another advanced strategy from the old warriors. Lord Aldrich sat with his paper high before his face, perhaps hoping no one noticed that he was taking yet another brief respite from his married life. Some of Wilberforce's more mature charges frankly napped in their chairs, killing time until the supper chime was rung.

Lady Lambert was pretending to read a book while actually monitoring the progress of her younger brother's chess lesson. Wilberforce felt sure that there could be no other explanation for the fact that Her Ladyship had not turned a page in a quarter of an hour.

Lady Madeleine was in the kitchen with Cook, going over menus. It was a duty she enjoyed, so Wilberforce graciously allowed her to believe she was in charge of it. Cook was her ladyship's most devoted minion. Therefore, the already superior fare at Brown's had actually improved, if that was possible.

Young Bailiwick lurked in the entrance hall, sighing repeatedly when he thought no one was near. The pretty Fiona endlessly dusted the newel post at the top of the stairs, hoping Bailiwick would look up, then hiding quickly when he did.

All the other footmen made sure their duties took them far away from Fiona and her tempting but dangerous smile. Wilberforce was glad to see that the young fools had some sense of self-preservation. It was about time some work got done around the place.

Sir Colin, Lord Blankenship, and Lord Strickland

were out tracking down the elusive Nanny Pruitt. Wilberforce wished them no luck whatsoever. Melody belonged to Brown's, and that, as far as Wilberforce was concerned, was that.

Little Lady Melody was playing in the attic.

Again.

And, contrary to Wilberforce's own rule, alone. Unless one counted the imaginary "queen in the tower."

Queen in the tower.

Missing carpets.

This morning he'd discovered that all the unoccupied rooms on the third floor had been stripped of their woven wall hangings. This was disturbing, for Wilberforce's father had established this collection of luxurious and beautiful tapestries nearly fifty years before. It was one of the things that distinguished Brown's chambers from other, more utilitarian rooms at other clubs.

The only reason Wilberforce had not immediately called the watch was the strange fact that the only occupied room to lack a tapestry was that of the Marquis of Strickland himself.

Wilberforce was a patient man. He took great pride in his ability to watch quietly on the sidelines of his charges' lives and make only the slightest and most subtle of adjustments when their plans began to go awry. For example, he'd recently exchanged Lord Aldrich's mattress for one much thinner and much lumpier. In less than a week, his lordship would decide to go home to his newlywed bride and make up whatever small spat had caused his recent defection from the marriage bed.

All for his lordship's own good, of course.

Queen in the Tower. Melody's game teased at Wilberforce's thoughts. Perhaps it was time to investigate this apparently endlessly fascinating diversion. Wilberforce turned on one heel and left the club room.

"Wilberforce!"

He halted at once and bowed deeply. "Lady Madeleine. How might I assist you?"

Her ladyship strode up to him with a strange expression on her lovely face. "Wilberforce, did Cook mention to you that there have been several small thefts from the larder?"

Wilberforce nodded. "Indeed, my lady. Since it seemed minor, I attributed it to, ah, a certain member of the staff who is currently undergoing some emotional distress—"

Lady Madeleine folded her arms. "You think Bailiwick ate it."

"That is usually the correct conclusion when food is in question, my lady, yes."

Lady Madeleine nodded. "I see. What about the fact that Bailiwick won't eat eggs? Not since Samuel used to tease him about 'giants eating babies.'"

Wilberforce blinked. "My lady, your powers of observation are most impressive. I had temporarily forgotten that fact."

"If it isn't Bailiwick," Lady Madeleine frowned, "then where is the food going?"

Indeed, Wilberforce thought. *Where is everything going?*

At that moment, Cook sounded the dinner chime. There was a general bustle in the club room, for no one ever missed a meal at Brown's. Even Melody came dancing down the stairs just then, one hand reaching high to hold the railing, Gordy Ann trailing from the other. There was a streak of dust on Melody's face.

Dust in his club.

She grinned at him. "Wibbly-force! I'm hungry! Are you hungry?"

Gazing up the stairs behind her, Wilberforce narrowed his eyes slightly. At the moment, he had work to do. Supper, then port and cigars for the gentlemen and sherry for the ladies. Orders to be written for the coming week. The children must be put to bed and the elder members as well. After he had performed his duties and settled his charges for the night, he would investigate this matter further.

Young Master Evan pounded past them, his overlarge feet not quite under his control. "Hurry up, Mellie, or I'm going to eat your carrots!"

"Nooo!" Lady Melody scrambled after Evan. Gordy Ann, apparently sensing the importance of preventing this, fluttered urgently behind her.

Lady Lambert joined Wilberforce and Lady Madeleine, smiling after the children. "She believes him every time. One day she'll notice that Evan has never voluntarily eaten a carrot in his life."

Wilberforce bowed his ladies into the dining room and set about his usual impeccable performance of his duties. The attic would wait.

For now.

Twenty-five

As soon as Jack could shake off Aidan and Colin, he made for Lementeur's establishment. Jack found the man serving a stout dowager tea and compliments and no doubt charging the woman her weight in gold for the privilege.

The woman didn't seem to mind.

Once he'd spoken to Button's man, Cabot, Jack stayed in the background as Button effortlessly fobbed the lady off on his extraordinarily handsome assistant.

Cabot leaned close, poured another cup of tea, and murmured something that made the woman, who was seventy if she was a day, bat her eyelashes and lick her lips.

Button whisked Jack away to his office, which was surprisingly ordinary and cluttered. Thousands of sketches of gowns were pinned to the walls, even layered several deep. Stacks of invoices and ledgers covered the ornate French desk, competing for space with inkpots and jars of brushes.

Jack was now quite convinced that for all his breezily avaricious manner, Lementeur worked hard for his living.

"My lord, what might I do for my favorite customer?"

Jack regarded Button helplessly for a long moment. How could he say it?

"Er . . . my friend needs another dress. At once."

Button smiled genially. "Of course. Might I ask . . ."

Please don't ask. Jack's encounter with Laurel on the floor had left him both heated and chilled with memories.

". . . was the gown in some way unsatisfactory?"

Jack cleared his throat and rubbed the back of his neck. Embarrassment was becoming almost familiar again. "I—ahem—the gown was . . . ruined."

A sly gleam flared in Button's eyes, matched by the merest twitch of his lips. "Indeed? How *delicious.*" He bowed. "I shall take it as a compliment to the chef, as it were."

Jack turned his gaze toward the ceiling, unable to meet Button's knowing eyes. "I don't suppose you have another one lying about?"

Button leaned back in his chair and tapped his fingertips together. "I believe I might have an appropriate garment on hand, but it means I must ask another valued client to wait. . . ." His voice trailed off expectantly.

Jack slid his gaze to meet Button's. "Cutpurse."

Button's puckish face creased in delight. "I'm so glad we understand each other, my lord." He stood. "Let me speak to Cabot for a moment. Please, allow me to get you some coffee while you wait?"

Jack wasn't sure what was in the coffee, but he drank four cups and ended up spending three times what any sane man should spend. Then, at the last moment, when his carriage was once more packed with more parcels than he remembered ordering, it seemed that the evening gown he'd asked for was actually ready as well. Such speed seemed rather miraculous, but for the fact that Jack was quite sure he'd paid for an entire regiment of seamstresses to work all night.

"Would you like to see it, my lord?"

Jack blinked owlishly. He'd been deluged with color and fabric choices for nearly an hour. Images of gloves and stockings and obscure little lacy things still clouded his vision. "Do I have to?" Was that a whimper in his voice? He cleared his throat manfully. "I'm sure it's perfectly adequate."

Button smirked. "My lord, it is just short of adequate for a royal marriage! I hope that you are escorting the lady somewhere worthy. A ball, perhaps?"

Nothing a lady likes better than a ball.

"Button," Jack burst out. "I need your help!"

Cabot slipped instantly away and Button poured Jack another cup of coffee. "My lord, I am of course entirely willing to aid you however I can."

"I want . . . I want to give her something. . . ." He shook his head. "Damn Bailiwick and his obsession with Fiona! I don't even know what I'm trying to say!"

Button tilted his head. "If I might advise you, my lord, I think you are trying to win a lady's heart. Through the observation of many happy couples, I've learned that the best way to win the lady is to truly understand the lady."

Jack blinked. "That doesn't help."

Button smiled. "Does it not? You love her, so—"

The words shot through Jack like an arrow. *You love her.*

The glittering obviousness of it nearly blinded him. *I love her. I don't simply lust after her. I don't simply want to make matters up to her. I don't simply want to keep Melody.*

I love her.

And then, with a flash of light like the sun coming up over a battlefield after a long night of war, he knew.

I always have.

Why else would he spend so many months pursuing a shallow girl he couldn't converse with for more than a quarter of an hour? Why else would he sit there, surrounded by other suitors, and not feel an instant of jealousy for her? Why else would he leave the parlor time and time again to seek out those serious blue eyes, wanting to watch the way they would blink dreamily up from some book, the way they would shyly light up when she saw him? Why else would he fight to keep a girl he could barely stand, if not to stay near that house and wait for Laurel to grow up?

His heart filled like bellows, only to deflate horribly an instant later.

Dear God, how he'd mucked it all up!

In her bedchamber where she'd been hiding out from her wedding day, Melody twirled about the room with joy.

"It's so romantic! He loved her always!"

Button followed Melody's giddy path, holding a string of pearls behind his back. When he got close enough, he continued the tale while surreptitiously continuing to dress her. He was so close. All she lacked now was the gown itself—

As he spoke he raised his hands to the back of her neck. "Once I gave him the gown, which I might add was one of my finest creations, he looked at me and said—"

Melody turned to him, her hands pressed to her cheeks. "Oh my goodness! Button! I'm the elf!" She laughed out loud. "The elf is me!"

Button sighed and smiled, dropping the pearls back behind him. "Yes, pet, the elf is you. And the magic climbing basket was the dumbwaiter and the troll whom the elf tricked into pulling her to the top was—"

"Evan!" Melody chortled. "Oh, wait until I tell him!" Then she remembered. Her giddy laughter dried up like a spring after a rockfall. She turned to Button, suddenly ashen with horror. "I'm not going to be able to tell him!"

Button smiled soothingly. "And why not? He's downstairs right now, along with everyone else."

Melody sat down on the sofa with a flounce. Her fantastically expensive silk underskirts belled about her, then settled. She sat there, an indescribable beauty clad in the finest of underthings, with her rich cloud of dark hair woven with pearls and satin cord and her face, her lovely, heart-shaped face that had long grown out of the round cheeks of childhood and let her exquisite bone structure emerge, gazing up at Button with the saddest blue eyes he'd ever seen.

"I can't tell him because I'm never leaving this room. Ever." She took a great shuddering breath. "Oh, Button, I can't go through with this!"

Button squatted down to look into her face, though it was hardly necessary. She had her father's height. "Mellie-my-love, my Mousie, my pet. *Why* can't you go through with it?"

She only shook her head and quickly looked away. "Just . . . finish the story, Button, please?"

Button sighed and sat beside her on the sofa. He

tucked her sad, lovely face into his neck, making a mental note to himself that he must change his surcoat before the ceremony for all the tears that had soaked into it this day, and carried on with the tale.

"His Lordship went back to the club with his purchases and . . ."

Outside Lementeur's, Colin and Aidan struggled to blend into the crowd. Aidan read a news sheet and Colin pretended to be vitally interested in a window display of ladies' cosmetic preparations. "Do y'think Pru uses all this stuff?"

Aidan glanced into the window. "Not a chance."

Colin frowned and looked at his friend. "Why not?"

Aidan blew out a bored breath and turned his news sheet to read the other side. Again. "Because Pru is dead stunning fresh out of the bath."

Colin nodded absently. "That's true. . . ." Then, "Oy! That's my wife you're talking about! How would you know something like that?"

Aidan rolled his eyes. "Because you carry on about it every time she takes a bloody bath, you dolt." He shook his head. "Mooncalf idiot."

Colin subsided, reassured. "Well, if I'm a mooncalf, then you're a panting pup. Every time Maddie walks across the room, you follow her with your eyes as if she's a sweetmeat and you need to dab at your chin. Sickening, it is."

Aidan grunted dismissively and Colin turned his gaze back to the window display, where he could see a reflection of the storefronts across the street. Amusing as such Aidan baiting was, Colin was more worried about what Jack was still doing in the dressmaker's shop.

"He's been in there for an hour. He usually lets Pru and Maddie pick out Melody's things anyway."

Aidan didn't look up. "Maybe he's feeling inclined to spoil her right now."

Colin shrugged one shoulder uncomfortably. "Can't say I blame him. Do you think we could stop by the confectioner's on the way back to the club?"

Aidan grunted. "No need for that."

Colin turned a scowl on him. "I think I have as much right to spoil her as anyone! I can buy her sweets if I like!"

Aidan didn't meet his gaze. "I already put an order in this morning," he admitted.

Colin's irritation left him in a breath. He knew Aidan felt as deeply as he did. "I don't suppose—"

"Heads up," Aidan hissed, and raised his paper high to cover his face. "Here he comes."

Colin kept an eye on the reflection and watched Jack climb into the carriage. They were close enough to hear the creak of the springs as he settled his large frame into the seat and to hear him order Brown's as his destination. Once the carriage rolled away down the Strand, Colin let out a breath.

"Well, he's gone. And you know what that means."

Aidan lowered his paper. "What?"

Colin shot his friend a dry glance. "It means we have to hire a common hack. Jack drove us out here, remember?"

Twenty-six

That evening, Jack frowned at himself in the mirror as he tried to tie his cravat. This was the first time in years he'd regretted his lack of valet.

"I ought to have had Button dress me as well," he muttered.

"I like Button! Button makes dresses for Gordy Ann!"

Gazing past himself in the mirror, Jack watched his daughter use his second-best cravat as a . . . shroud? Possibly, for Gordy Ann looked rather like an Egyptian mummy at the moment.

Or possibly an insect cocoon. Sometimes it was difficult to follow Melody's train of imagination. "Gordy Ann looks . . . splendid." That should cover any number of possibilities.

"Splendid!" Melody seized the word and practiced it. "Splendid Gordy Ann!"

Melody sat on the bed with her little feet wide apart and her little brow furrowed in concentration as she rewound the cravat and held it up for his inspection. "Papa, look! Look at Gordy Ann!"

Jack turned away from the mirror to fulfill his parental duties. "Indeed." He nodded solemnly. "I have never seen Gordy Ann look more . . ." He was running out of superlatives. "Splendid," he said again, somewhat weakly.

Melody found that entirely satisfactory. "Splendid!"

As Jack turned back to the mirror and his inexplicably reluctant cravat, he pondered the fact that "splendid" now no longer sounded like a word at all.

That would have made Laurel laugh once upon a time.

Jack found himself positively panting to hear Laurel laugh again. He wanted to see her smile more than anything—a real smile, the wide, glowing one she'd blessed him with last evening when he'd given her Melody for the night.

He hoped that his little Bailiwick-inspired plan worked. The fact that not long ago Jack would have thought any plan conceived by the enormous underfootman should be avoided at all costs did not escape him. However, he knew when he was bested, and Bailiwick looked to be far closer to getting his love than Jack himself was. A man had to know when to bow to the master.

Melody was rocking the strangulated Gordy Ann and singing her favorite pony song. Madeleine had a theory that the frequency of this song was a hint. Pru refused to believe Melody was subtle enough for hints. She said the child was more likely to point at ponies and ask directly. Jack merely awaited the signal, for he had already purchased a stout, gentle little pony gelding whose markings exactly matched those of Evan's sleek mount, Ramses.

Melody was going to love it. Evan was going to die of horror.

It occurred to Jack that he probably ought to inform

Colin and Aidan of his surprise, before Melody ended up with three ponies.

"You have a lovely voice, Lady Melody."

"I know."

Jack turned to look at her over his shoulder. "Lady Melody, one says 'thank you' when one receives a compliment."

"Thank you," Melody repeated automatically. Then, "What's a commple-mint?"

"Compliment," Jack repeated carefully. "It is when someone says something nice about you."

Melody unwrapped Gordy Ann to begin again. "Mama sings the beautifulest."

Jack's hands stilled. "Does she?" Had he ever heard Laurel sing? No. She had always stayed in the background, uninterested in competing with Amaryllis for attention.

Seized by a sudden desire to hear Laurel sing, Jack lost track of his cravat tying once again. "Blast!"

"Blast!" caroled Melody. "Blast! Splendid! Commple-mint!" Then, absently as she played with her rag doll, "You and Mama should get merry, Papa. Then Mama could come out of the tower."

The room seemed to turn. Jack leaned his hands on his dressing table and took a deep breath. He was too full of conflicting emotions, incredible as that seemed. He was nervous and eager and worried all at once, while beneath that, happiness and pure male panic swirled together rather sickeningly.

I love her.

Of course, that ringing, bell-like thought was always followed by the heavy, gloomy reverse.

She hates me.

He finished with his cravat and pulled on his evening coat. Turning to his daughter, he held out his arms. "What do you think?"

She clapped her hands. "Splendid, Papa! Gordy Ann thinks you look splendid, too!"

Jack swallowed and hoped that once he got upstairs to the attic the opinion would be unanimous.

Laurel lighted another candle of the ones that she'd found with her breakfast tray that morning and turned back to the book she couldn't put down. It was more of a bound manuscript than a published novel, scribed in a clear masculine hand.

There's a book I shall lend you. . . . My Lady's Shadow.

Laurel could scarcely turn the pages fast enough. It was a thrilling tale of a brave and clever woman who sought to outrun a mad wolf who had taken her scent and would not leave her trail.

On the chase, the woman found love and succor with a feudal lord, but even the lord could not prevent the wolf's fanatical pursuit. The heroine was dragged into the wolf's den and imprisoned there.

Even as Laurel read, the lord's child fell into the jaws of the wolf. Laurel's breath caught and she slammed the book shut. *My Lady's Shadow.*

Madeleine. Aidan. The Badman.

Melody.

Laurel gazed into space. "I think I might be ill," she whispered to the empty room.

This was the wolf's den. That was why Melody had been reluctant to exit the dumbwaiter that first day, why she'd needed reassurance before she'd spent the night in the attic.

Laurel stared down at the book. She couldn't bear to read another word.

Neither could she bear to stop.

Reassuring herself that Madeleine, Aidan, and Melody were fine now and that Jack had solemnly vowed that the Badman was most thoroughly and completely dead, Laurel opened the book and began to read once more.

When Jack tapped at her door she nearly died of fright. "Come in," she called breathlessly.

Jack entered, carrying something as usual. Laurel gazed up at him, her eyes wide and blinking as she was torn from the story. "Wimbledon just shot the wolf!"

For some reason, Jack paused to gaze at her for a long moment. Then he ripped his gaze away and strode to the bed. "His name is Wibbly-force, actually—or rather, Wilberforce." He placed the large box on the bed and returned to the door. "I'll be back for you in half an hour," he told her. "I . . . I hope you like it."

It wasn't until Jack had left the room and locked the door behind him that Laurel realized that he wore full evening dress.

And he looked bloody wonderful in it, too.

Though the box on the bed showed no marks on the outside, it was the same color and style as the ones labeled: *L.* Only Lementeur could have enticed Laurel away from the book before she was finished. However, beneath all her cleverness, she was still very much a girl. She bit her lip and ran across the room.

When she lifted the lid, her breath left her in an

exhalation of bliss. With shaking hands, she reached into the box. Someday, somehow, if she ever met the great Lementeur in person, she was going to cover his face in kisses!

It was a dress.

Better call a swan a duck than to call this confection of sky blue silk a mere dress! Laurel stripped down to nothing, then pulled on the stockings that were so finely knitted that she could see the pink of her flesh through them. She knotted the garters above her knees and smoothed the stockings with a wondering touch.

She'd never had anything so fine—and she'd only just begun!

The blue gown was cleverly made. She was able to reach the buttons because it dipped dangerously low on her back. The tiny sleeves were little more than useless puffs to drape over the points of her shoulders, yet the gown was so perfectly fitted that it could never slip.

How had anyone been able to make such an ideal gown for her with only a couple of old dresses to measure from?

She ought not to accept. It implied . . . oh, never mind! She'd already borne his child! How much more improper could things get?

So she donned the gloves without a single twinge of guilt, smoothing them high over her elbows.

She was panting for a mirror. How could she be expected to do her hair? She wasn't even sure she'd buttoned herself up properly!

There was a tiny silk bag left on the bottom of the box, much like the one the garters had come in. Was it a spare?

No. It was a lovely little hand mirror. She held it up to the light, running her fingertips over the gleaming metal. It warmed to her touch at once. There was only one thing that did that.

Solid gold.

Blinking, she looked at the generous array of lovely things. If it were any other man, she might think he was trying to buy her. Jack, no. These were gifts, plain and simple, purely to give her pleasure.

A woman could get used to this.

The bag also contained a small gold-handled brush. There wasn't much Laurel could do with her hair, for she only had the pins she'd worn the day she'd come to Brown's. Feeling daring, she decided to simply brush her long, curling hair into a dark, silken cloud and let it cling to her bare shoulders and swing sensuously over her bare back.

The box was empty of treasures at last. *Hmm.*

No underthings. None at all, other than the stockings, and those only made her look more naked!

This Lementeur was a very naughty fellow indeed. Not that anyone would see, of course.

Her fingers stilled in the act of caressing the folds of the gown yet again. No one would see her except for Jack. What were they going to do, sit down at her little breakfast table and talk, dressed in ballroom finery?

At that moment, a tap came on the door. "Come in," she called out, unable to resist assuming a slight pose. Chin up, breasts high, her hands clasped demurely behind her back . . . she couldn't help it. She was a woman, wasn't she?

His face when he entered and saw her standing there was absolutely priceless. The last shred of his haunted remoteness burned away as his eyes flared with appreciation. "You look . . . you are . . . stunning."

It mattered, damn it. It mattered to her that he thought she was attractive. In all her life, she had never cared what any man thought of her but for Jack. That didn't seem likely to change any time soon.

She dipped a curtsy. "Thank you. You look rather devastating yourself, my lord."

Her compliment was meant to be light and social, but his eyes widened. "Thank you," he said seriously. "The cravat gave me fits for half an hour."

Laurel bit her lip and did not smile, but she could see that his neckcloth was just a tiny bit . . . wonky. Jack, nervous?

She would not be charmed. Instead, she folded her arms and tilted her head. "Now what are we to do? Change back?"

He gazed at her for a long moment, his brown eyes going nearly black with desire. Laurel became very aware of the strategic tightness of her bodice and the very telling lack of underthings.

Lementeur, you and I are going to have to have a little talk.

Just when Laurel was afraid Jack meant to ruin another gown on the floor—*heavens, what a marvelous idea!*—he held out his hand. "Come," he said.

He'd said that to her once before. Now, as then, she came. Putting her gloved hand in his, dipping her head to hide her flaming face, she let him lead her from the attic.

But when she thought they were about to head down the stairs and into the club, he turned to take her to the large window in the main attic.

It was much like the one in her cell. In fact, it was in

the same wall and had the same view of St. James Street. Jack let go of her hand long enough to open the center panel of the window wide.

Then he climbed through it.

Twenty-seven

Laurel's eyes widened and she stepped forward hurriedly to reach out to Jack. "Don't do it, Jack! It isn't worth it!"

He looked back at her in surprise. Then he smiled, a quick flash of white teeth in the moonlight pouring down upon them. "Don't worry. I'm not planning to end it all."

It was the first smile she'd seen in years. Not since before he went away to war.

Her heart melted into a simmering little puddle, quite against her will. He was yet so beautiful, even shadowed as he was now.

He became vastly less attractive when he held out his hand through the window. "Let me help you through."

Laurel stepped back. "I hardly think so!"

He reached for her. "It's all right."

Laurel put her gloved fists on her hips. "My dear marquis, I'll have you know that there are certain laws of nature that cannot be denied. One is that it will inevitably rain on the first day you wear your new bonnet. The other is that what goes up must always fall down!"

Jack blinked at her. "Aren't you even a tiny bit curious, Bramble?" He flashed her another smile. "I double-damn dare you!"

The nickname caused a repeat melting. She was going to have to do something about that very soon. The dare, however . . .

Hiking her priceless skirts high, she grabbed his hand and stepped through the window. Keeping her eyes ruthlessly on the ledge at her feet and at the handholds he helped her to, she somehow managed to climb the slanting edge of the mansard roof to the flat top above.

Dusting her gloves irritably, peering at the stains in the moonlight, Laurel shook out her skirts and looked up.

She gasped. "Oh, my heavens!"

It was beautiful. Jack had lighted dozens of candles and placed them all around the roof. Some were lanterns and some were in candelabras. Some appeared to be simply stuck into a puddle of wax on the stone. The effect was madly beautiful, like a fantasy ballroom with no ceiling but the sky.

Laurel turned and gasped again. The moonlight streamed down upon the city of London, laid out before her. She could see St. James's Palace, fully lighted as the Prince Regent always kept it during the Season. She could see rooftops and the golden squares of windows in buildings as far as the eye could see.

"I never realized the city was so huge," she gasped. "It looks like a fairyland from here!"

Jack, who had not yet released her hand, led her to the center of the roof. Then he left her, hurrying over to one side. He bent over something she could not see.

A sweet chiming sound filled the night air. Jack came back to her and bowed. "May I have this dance, dear lady?"

Laurel stood in the circle of candlelight and stared at this amazing, bewildering man. "You wish to dance with me? To a music box?"

Jack straightened. He looked a little worried. "I hoped . . ." He stopped, then cleared his throat. "You never had the opportunity to attend a ball," he said huskily. "That was my fault."

A ball? For her? She gazed around at the shimmering fantasy rooftop. The silvery chimes of the music box danced on the moonlit night.

It was hands-down the most romantic thing she'd ever seen.

Her heart was never going to unmelt if he kept this sort of thing up. Swallowing back a ridiculous little sob, Laurel curtsied to Jack in return. "Why, thank you, my lord. I would dearly love to dance."

She put her hand in his. He swept her into his arms.

At last.

She'd dreamed of dancing with Jack when she was young. She'd fancied that they would whirl about the dance floor, entranced in each other's eyes, and the entire world would disappear.

Laughing out loud at her own prophetic fantasy, she let her head fall back as Jack whirled her around and around, skillfully guiding her in the steps she'd never had the opportunity to try out.

"Sing the words," Jack urged her.

Laurel laughed and looked away. "I think not."

"Sing. Melody told me your voice was the beautifulest." He gazed down at her with eyes dark and admiring, just as she'd once dreamed he would. "I want to hear you sing," he said huskily.

It seemed she could never refuse that tone of intimate command.

She could scarcely believe it when her lips opened and the words came out, shyly at first and then with more confidence. It was a love song, this silly music box tune. A sentimental favorite of hers.

> *"Alas, my love, you do me wrong*
> *To cast me off discourteously.*
> *And I have loved you oh so long,*
> *Delighting in your company."*

They didn't even notice when the music box wound down, nor when the candles guttered and failed. They danced until the moon went behind a cloud and then they danced in the dark, wrapped in each other's arms, lost in each other's eyes.

When Wilberforce had put all his charges to bed, both young and old, he consulted with Cook briefly to approve the menus that Lady Madeleine thought she had already approved, and made a brisk circuit of the main rooms of the club with Bailiwick, pointing out several minor matters that needed seeing to.

The mantel in the "family parlor" was looking a mite sooty and there was a new scratch in the wood parquet floor that needed polishing out. Wilberforce squinted at it for a long moment. Bailiwick shifted uncomfortably.

"It were spurs, Mr. Wilberforce."

"I am quite aware of that, Bailiwick. I am only pondering whether the aforementioned apparatus resided on Master Evan's boot or perhaps . . ."

He waited.

Bailiwick drooped. "It might've been mine, Mr. Wilberforce."

Wilberforce was perfectly aware that the mark came

from Evan's spurs. The boy had affected a pair of them only last week, although he would never dream of actually using them on his beloved Ramses. He had insisted that Bailiwick wear them as well, sending half the staff running around London trying to find a pair that would fit the young underfootman's massive boots. Bailiwick's spurs still hung next to Balthazar's whip in the mews, neither ever having been used.

Wilberforce merely wished to ascertain whether Bailiwick remembered his primary purpose on this earth. He was to serve. Service was an ancient and nearly holy occupation, in Wilberforce's mind. Service, to him, was an art and a science, and he was the high master of both.

Nodding in satisfaction that Bailiwick did in fact recall his proper mission in life, Wilberforce offered the young man his highest praise. "That will do, Mr. Bailiwick."

Even in the doldrums of his languishing passion for Fiona, Bailiwick brightened at such a florid compliment. "*Thank you,* Mr. Wilberforce!"

Wilberforce nodded and turned away. All was right in his kingdom.

It was time to investigate the attic.

Once through the door in the upper hallway, he saw little to dismay him on the stairs. Climbing higher, he saw by the light of his candle that the main attic chamber was much as it should be, although he thought he might send the abrasive young Samuel up there to give the relics a thorough dusting and inventory.

Then Wilberforce noticed a strange fact. There was dust everywhere in the attic, a thick layer that covered everything like a sifting of fine flour.

Everywhere except in a clearly defined path that led directly from the top of the stairs to the attic laundry chamber where Lady Madeleine had once been imprisoned. That must be where Melody was spending her days.

Crossing the chamber, Wilberforce felt in his pocket for his other master key. When he put his hand to the latch, however, the door simply opened. Melody had not locked up behind her—

It was difficult to surprise a man of Wilberforce's experience. He'd endured decades of churlish members, demanding members, and even a few insane members. Still, his elegant features registered actual shock as the door opened onto Ali Baba's cave of treasures.

The room was filled with color and comfort. This was no child's hideaway, not unless the child had an army at her disposal. Had Bailiwick helped Melody create this luxurious chamber? Had it been the marquis himself who had raided his own room for Melody's comfort?

And why in the world would Melody need a bed?

Abruptly aware that his jaw sagged in disbelief, Wilberforce snapped it shut and assumed his usual imperturbable expression, grateful that there was no one about to see him lose control so outrageously.

How to handle this strange thievery? There was no actual crime of course, for it appeared that nothing had left the club at all. There were the tapestries and all the carpets and the fine rosewood furniture, right before his eyes.

Actually, there seemed to be no harm at all in it. If his lordship knew of Melody's secret chamber, then there was no reason to interfere with her play. He might have a word with Bailiwick, just in case the young man had known of it and neglected to inform Wilberforce, but that was no concern of his lordship's.

With a decisive nod, Wilberforce turned and left the chamber as he had found it.

However, he would keep a very close eye on matters, to be sure.

Wilberforce would have been very surprised to know that in the main attic chamber he had failed to notice that the center panel of the large window stood ever so slightly ajar.

Wilberforce was not the sort to miss things.

Laurel gasped and shut her eyes and trembled, yet somehow she still managed to make her way back down the angled bit of roof and across the narrow ledge to the attic window. Jack kept her hand tightly in his the entire time and helped her, giggling with relief, back through the window into the attic.

She tripped over the windowsill and tumbled with a tiny shriek into his arms. Gasping, she clung to him, then recalled that she had only to fall to the floor. She snickered. "Only I would be clumsy *after* the ledge."

Jack didn't set her on her feet again as she'd expected him to. He held her there, close enough to hear his heart pound. "I would never let you fall," he whispered.

If her heart melted one more time she was going to have to keep it in a jam jar on a shelf. Her lips parted as she gazed into his shadowed eyes. *Kiss me.*

He kissed her, so softly at first it was no more than if a butterfly had rested on her lips. She grasped his lapels in her gloved hands and leaned into the kiss, deepening it. He let her, returning her foray into his mouth with a questing tongue of his own. His hands came up to cup her jaw and he tilted her head to better explore her mouth.

They kissed long and slow, until Laurel lost her breath and hung dizzily in his arms.

At last she pulled away, gasping. "Stay—stay with me tonight."

Even as the words came from her lips, she had no idea why she'd said them, nor did she have any wish to call them back. Time was running out, this time of secret days and nights. She could feel the clock ticking away until the moment when the world would intrude once more.

One night, she told herself. *One last night and then I will take my daughter and go.*

One glorious night with Jack, to match that other astonishing night. Two memories to keep with her always.

Together they stumbled into her chamber. Laurel staggered to the center of the room, hardly noticing when Jack paused to lock them inside.

Twenty-eight

Once he had locked them in, Jack dropped the key into his weskit pocket and walked slowly toward his magnificent, outrageous Laurel.

This time he would not take. His overpowering need on this night was to make sure Laurel understood.

I know what you have lost.

Her girlhood was stolen from her, her debut passed over to give birth in secrecy and loss. She experienced nothing that a young lady should—no beaus, no balls, no dancing the night away in beautiful gowns. There was only betrayal from everyone who should have been most kind to her. The world had been taking from Laurel for far too long.

It was time for him to give.

He had so much to make up for. So many years lost to being foolish and blind. So many times he could have seen the truth and he'd turned away from it.

Most of all, he needed Laurel to feel how much he loved her, not just wanted her, not simply needed her.

He stood behind her and slowly scooped her hair from her back and swept it over her shoulder to fall down the front of her gown. That left her delectable back bare to his hands and his lips. She stood quite still with her head bent as he kissed his way down her delicate spine until he reached the tiny buttons.

He managed them rather well, considering he was a bit out of practice undressing women. Though they shook a bit, his hands were sure as they spread out over her shoulder blades like wings, then pushed the silly little cap sleeves off her shoulders.

The gown slipped dramatically away and she was quite suddenly naked before him.

Thank you, Button!

Jack moved up close behind her and laced his fingers into hers by her sides. For a long moment he simply buried his face in her neck and breathed her in. Never, never would he get enough of that sweet, clean scent.

She shivered slightly as his hands slid slowly up her arms to her shoulders. He pulled her to him, savoring the roundness of her bottom against his groin. Tipping her head back on his shoulder, he let his hands explore the changes the years had wrought in her.

Her breasts were full and heavy in his palms. Her body swelled beautifully from her tiny waist, providing him with tempting hips and full, soft thighs. She was rounder all over now and he relished it.

She melted against him. He recognized that desire in her. She was ready to be conquered and dominated. How wrong he'd been to introduce her with such play. If it was possible to rewrite that night of taking, he would try to do it over again tonight.

Tonight they would come together as equals, as lovers, as two hearts showing their true feelings with their bodies.

His cock surged as he ran his palms down over her

belly and down, brushing those dark curls with his finger-tips.

Laurel didn't know what to do with the flood of emotions his gentle touch ignited within her. He'd done so many things to her in the past, even in the past few days, and yet never once had she felt such tenderness from his touch.

What had happened to him? He was not the cock-sure Jack of old, nor was he the shattered, beautiful man who had emerged from battle.

This Jack was someone new. Something of the old, something of the broken, which likely would never be completely gone, nor would she wish it. Within herself, the broken bits were part of her now, part of her world. Even Melody was a part of them now.

And now, inside Jack, coming from him in a deep and silent rhythm that seemed to resonate in the very deepest parts of her, was something new. He was no longer lost, no longer drowning, no longer swept away in a maelstrom of terror and loss.

Jack had somehow found his land legs at last.

It only made him all the more beautiful to her.

She tried to turn to him, to explain what she had only just realized, but at that moment his tender ques-tioning fingertips had found their way between her damp labia.

With a gasp, every thought she had left her head.

There was only his sweet, seeking touch, only his breath on her neck, only his big, warm, solid body be-hind her.

He surrounded her, enfolded her. She felt like a trea-sure, guarded and protected in his arms.

Something of the old trust survived, for she simply

let her head fall back upon his shoulder, permitting him anything he wished.

Evidently, he wished to please her.

His fingertips stroked up and down her slit, testing the dampness and spreading the slippery nectar up and down, up and down, a little deeper on each pass. She lightly rested her hands on his clothed forearms. He was still in evening dress. She was naked but for her stockings and the ribbon she wore about her throat. The difference plucked every erotic chord in her body.

His teasing fingers slid softly up to and around her clitoris. She jumped and shivered, but he did not stay. He went back to the slipping sliding rhythm. Each time his fingertips crested her slit, he gently caressed her clitoris in sweet little circles, then left it again. Her body grew slowly heavy with desire, a deep throb of want beginning inside her.

Her clitoris hardened like one of her nipples, which were already diamond points in the waves of chill that shivered her body, though the room was warm.

There was no sound in the chamber but the occasional crackling of the coals in the hearth and her own breathing, which was quickened with each inhalation.

His own breath was silent and hot on her neck, warming her shoulder and breast. Then she felt his fingers slip deeper within her. She gasped and gripped his forearms with her hands, pressing back against him in reaction.

She felt his cock rise then, a thick prisoner within his trousers, pressing just above her bottom. Once she had taken his cock inside her, had sucked him deep into her throat, had allowed and enjoyed every single inch of it.

Now she shivered. If she should lose herself to that passion again, she might never come back.

If she didn't, she would regret it for the rest of her life.

She wanted Jack. She'd always wanted Jack.

Whether or not she could keep him was a question she preferred to reserve for another night, one of the cold and lonely ones that filled her future.

Her knees gave a little as her growing desire weakened them. Jack wrapped one arm about her waist and held her close while he continued his leisurely caresses. Slowly, slowly, he taught her patience. Slippery wet now, his big fingers stroked into her, then withdrew to draw delicate circles around her clitoris, ever smaller spirals until it throbbed to his touch. Dipping deep, taking her slowly and gently, one finger, then two, then back to her clitoris, circling, circling.

Her head tossed restlessly on his shoulder. He shushed her impatience and kissed her neck as he touched her, his lips finding that perfectly sensitive place at the base of her neck. Slowly, sweetly, in and out, up and around. His other hand joined the first so that she could have both together. Her knees wanted to widen for him. She wanted to fall beneath him and be filled with him. She wanted his hands on her breasts so badly that she put her own there instead, squeezing her full breasts, knowing that he watched as she teased her own nipples.

She heard her own voice, wordless little whimpering cries of want, tiny sighs of pleasure. The solid room absorbed the sound. She could scream in this room if she liked.

In and out. Around and around. His fingers drove her higher with such gentle ease that she was scarcely ready for her orgasm when it fell upon her. With a cry, she shattered in his grasp, bucking her body into his fingers, rolling her head on his shoulder, crying out his name again and again as she tumbled from the height, falling, flying, fluttering down, her heart pounding, her breath rasping in her throat.

Her legs gave out. He caught her, lifting her effortlessly in his arms. Still panting, she wound her naked arms about his clothed shoulders and held on, feeling her heart find its rhythm again, coming back to herself in little moments.

She could feel the buttons of his weskit against her ribs and breast. She could feel his clothed arms about her naked body. It excited her, yet she also wanted him naked as well.

He carried her to the bed. She thought he would lie down with her, but he did not. Instead he laid her gently down. Then he knelt beside the bed and pulled her gently toward him, his big hands wrapped around her knees.

She slid easily across the coverlet, her arms limp above her head, her body still humming with pleasure. When he pressed her knees wide apart, his hands spread over her thighs, she opened willingly, for she had no will left at all.

When he dropped his mouth upon her, she gasped. *Oh, sweet heaven!* She'd thought his hands talented, but they were nothing compared to his wicked, teasing tongue! He licked her slit, up and down. Then he dipped inside, thrusting his tongue deep. Then, he slid his big thumbs together up her wet valley and pressed her labia apart so that his mouth could service her clitoris.

Laurel grabbed double fistfuls of coverlet and held

on for dear life as the pleasure stole her away like a hurricane wind. His mouth, his tongue, even the evening stubble on his cheeks and chin, his big gentle fingers, probing and pressing, his wicked, skillful tongue, lapping and licking, touching, probing, slippery and blunt, over and over and over her clitoris, until her hips pumped without her will and her head tossed so her hair covered her face.

He took her there and kept her there, suspended in constant exquisite ecstasy, yet not high enough to fly over the edge. She begged and pleaded. She said wicked, exciting words, trying to drive him to lose control, to enter her, to take her hard and fast and make her come at his command.

He would not but only drove her onward, only made her nearly weep for it, until the moment when he abruptly sucked her rigid clitoris into his mouth like one of her nipples and thrust two fingers inside her, thrusting again and again.

She shrieked in relief as her orgasm shuddered through her like a thunderbolt. It went on and on and she rode it helplessly, clinging to Jack's clothed shoulders, driving her hands into his thick hair, flinging her arms wide to pull helplessly at the coverlet.

At last it left her, lying there like a bit of flotsam on the beach, abandoned by the waves. Her breath wheezed in her lungs and she shuddered on and on, unable to stop until he climbed onto the bed and pulled her into his arms, holding her tightly, giving her something to hang on to as she slowly regained herself once more.

He murmured things into her hair, though she did not truly hear them. Comforting things, nonsense things. "Laurel, sweet Bramble, shh, hold on. Shh, just breathe."

Then she thought she heard him whisper, "Marry me, Bramble."

With a gasp, she drew back to look at him, seeking to meet his gaze, but he would not look at her. He gazed anywhere but into her face as he smoothed her hair upon the pillow and used his handkerchief to dab at the perspiration on her face and between her breasts.

She opened her lips to question him but then realized that she might not be able to handle the answer. Closing her eyes, she turned her face away and allowed him to tend to her instead.

Her heart returned to its normal pace, but for the occasional skip when she remembered those maybe-whispered words. Her breathing became inaudible once more though her chest went tight as she played those lovely, terrifying impossible words back in her mind.

Marry me, Bramble.

No, she did not want to hear him repeat them. She did not want to have to answer. Words were meaningless sounds, anyway. Instead, she wanted to feel everything she could possibly feel tonight. Abruptly she rolled into his body, pressing her breasts and belly and thighs against him. Driving her hands into his hair, she pulled his face down for her kiss, deep and hard and sure to keep any more words from hanging in the air between them.

Twenty-nine

Jack kissed Laurel back, letting his big hands slide down to her buttocks, where he held her tightly to his erection as they ravaged each other's mouths.

Jack's cock was so hard he was quite sure his trouser buttons were in danger of flying across the room like bullets, but he was determined that this night would be for his lovely Bramble's pleasure. When Laurel pushed on his shoulders, he obediently rolled back onto the bed, pulling her over him. Her beautiful mass of dark hair covered both their faces, hiding them, keeping their passion secret and safe. Her breasts pressed to his chest, full and heavy, her nipples so hard that he felt them even through his weskit and shirt. She straddled his body, her cunt wet and hot over the fabric stretched across his cock. It was torture, sweet and painful, to feel her so close yet be unable to enter her.

Torture, perhaps, that he deserved.

She sat up at last, mounted upon him like a lovely Godiva, her hair flowing over her full breasts, her mouth swollen and pink from their kiss. She ran her tongue over those full lips, making Jack's cock throb in response.

Then she began to work at his lopsided cravat. Jack let her, watching her face as she concentrated on the mangled knot, watching her breasts jiggle delightfully as she tugged at the stubborn linen.

He slid his hands up her open thighs slowly, then merely rested them upon her shapely hips. This was Laurel's command. He was naught but a sailor on her ship.

At last she smiled triumphantly and tossed the cravat from her with a flourish. "I outwitted it!"

In mere moments she had undone his weskit and pulled his shirt from his trousers. Taking his hands, she made him sit up so she could remove his upper garments. Naked from the waist up, lying beneath her, Jack wanted nothing more than to suck madly on her breasts while he drove himself into her hot, wet body again and again, but he forced himself to wait.

It was but the work of a moment to undress him. Smiling, she ran quick, questing hands over his body, making him shiver.

The rest of his clothing melted away without nearly so much effort and then she was upon him. She only faltered for a moment, when he maneuvered her thighs astride him. "Like this?"

He ran his hands up her rounded thighs. "You shall decide," he said softly. "It is your will."

Her tongue flicked across her lips as she considered this and Jack thought he might die a little if she hesitated much longer. Then she lowered herself upon his cock, enveloping him in wet, sweet heat, inch by agonizing inch, until she rested her hands upon his chest, entirely impaled upon him.

Gasping slightly, she followed his urging to rise and fall. Her pace was slow and torturous to him, arousing him beyond bearing, yet he made no move to hurry her.

His hands were upon her only to aid her pleasure. He teased her nipples hard, pinching and rolling tenderly. She tossed her hair back and increased her pace then, riding him at a gallop.

She was so beautiful above him, wild and commanding and openly sexual, confident in her beauty, sure in his desire for her.

When he slipped his fingertips into the wet crevice where they joined, she cried out loud. Desperately holding his own ejaculation back, nearly biting a hole through his own lip, he used every bit of concentration he had to tease her clitoris into giving her an orgasm.

She rose and fell, faster and faster, arching and glistening with sweat, so beautiful, so perfectly animal with her hot gaze locked on his and her lips parted with her panting breath.

When she came, she cried out his name. The feeling of her cunt throbbing about his cock was too much for Jack and he lost control with a roar, grabbing her hips with hard hands and thrusting once, deep, spilling his seed into her even as she trembled and gasped above him.

Carried by lust, tangled by love, they rode the moment together, skin to skin, hard into soft, heart to heart, gasping each other's breath into their lungs.

Laurel lay wrapped in Jack's arms, her silken hair trailing over his chest and stomach, her smooth thigh overlying his hairy ones. He wanted it to go on forever, this moment out of time, this moment that might have been theirs always if things had not gone so horribly wrong.

It broke his heart to know that she'd heard him and pretended she had not. How badly he had damaged her beautiful, loving soul that she could not believe in what was freely offered to her.

He stroked one hand down the curve of her waist. "Will you wed me, Bramble?"

He felt her freeze even as he said the words. Her sudden stillness reminded him of a rabbit trying very hard not to be spotted by a hawk.

"Bramble?"

She shivered at the nickname. Then she pulled away from him, drawing the coverlet with her. She ended up as far as she could get from him and still remain on the bed. She was covered from breastbone to feet with the cover and she clutched it to her as if she feared he would rip it from her body.

"I . . ." Her breath sounded panicked, as if she fled a great beast. "I *can't.*"

Jack sat up and gazed at her with the sheet just puddled at his hips. "What is it? What has you so terrified?"

She shook her head. "No. I'm fine," she said tightly.

He reached a hand to her. She drew back. "Laurel, you are shaking with fear. What is it?"

Brushing at her face quickly, she raised her chin and looked away from him. "Do you know what my parents did when they learned I was with child?"

He nodded. "They told you she died."

She laughed, a small sound like breaking glass. "They locked me in my room."

Jack frowned. "Well, I can imagine they were upset—"

Her face came up and her eyes were hot and full of hatred. "They locked me up for more than *six months!*"

"Oh my God." Jack's gut went cold. "Oh, Bramble—"

Then it hit him. *Oh no.*

He had done the same.

"They said they would let me out if I told them who the father was. They said they would let me out if I drank the nettle tea and lost the baby. They promised me that everything would go back to being the same if I let some old witch kill my baby with a knitting needle!"

You told her you would let her go if she gave up Melody. It might not be what you said, but it was what you meant and she knew it.

"My mother! My father! The last two people in the world I could have dreamed would harm me!"

And me. Don't forget it was I who left you there.

"So you might forgive me, my lord," her voice was choked, as if her throat were too tight to speak, "if I don't believe a bloody word anyone says to me while they've locked me in a room!"

Jack passed his hands over his face. It occurred to him from a strange distance that he might like to vomit soon.

Her breath hitched in her throat. He could feel the depth of her trembling through the bed itself.

He cleared his throat. It was time to give her everything. "I found the midwife who delivered Melody," he told her. "Your parents ordered her to kill the baby, but she kept her instead. For three years she blackmailed your mother and father in order to support Melody in secret."

Laurel gazed at him with wide eyes. "She . . . she seemed kind . . . that night."

Jack nodded. "I think she was. She is dying, or I think she might have kept Melody forever. She loves her very much and Melody seems very attached as well."

Laurel let out a breath. "That's good, that she loved her."

This part would not be so simple. "Nanny Pruitt tried to find you when she learned she was ill. She spoke to Amaryllis, thinking you were one and the same. Your sister sent her packing, empty-handed. That was . . . more than three months back."

Laurel's gaze flared with the blue heat of the center of a flame. "I have no sister."

"Nanny Pruitt remembered that you said, 'He's at Brown's.' She left Melody here with naught but a note pinned to her coat. I imagine she was frightened of being found out for blackmail."

Laurel pulled her knees up high and wrapped her arms about them. "Perhaps I should have told them," she murmured. "They might have been able to find you when I could not."

Jack shook his head. "They would not have. I had been at sea for more than three years, never stopping for more than a few weeks in any port. Of the many letters sent to me, only the merest few reached me at all."

Laurel closed her eyes, remembering. "I wrote you letter after letter, but then I burned them. My mother kept a tight rein on her staff. The letters would never have made it out of our house."

"Why didn't you tell them?" he whispered.

She dropped her face into her knees. "I was so horrified when they locked me up, when they beat me—I couldn't bear to cooperate with them. Then, later, when I cried and begged and pleaded . . . when I became a silly, desperate coward and promised to tell them everything, to do *anything,* my mother sneered and said it was too late. I was already becoming large. There would be a scandal no matter what and there could be no scandal allowed to interfere with Amaryllis's wedding to her precious earl."

Jack felt his chance to love her dying with every word. She'd spent so long betrayed. Could she ever bring herself to believe again? How could she ever trust him with such overwhelming evidence to the contrary? It was no wonder she thought she could not count on anyone but herself.

She rocked slowly back and forth in silence for a moment. "My parents could not have designed a more thorough punishment. Don't you see? By locking me away, by keeping me so alone, the child inside me was my only companion. I spoke to her, sang to her, told her every story I could remember. Sometimes when I wept, she would dance in my belly and distract me from my self-pity. When I slept, she would wake me in the night and we would curl up together as I would whisper to her of all the places I would show her and all the wonderful things we would do."

She brushed at her eyes again. "She was particularly fond of adventure stories. I know it sounds mad, but I swear to you that I could always calm her kicking by telling her tales of—"

"Pirates."

Her eyes widened. "Don't tell me that's still true?"

"She tells them to me more often than the other way about, but she wants nothing to do with any story but 'Captain Jack and the Wily Crew of the *Dishonor's Plunder.*'"

Laurel looked at him with a brow raised. "I believe I've met this pirate."

Her faint teasing tone only made him feel worse.

"Really?" He glanced aside. "I haven't seen him for years."

"No," she said thoughtfully. "I don't suppose you have."

It was blindingly obvious that it was no use, but he had to try. "Bramble, I love you."

She drew back, suspicion flaring in her eyes. "Lies will not help, Jack. You do not love me. Until a few days ago, you'd forgotten me!"

"Never! I simply—didn't know who it was I remembered." He sounded ridiculous. She gazed at him with wary eyes. "It was the dress, you see. . . ." He tried to explain, to tell her about Lementeur's words and how he'd realized the truth. "I was so blind. It was always you, Bramble. You were the reason I came to that house again and again. You were the one I truly wanted to see, to talk to. You have always been the one whom I loved!"

She stared at him silently. He continued, his words halting but determined. If he had to rip himself open and serve himself up on a plate of eggs and bacon, he would do it. Anything to take that dark suspicion from her gaze.

"I love you, just . . . you. I love the way that you see right to the center of things, the way that you see people for who they really, truly are!" *See me, my love; oh, please see me!* "I love your beautiful face and your sweet body and I love your true heart! I love the girl who wouldn't give in and I love the girl who gave in."

She flinched.

He stumbled on. "I love the look on your face when you hold Melody. I love the way that you lose yourself in a book and can barely remember your own name when you're interrupted. I love the way that you live,

Laurel Clarke, the way that I have never seen anyone live—full speed ahead, damn the pirates, honest and uncompromising with the truth." He slid naked from the bed to kneel at her feet. "This is the truth, Laurel, my thorny Bramble, my love—this is the only true thing that I know. I love you. I will always love you. How can I prove it to you? What can I do to make you understand what you mean to me?"

Laurel hugged the covers to her chilled belly and stared at Jack. She had never seen this Jack before. She had never seen this man who spoke so passionately, who pleaded so clumsily and endearingly before her.

He was rather wonderful—

If he was real.

However, this was not a natural courtship, this bizarre seduction of tapestries and ball gowns and locked doors. She could not allow herself to believe anything she was feeling under this sort of duress.

If she trusted this, if she gave in to him and he failed her, she did not think she could ever recover herself again. Like a leg too often broken, her heart would never work properly again.

She swallowed hard. "I want Melody. I want to leave this place. I want to go far, far away from here and never return."

His face went tight. "You wish to leave me?"

Forcing herself to become iron, Laurel met his gaze unflinchingly. "You asked what I wanted. Will you give me that?"

She saw the light die out of his eyes then. The passionately pleading man went away. It was dark Jack who stood up, un-self-consciously naked before her, as detached from the world as ever.

"That is the one thing I will not do," he said flatly. Then he turned and gathered up his clothing. Still naked, he strode from the room.

Laurel heard the lock turn. The clunking sound was like the first shovelful of soil into the grave of her hopes.

He would not give Melody up, not ever. Laurel would have to flee with her daughter and live like a fugitive for the rest of her life, scarcely able to pay for a roof over their heads.

It was not enough to stop her, but her heart wept that she must do that to Melody.

Laurel would not admit to herself that her heart wept that she must do that to Jack as well.

Thirty

The mighty Marquis of Strickland paced his room, helpless in the face of his tangled feelings. The entire world was sleeping, even the fast-living, dancing-till-dawn *ton*. He was the only one who could not bear to shut his eyes and enter the world of dreams.

He leaned one shoulder against the side of his window embrasure and gazed out at the moonlit garden. What was he to do?

If he kept her, she would never trust him.

If he set her free, she would run as far as possible and never return, taking his daughter with her.

He rubbed his face with his hands, trying to force a solution into his brain. How could he get the family who he wanted? How could he make her understand what she meant to him—what both of them meant to him?

When he raised his face from his hands, he noticed a corner of linen poking up from beneath the bottom of the draperies. Bending, he reached for the grimy, knotted thing. Contemplating the stitched-on "eyes" of Gordy Ann, he carried her to join him in his wingback chair by the fire.

"What do you think?" He hadn't been exaggerating when he'd called Gordy Ann a good listener. There was none better. "What am I to do?"

She flopped limply in his grasp, knot-head rolling back. He gave her a gentle shake. "Come on. I need a bit of help here."

No reply. Well, how could he blame her when he had no answers himself?

If he squinted, he could still see how Colin had tied a fine cravat into the dandified pattern known as the "Gordian Knot" style. How Melody could have discerned a doll from that was anyone's guess, but just like everyone else at Brown's under the influence of Melody's ferocious imagination, Jack had quickly come to see Gordy Ann as a doll, not a neck cloth.

He held her up by a single grimy "arm" and frowned at her. "You need a bit of a scrub, old thing." He tossed her over to the little Melody-size chair opposite his and contemplated Gordy Ann's flopped form impassively. "You are no help whatsoever."

Stretching his arms over his head, then rotating his neck, did nothing to ease the tension within him. "'And Alexander the Great saw the Gordian Knot,'" he recited the story beneath his breath, "'that not even the finest minds of the world could untie. He raised his sword and with a great cry, cleaved the knot in two . . .'"

Slowly his voice faded to a whisper. "Cleaved . . ."

What do you do when there is no solution to a knotted puzzle?

Cleave the puzzle in two.

What if the puzzle is your own heart?

In the purple hour just before dawn, Laurel slipped from Jack's guest room to creep back to her own bedchamber. She'd scarcely been able to walk when she'd risen from Jack's bed, leaving him quite unconscious with satiation. Her knees might never be the same.

It was a chilly, breathless game to sneak back through her house in her nightdress. Some of the servants were surely already up, for there were guests in the house.

Once back where she should be, safely unseen, she leaned back against her closed door and took a deep breath.

Her room looked odd. It was the room of a child, full of books and drawings and hair ribbons. It felt wrong to her now.

The world would never be the same. She would never be the same. This night she had explored a part of herself that she'd never known existed.

When she was small, she'd had a governess who was one of the only people in the world who preferred her to Amaryllis. The woman had seemed stern and exacting, but upon realizing Laurel's love of reading and knowledge she'd warmed to her completely.

Still waters run deep, *her teacher had told her once, when she moped about being outshone by her sister.*

"Still waters," Laurel whispered to herself now. It was so true. In this house where no one thought of anything but rank and wealth and how to get more of it, she had spent her days simply trying to live alongside her family, thinking that if she could only understand them, she could learn how to make them understand her.

How could she have understood the depths that lay within her?

Now she realized for the first time that she was a person all in her own right. She had taken a step, opened a door, and was now miles away from the young woman she'd been yesterday. The concerns of her family seemed like the wind in the trees, not worthy of her notice.

She would wed Jack as soon as possible. She would leave here with him and live with him and love him always. He would take her away and take her to bed every night and they would work dark and beautiful magic there, transformative magic. She would be his wife, best friend, and lover.

He would be her everything.

Abruptly she yawned. Pulling her aching, exhausted body upright once more, she staggered to her bed. As she sat on the mattress, she winced.

Well, perhaps they would not do this every night. Surely once or twice a week they ought to sleep instead. Giggling at the thought of her shimmering, jewel-toned future with her Jack, she fell back onto her pillow and slipped into the heavy sleep of the most thoroughly satisfied.

It was only four hours later that she ran to the front door in her dressing gown, clutching her wrapper about her, and watched Jack being thrown from her house onto the gravel drive outside.

Wide-eyed, she turned to her sister, who stood watching the drama unfold with haughty disinterest.

"What has happened? Why has Papa done this?"

Amaryllis's sharp eyes swept over her and Laurel became aware of her tangled hair and her kiss-bruised mouth. She pulled the neck of her wrapper high to hide the rash of stubble burn on her neck. Amaryllis's eyes glinted malevolently as she turned back to where Jack stood, cursing and shouting in the drive.

"Jack refused to release me from our silly little engagement. He thought I should choose him instead of

my darling earl! Can you imagine?" She smiled archly at her sister. "He begged me to wed him straightaway. Poor Jack. I was bored with him weeks ago."

Amaryllis sauntered away, leaving Laurel to stare out at the drive where two Clarke footmen were forcibly shoving Jack onto his saddled horse and whipping it until it raced from the estate, Jack clinging to its back.

He would come back. Laurel dashed the tears from her eyes and lifted her chin. She trusted Jack with her life. He would never leave her now.

As soon as he calmed his horse, he would come back for her. It was all a misunderstanding. Papa had thought Jack wanted Amaryllis when it should have been perfectly obvious he truly loved Laurel instead!

Putting a hand to her face, she felt her tangled locks hanging over her brow. Oh, heavens! She looked a mess! She ought to go and dress. Jack would be coming for her soon!

He'd as much as told her he loved her last night! Hadn't he?

In the early-morning hours Jack moved carefully past the bed containing sleeping Aidan and Madeleine and entered Melody's nursery. Pulling her limp and warm from her bed, Jack took her to the chair and held her in his lap while she slept.

She wiggled into him, little elbows pressed firmly into his belly. On her small bed, the kitten woke and shook his oversized head. Then he proceeded to cleanse his bottom, one scrawny mutton leg high in the air, toes spread wide.

Jack held his tiny daughter, listening to her wispy breathing. She was growing so fast. Her feet had begun to hang over the side of his lap. He kissed the top of her shining head and breathed in that clean, childish scent that she would not keep for much longer.

Finally, she stirred in his lap. Her big eyes blinked open, unfocused and confused. She gazed at her bed for a long moment, possibly wondering why she wasn't in it. Then she looked up at him, her baby cheeks flushed and round. Her eyes were Laurel's eyes. They would remind him forever of the love he'd ruined with his own two hands.

"Papa, did you sleep in my bed?"

Her bed was not much more than a yard long. Jack imagined himself bent like a kipper in a jar, stuffed into the tiny bed. "No, Lady Melody, I—" *did not sleep.* "I did not sleep in your bed. I only wanted to say good morning and say hello to your very fine cat."

Melody scrubbed at her eyes. "Papa, I can't find Gordy Ann. She went away."

Jack reached into his pocket and extracted his secret confidante. Melody grasped her with a sigh of relief and tucked her beneath her little chin. "She came back!"

"Oh, thank goodness," said a husky voice in the doorway of the nursery. Lady Madeleine stood there in her dressing gown and mussed hair. "I rose early to start the search once more. We were up late in a panic, I can tell you. Colin even vowed that he could tie another cravat, but Aidan didn't believe him."

Jack nodded at Gordy Ann. "I think she's become something beyond a simple cravat now, don't you?"

Madeleine blinked at him. Then she shook off her surprise. "My apologies, my lord. I simply cannot get used to you actually answering me."

Jack tilted his head. "Then why did you continue to speak to me as if you expected one?"

She shrugged. "I hoped, I suppose. And . . . well, it seemed rude not to."

The corner of his mouth twitched. "My friend is a lucky man."

She flashed a lovely smile and dropped a casual curtsy. "Thank you, my lord."

Melody looked up. "Did Papa say a commple-mint, Maddie?"

Madeleine smiled at the new word. "Indeed he did pay me a compliment, Mousie."

"Commple-mints are nice things." Melody snuggled into Jack. "Papa, say a nice thing to Gordy Ann."

Jack gazed down at the filthy linen knot-head. "You've been a good friend to me, my lady."

Satisfied, Melody yawned, much like the kitten had. "Gordy Ann says thank you, Papa."

Madeleine gazed thoughtfully at them for a long moment. "Something is different, isn't it? What did you learn yesterday?"

Yesterday seemed like a dozen years past. Jack gazed at Madeleine. "Melody is indeed mine," he told her. It didn't matter any longer.

Her eyes widened, then filled with joy. "Oh! But that is wonderful! I must tell Aidan! And Pru!" She turned and bustled back into her room.

Jack preferred not to take part in any further discussion on the matter, so he plunked Melody back into her little bed, making the kitten jump in surprise and making Melody giggle. Then Jack slipped quickly away while Madeleine was hidden in her bed curtains.

"Aidan! Aidan, we may keep her! Isn't that wonderful?"

Was it wonderful? Or was it simply another betrayal?

Sometime later that morning, when everyone had heard the glad news and had raised their coffee high in a toast, despite the fact that Jack had missed breakfast, Evan wandered through the parlor.

"Where's the monster?" he asked his sister casually.

Pru put down her book and frowned. "Do you know, I haven't seen her for a while."

Evan rolled his eyes. "Hiding again."

It soon became clear that if Melody was hiding, it was not in any of her usual haunts. Feeling a bit guilty, Evan even checked the dumbwaiter, only to find that someone had secured it down in the cellar and it would no longer move at all.

Wilberforce came upon Lady Madeleine and Lady Lambert checking the window embrasure at the end of the upper hallway. Bailiwick was farther down, peering into the large Ming dynasty vase on the hall table. Lady Lambert frowned at him. "Have you seen Melody, Wibbly-force?"

Wilberforce gave Lady Lambert a long-suffering gaze, but she didn't even realize she'd said it. "I believe Lady Melody is prone to playing in the attic."

Lady Madeleine shook her head. "I don't think so. She doesn't like it up there any more than I do."

Wilberforce bowed. "I do not wish to contradict you, my lady, but I believe she plays there daily."

Lady Lambert turned to regard the door at the opposite end of the hallway. "Really?"

Thirty-one

Laurel's eyes went wide and she sat very still as her door opened and an unfamiliar man stood in the doorway. He blinked at her for a long moment, his patrician face revealing nothing but bland surprise.

Then this elegant figure in livery backed out and bowed two ladies through the door. Two heads, one dark and the other red, peered from opposite sides of the door.

Laurel stood and smiled. "Good morning, Lady Madeleine, Lady Prudence."

The redhead straightened and stepped into the room. "Lady Lambert," she corrected absently as she gazed about her in astonishment. She waved a hand at Lady Madeleine. "Born posh." Then at herself. "Married posh."

Laurel smiled nervously. "Thank you for your clarity." She held out her hand. "I am Miss Laurel Clarke."

Lady Madeleine entered, shrinking away from the walls and staying near the door. "You are a *prisoner* here?"

Laurel dropped her hand. Polite social conversation did seem a bit silly. "I am—" What was she? Prisoner or guest? Victim or lover? Abruptly she was no longer sure. The reality of these people seeing her and seeing her locked cell seemed to flip some sort of switch in her mind.

Icy realization doused her. Nothing she'd felt or believed in this room could ever be considered real. In a mere matter of days she'd come to feel at home in her attic cell. Her mind had slipped sideways into receptiveness so quickly, it made her wonder if she were perhaps a little bit mad.

She stumbled in her explanation. "I am—"

"Mama!" Melody bounced into the room, waving Gordy Ann in the air joyously. "Can Maddie and Pru play 'Queen in the Tower' now, too?"

Lady Madeleine pressed a hand to her throat. "'Mama'?" she whispered. "Oh, sweet heaven, how could he?"

Lady Lambert made a face. "Jack, you idiot!" There were a few other choice words beyond that, but Laurel pretended not to hear.

The tall, haughty servant stepped forward and bowed. "Madam, I am Wilberforce, head of staff here at Brown's. Is there anything I may do for you?"

Laurel only stared at him, at Lady Madeleine's white-faced shock, at Lady Lambert's open cursing, down at Melody, who had her arms wrapped around Laurel's shins and who smiled up at her happily.

She looked back up at Wilberforce. "I could truly use a cup of tea."

It took several pots of tea, served to them by a footman so vastly tall that he was forced to duck beneath the attic beams. Laurel told Maddie and Pru, as she was commanded to call them, every detail of her arrival and subsequent incarceration. Well, not every detail. She left out the intimate bits and she kept quiet about her master key, not wishing for them to realize how she'd roamed the club at night, poking into their rooms.

Wilberforce had taken Melody away, luring her with the promise of lemon seedcakes, so Laurel could speak freely. Pru moved restlessly about the room. "You should pack at once," she said firmly.

Madeleine still did not seem comfortable in the room. She kept looking about her nervously. Laurel finally took pity on her. She leaned close. "I've been assured that the Badman is completely and entirely dead, several times over in fact."

Madeleine shot her a dark glance. "Is he? Jack knew of my imprisonment. The fact that he would use this room so—" She shook her head. "It's simply four walls and a window." She swallowed. "And a door. Did you know there was a peephole drilled into the door?"

Laurel had not. She sprang to her feet and strode to the open door, pulling it to and fro to examine it. "No. I can see where there was one, but it has been filled in quite permanently."

Madeleine's brows gathered. "Well, I suppose we can give Jack one mark for decency."

"Ha!" Pru stopped her prowling in the center of the room and turned to them. "You must leave at once."

Laurel blinked. And here she thought they were getting along so well.

Madeleine stood. "Yes. At once." She brushed at her eyes. "I shall tell Fiona to pack Melody's things." She dashed from the room, but not before Laurel heard a sob break from her throat.

Pru was white-faced and grimly determined. "I love Melody like my own, but I will not stand for this sort of high-handed, bloody-minded—"

Laurel held up a hand to forestall more cursing, no matter how appropriate it might be. "You'll let me take her away?"

Pru blinked at her. "Of course. You're obviously her mother. One need only look at the two of you to see that."

"But . . . you all love her so—"

Pru flinched but would not budge. "And you love her or you would not have come to Brown's in the first place. She adores you, as well."

Laurel gazed at Pru for a long moment. "You're terribly fierce."

Pru slid her a glance, her green eyes damp. "No, I simply look it." Then she turned away and grabbed up Laurel's old valise from the top of the wardrobe. "Pack. I shall send Bailiwick to arrange transportation. Where would you like to go?"

Laurel looked at the four walls, the window, and the door with the lock. Seeing it with the eyes of the others, she shuddered inside. What had she almost done?

"Far," she said huskily. "Very, very far away."

Colin and Aidan couldn't believe it.

Colin ran a hand over his face. "He didn't. He *couldn't.*"

Pru grimaced. "He did."

Aidan's jaw worked grimly. "I had no idea he was so far gone."

Colin looked at his friend. "We could have prevented this."

Aidan looked back at him. "We could have, but we didn't. We wanted to believe he could come back to us."

Madeleine couldn't stop her eyes from leaking. "She's taking her away. Far away, she said."

"Can you blame her?" Pru wasn't any drier. "She must be traumatized!"

Madeleine bit her lip. "I think . . . I'm not sure, but when I was in the room . . . I think he slept with her there. I saw his cravat on the floor beside the bed."

Pru clapped a hand to her mouth. "The bastard!"

Colin leaned back against the wall. "I feel sick," he muttered.

"I," Aidan bit out furiously, "would rather that Jack felt sick!"

Madeleine wrapped her arms about her midriff. "I spoke to him only this morning. He seemed very calm, very . . . resigned."

Pru looked up. "Resigned? To what, do you suppose?"

Madeleine shrugged one shoulder tentatively. "I don't really know, but . . . well, the door to the attic chamber wasn't actually locked, you know."

Colin straightened. "It wasn't?"

Madeleine shook her head. "No. Wilberforce simply opened it and we saw Laurel sitting there. She seemed as surprised to see us as we were to see her."

Aidan's scowl cleared. "He let her go."

Colin brightened. "Of course he did!" He turned to his wife, who looked highly doubtful. "Don't you see, Pru? He'd decided to let her go! That's why he went to Melody so early this morning. He was saying good-bye!"

Pru blinked. "Oh, that poor man."

Madeleine stared at her. "Pru, you've always mistrusted Jack."

Pru waved a dismissive hand. "Well, I don't now and there's no point in bringing up the past." She turned to her husband. "You have to find him. He'll think we hate him!"

Colin blinked, confused. "But you do—"

Pru shot him a narrow glare. Colin subsided. "Yes, my treasure." He turned to Aidan. "We're under orders, old man. What are you waiting for?"

Madeleine was less sure. "Do you know where he would go? He doesn't really seem to know anyone but us anymore."

Aidan looked thoughtful. "Oh, I think I have an idea."

Jack ended up at Lementeur's without really recalling the journey or his reason for coming. He simply entered the place and loomed darkly in the greeting area. Cabot took one look at Jack and rang for his employer.

Button did not bother with niceties and teasing conversation. He took Jack back to his office and poured him a whiskey.

Jack shook his head. "I do not drink."

Button pressed the glass into his hand. "This isn't for pleasure. This is so you don't crack right down the middle and fall into pieces on my floor."

Jack took the glass and tossed back the whiskey, simply to shut the smaller man up. Button removed the empty glass and refilled it.

Jack drew back. "I dare not."

Button shot him a look. "This one's for me." The dressmaker tossed back the whiskey like a teamster, then wheezed for a moment. "That's better," he choked, then put the decanter away. Sitting down opposite Jack with a sigh, he put his elbows on his knees and leaned forward.

"Tell me."

Jack told him everything. It seemed Laurel was right. There was no shutting him up these days. "I let her go," he said at last. "I couldn't betray her again."

Button rubbed his face. "And little Melody? Will Laurel take her away?"

"Oh yes," Jack said faintly. "I rather think so." The pain in his heart was the natural result of slicing it in half. In a just world, Laurel would have simply taken the whole thing with her, instead of leaving him with a twitching, gasping remnant.

Button leaned back and let out a sigh. "All those happy couples. I suppose it was only a matter of time before I lost one. After all, it seems even I am not perfect."

Jack wasn't really listening. He was too busy dying by inches. He was alone. Even now, he was sure that the unlocked attic door had led to Laurel announcing herself to the members of the club. After this, even his friends would cut him off. He certainly wouldn't blame them for it. All the time he had spent running from the ties of friendship, how could he know how much it would hurt to break them?

How he wished he could have simply continued on in his gray, numb world!

Really? And missed out on Melody? Missed out on Laurel, warm and sweet in his arms, dancing and singing on the rooftop? Missed out on knowing real love at last?

No. Every moment had been like a moment in heaven.

However, the next forty or so years of his life were going to be pure unadulterated hell.

When Colin and Aidan burst into Button's office a

few minutes later, Jack simply accepted that hell was going to begin a bit sooner than anticipated.

Wilberforce found his youngest footman on the landing of the servants' stair, gazing out at St. James Street through the small window set high in the wall.

Bailiwick cast his superior an agonized glance. "She went."

Wilberforce knew that it wasn't only the loss of his little Milady that saddened the young giant. Fiona had left this day as well.

It was painful to watch such a big fellow cut off at the knees.

Fiona had come to Wilberforce that morning. Her chin was high and her shoulders were back, but her face was pale and her eyes red from weeping. "I guess I ain't for London Town," she'd told him. "I be sorry to leave their ladyships, sir, but the city air just don't agree with me."

She'd done a fine job in her week at Brown's, so Wilberforce gave her every penny of her pay and a bonus besides. Now, looking at Bailiwick's misery, he thought perhaps he ought not to have made it so easy for the girl to go.

Fiona had stayed long enough to see little Melody off with her mother. Then she had taken a proper long time to pack her small valise and then she'd lingered in the kitchens saying farewell to all the fellows on the staff.

All but one.

Bailiwick had not been able to say good-bye.

"Bailiwick!" Enough was enough. Wilberforce had

coddled the lad for far too long. "The girl left because you practically threw her out the door."

Bailiwick turned his stunned gaze on Wilberforce. "Sir? But I—"

"You turned her away."

Bailiwick wiped his nose on his liveried arm. Wilberforce chose not to wince.

"I didn't! I wanted her to see that I wasn't like them blokes!"

"She saw that unlike the others, you weren't interested in her at all."

Bailiwick blinked. "But . . . I got her the job and all. I carried her parcels. I was goin' to give her a gift!"

"A romantic gift?"

Bailiwick shrugged. "It were a set o' silver brushes, for to use on the ladies. Like her tools."

Wilberforce considered the young man with no hint of his exasperation on his face. "Is that a romantic gift in your vast experience?"

Bailiwick's face crumpled. "Don't have experience, sir. Never set my sights on a girl before."

Poor Bailiwick. Well versed in love and devotion of every kind but the romantic sort. Poor Fiona. Experienced in every way except in love itself. They were an impossible couple. They were made for each other.

This would not do. The world was awry. Wilberforce prided himself on setting the world straight.

"Why didn't you ask her to marry you?"

Bailiwick blinked. "Underfootmen don't get married, sir. We have to live in-house. Ye can't have a wife in-house!"

Wilberforce gazed through the small window at the street outside. "This is a gentleman's club with ladies and children in residence. And a kitten. And soon, I suspect, a puppy for young Master Evan."

With a slight lifting of his chin, Wilberforce repressed a single moment of longing for those peaceful, organized days of old. Those boring, dreary days that had threatened to last the rest of his natural life. "Bailiwick, I have come to understand that this is a special place in the world. Rules are what we make of them, here at Brown's."

Bailiwick sniffled. "I don't understand, sir."

Wilberforce turned to the vast young man. "Bailiwick, you have served our gentlemen and their families very well. You have shown dedication and bravery well beyond your terms of service. You have, in fact, done more to promote the well-being and happiness of our members than all the other footmen put together."

Bailiwick blinked under this barrage of praise. He looked a little faint, actually. "Sir!"

Wilberforce held up a hand. "Do not interrupt. Since you are such a valuable employee and since it is integral to the smooth running of this establishment that you are satisfied with your station, it behooves me to raise that station to better implement our members' needs and pleasure."

Bailiwick's face was a priceless mixture of confusion and trust. He looked like a mystified hound. "I don't know what that means, sir."

Wilberforce gazed at him for a long moment. "It means that you have been promoted to head footman and that you might indeed marry, as long as your bride is also an employee and lives in-house." That should keep the other footmen from clamoring for equality.

Wilberforce serenely folded his hands before him.

"You may move into a proper chamber and there will be a raise in pay—" He held up a single finger. "A slight raise in pay." There was no need to go mad, after all. One needed to keep a few carrots back, didn't one?

Bailiwick stood there for a long moment, looking like a great stunned ox. Then Wilberforce found himself swept up in a massive bear hug that actually lifted his feet from the ground. Before he could remonstrate with his giant employee, Bailiwick had plunked him back onto his footing and was galloping down the servants' stairs.

A bit of dust sifted down from the ceiling beams at the seismic shifting of the big man's footfalls and landed on Wilberforce's liveried shoulders. He brushed at it, frowning ever so slightly.

Dust. In his club.

The three men crowded into Button's office made for little room to shift one's elbow, but Button wasn't about to give them their privacy. He did not intend to miss a single moment. He remained quietly, mostly, in his chair and let Aidan and Colin corner Jack in his. Brandy had been poured, but no one was interested in drowning their woes. No, today the woes were alive and kicking and putting on a most intriguing performance.

Aidan leaned forward in his dainty chair, planting both elbows on the table as he glared at Jack. "You kidnapped Melody's mother!"

Colin nodded forcefully from his own elegant little perch. "And then you neglected to tell us about it!"

"You two have your ladies. You didn't need to worry yourselves about my problems." Jack leaned back in his chair, the picture of defeat. "What does it matter now?"

Colin looked at Aidan. "You hold him down. I'll bite him."

Aidan snorted. "At this moment, you couldn't pay me to lay a hand on him. Revolting coward."

That insult prompted a sign of life at last. Jack's jaw visibly clenched and his voice dropped to a growl. "Blankenship, you're not too big to knock down. I could use a fight right now."

Colin threw out his hands. "Then *fight*, by God! Fight for Miss Clarke, fight for Melody!"

Jack ran a hand over his face. "I suppose I could find her."

Colin nodded enthusiastically.

Jack looked up at him. "I suppose I could grab her hand and not let go."

Colin clapped his hands once. "That's the ticket!"

Jack tilted his head and gazed sourly at Colin. "I suppose I could lock her in a room until she agrees to marry me."

Colin deflated. "Oh. Well. No."

Aidan let out a breath. "So you did ask. You asked nicely, didn't you? You know, with all the proper emotional intensity? That part is required, I learned."

Jack looked down at his hands. "I ripped myself open and spilled my guts at her feet."

"My, my." Button fanned himself. "How romantic."

Colin rubbed the back of his neck, thinking. "So she really doesn't want to marry you."

Jack shot him a dark glance. "Can you blame her?"

"Then we have to negotiate some other arrangement. Some way for us to keep Melody, or see her often . . . or at least once in a while . . ." Colin was pale with panic. He looked at Aidan. "Think of something, damn you!"

Aidan let out a breath. "Jack, Colin is right. The three of us have considerable wealth and power. There has to be some way to coerce the lady into sharing custody. After all, you'd be in your rights to extract Melody from her care completely."

Colin sat upright. "Now, hold it right there—"

Aidan waved a hand. "I didn't mean we should, just that we *could*. Surely Miss Clarke is aware of that?"

Colin considered the idea. "I shouldn't like to make her afraid, but if we could simply make her come to her senses! Present her with some options! After all, Jack would be able to provide Melody with a brilliant life of privilege and high social standing."

Jack looked thoughtful. "I should like nothing better, but I don't even know where Laurel has gone."

Aidan folded his arms and regarded his friend with fond exasperation. "Wilberforce sent her off in a hired carriage. To the docks. To a ship."

Jack looked up, hope sparking in his eyes. "Wilberforce wouldn't put Laurel on just any ship."

They stood, three large men ready for action. They stilled, however, when Button raised a languid hand.

"I can see we are about to be honored with a diverting exhibition of manliness, and I am never averse to such an amusing display of . . . plumage, but I have one question. Precisely how do you intend to convince the lady to cooperate, my lord?"

Jack's eyes were as dark as night. "I don't."

In the yard of the mews, Bailiwick struggled to control Balthazar's uninhibited attempts to avoid being bridled.

The giant white horse was resentful and scheming at the best of times, but Bailiwick loved his valiant, willful friend.

Nevertheless, Bailiwick currently wished he could fling a saddle on Evan's faithful Ramses and be done with it. Ramses, thankfully, had no idea of such feelings or the mild-mannered gelding would have fainted dead away at the notion. No horse could carry Bailiwick except the mighty Balthazar.

At the moment, however, Balthazar wasn't in the mood. As he battled with his obstinate horse, Bailiwick felt Fiona traveling farther away with every breath he took. His chest tightened correspondingly. At last he muscled the great, bony white head close to his and glared into Balthazar's wicked brown eye.

"She's gettin' away, you big lout! Fiona's leavin' me and you're me only hope for gettin' her back! So open your bloody great teeth and *take the bloomin' bit!*"

Slowly, Balthazar dropped his long white lashes low on his eye and opened his mouth wide. Bailiwick didn't waste a moment. He thrust the metal bit deep behind Balthazar's huge yellow teeth and quickly fixed the buckle of the bridle behind the velvety ears that now tilted urgently at him as if to say, "Hurry up! We've a girl to catch!"

Once the bridle was on, Balthazar began to trot from the yard. Unfortunately, he had neither a saddle nor Bailiwick upon his back.

Still holding the reins, Bailiwick ran alongside, then threw himself bodily across Balthazar's back. "That's right, lad! We don't need the bloody saddle!"

Sometime between flinging his leg over the great wide back and sitting up straight, Bailiwick found himself traveling at a full gallop. Since Balthazar's stride was half again the length of a normal horse, that gallop was frighteningly impressive.

Bailiwick only grinned into the fierce wind of their passing. "I'm coming for you, Fiona!"

Though Fiona had ridden away seated on the back of the tinker's wagon hours before, nestled between dangling, banging pots and pans to be repaired and re-sold, the wagon traveled slowly. Balthazar traveled like a wildfire before a gale. Dodging carts and carriages, deftly bounding around and occasionally over startled pedestrians, Balthazar carried Bailiwick through May-fair and into the western part of the city in less than a quarter of an hour. Bailiwick felt bad about those folk at the market and he was sure Wilberforce would somehow hear about the baker's cart and all those loaves crum-bling beneath great speckled hooves, but now they had reached the outskirts of urban restraint and there was nothing and no one before them on the open road.

There was no need for spurs. Balthazar set sail be-fore the wind. Bailiwick leaned low and held on tight.

Far down the road, hours outside the city, Fiona shifted her sore buttocks on the hard seat and let out another sigh. She was no stranger to bumping down the road in some highly inconvenient conveyance. She'd been doing it most of her life, after all. However, there was a splinter of wood digging into her thigh and she was getting full dust seated facing backward with her feet dangling off the end.

Brown's had been so nice, so clean and comfortable and merry. The ladies were lovely to her and she'd never eaten food like that in her life! Three times a day, too!

"It's just as well," she told herself out loud, "for ye'd be gettin' fat as old Pomme's wife and who'd look at ye then?"

Bailiwick. Her sweet Johnny would look at her. Her big, bashful giant would watch her walk past with a shine of hunger in his eyes that nearly took her breath away at the memory of it. She'd wanted to find out what that hunger meant, but he'd pushed her away like he couldn't bear the touch of her.

The first time she'd seen her handsome Johnny, she'd been cornered on the road with two of her friends, the victims of a bandit's filthy sense of humor. Along had come Johnny Bailiwick, thundering down the road like an avenging angel mounted on a great white steed. He'd ridden through that band of ruffians like a ball striking the bowling pins, sending them spinning off in every direction. Fiona smiled a bit damply at the memory. She could almost hear those mighty hoofbeats now.

Ba-ba-da-dum. Ba-ba-da-dum.

Fiona raised her head, startled. She *could* hear hoofbeats!

Ba-ba-da-dum. Ba-ba-da-dum.

As she gazed back down the road toward the sound, squinting into the afternoon light, she thought she might see a postboy on a courier horse, or even a lord out for a gallop. Never did she think she'd see her Johnny, racing up the road on his great white steed!

He looked so big and handsome, like a knight out to slay dragons! Inside Fiona's hardened, road-wise shell, her girlishly romantic heart thudded like she rode a dangerous mount of her own!

Johnny came after me.

The tinker, startled by what sounded like an army

flying down the road behind him, pulled his elderly draft horse to one side of the road to wait for it to pass. As soon as the wheels slowed, Fiona bounced herself off and landed on her feet in the dust, fixing the strap of her bundle diagonally across her bosom. She set off into a run, her bright skirts flying like a flag at a jousting match.

Balthazar didn't even slow his pace. Fiona smiled into the oncoming equine storm and held one hand trustingly up in the air.

Johnny's big hand came down and wrapped itself around her upper arm. With Balthazar's next great leap, Fiona found herself lifted into the air to come down seated across the big horse's withers, wrapped in her big Johnny's arms. Turning into him, she twined her arms about his neck.

Balthazar slowed at last, his relentless gallop softening as he moved in a great circling turn. Bailiwick leaned back to gaze down into Fiona's beautiful face. "I love you," he said bluntly.

Fiona smiled up at him. "Aye, and I love ye too, ye great fool."

Bailiwick scowled down at her. "No more of your flirtin' now. You're mine, you hear? My woman! My wife!" He brought his mouth down on hers for a bruising kiss. Then he lifted his head. "Now don't you ever forget it!"

Fiona gaped, her mouth opening and closing. "W— wife?"

Bailiwick lifted his chin. "I got no ring for you now, but I've been promoted, I have. I'll have the finest gold ring you every saw, as soon as I become head footman of Brown's!"

Fiona only blinked at him. "Wife?"

Bailiwick frowned down at her. "Yes. Wife. Be there somethin' wrong with that?"

She licked her lips. "Not sneakin' about? Not climbin' back into me cold bed alone afterward?" She frowned slightly. "Will ye be wantin' children, then?"

Bailiwick cleared his throat. "Yes. Or no. Whatever you'll be wantin'."

"Whatever I'll be wantin'?" Fiona smiled, then wrapped her arms about his waist and pressed her ear to his pounding heart. "Mr. Johnny Bailiwick, there'll be children spillin' into St. James Street and all, there will!"

Bailiwick's arms tightened around her until she could hardly breathe. Who needed breath when she had her own personal knight in shining livery?

Johnny's deep voice rumbled through her body, making her close her eyes in pleasure.

"Will you be wantin' to start those children soon, Fi?" Johnny's big hands tightened on her waist. "Because Balthazar's a big horse. You could practically lie down on top of a horse this size."

Thirty-two

In the slanting afternoon light, Laurel stood on the docks with her daughter's tiny hand in hers and their rather pathetic pile of belongings beside them. Most of it was Melody's. They'd had to leave many of her toys behind and some of her beautiful dresses, but there was no use for lace dresses where they were going.

Laurel had emptied her small account and purchased passage for two to the farthest, warmest destination the shipping office could provide that day. As she waited for the purser to find her and help her and Melody onto the ship, Laurel watched men carrying crate after crate past them, over the plank and onto the waiting ship.

It wasn't until a dozen had passed that Laurel's gaze actually focused on to the name stenciled on the sides of the crates.

Honor's Thunder.

"Why does that name sound so familiar?" she murmured to herself.

"Because it is my flagship," came a deep voice behind her.

Laurel whirled to see Jack, looking dark and dashing in a wool sailor's coat, a seaman's cap upon his head. He gazed at her as the wind off the Thames whipped her hair from its pins and teased it around the sides of her bonnet.

He looked so handsome Laurel's heart couldn't decide whether to stop or beat double time.

"What—what are you doing here?"

He looked past her at the ship. "Wilberforce told me where you'd gone. He can be quite devious sometimes." He turned his gaze back to her. "He recommended this particular ship, didn't he?"

Laurel nodded. "It is yours. It's the *Dishonor's Plunder,* isn't it?"

Jack smiled. It was a sad, barely there thing, yet her heart sang to see it. Jack was coming home at last. She was glad of it.

He would need everything that lay within him to withstand the loss of his daughter.

"It isn't my ship," Jack said evenly. "It is yours."

Laurel blinked. "What does that mean?"

He looked down at Melody and smiled. The love and sadness in his eyes made Laurel ache. "I give her to you," he said quietly. Then he raised his gaze to meet hers. "I give it all to you. Melody. My ships. Everything in my accounts. I would give you Strickland itself if it were not entailed, but you may live there undisturbed by me, if you like."

Laurel couldn't take his words in. "I don't understand. What do you mean?"

"It might be easier if you took my name, but I promise it would be marriage in name only. Still, it would afford you all the protection of my rank and Melody would become legitimate."

Laurel felt dizzy. "Jack, shut up! Tell me what you *mean!*"

He took three steps toward her, just close enough to reach out to touch her flying hair. "I mean," he said softly, "that everything I have is yours. Take it. Be happy. Be . . ." His voice failed him for a long moment. "Be free."

The purser came then. He nodded deferentially to Jack. "Ready when you are, miss."

" 'My lady,' " Jack corrected him. "Ready when you are, my lady."

Then Jack knelt and kissed Melody quickly. "You're going to have a marvelous journey, Lady Melody."

"Are you coming, too, Papa? Can we skewer some pirates?"

Jack faltered then, for the first time. He looked away for a long moment, entirely unable to speak. Laurel ached for him. Then he mustered up a near smile and kissed Melody again. "No, little one. I am not. You'll have to fight Black Pete without me this time."

Then he stood and backed away along the docks. The fog was naught but wisps and he stood out like a dark statue in the white.

Their luggage was already being put on the ship. Laurel picked Melody up and turned away from Jack, walking with determination to the boarding plank, over it, and beyond.

If it was true, she had the entire world before her now. If Jack's word was true, she had everything she could ever want.

On the ship, they were shown to a small but comfortable cabin. Melody ran about, exploring every nook and cranny, Gordy Ann tucked in her armpit.

Laurel sat on the bunk, which probably would have been small for a man but would easily accommodate herself and the twelve-monkey marching band for the next several weeks. Weariness drained her at the thought.

What are you doing?

I am taking my daughter away, just as I planned.

But why?

Because . . . because I am done with someone else deciding my destiny. I am done with being manipulated and lied to and stolen from—

I give it all to you.

His face as he'd stood there in the mist . . . the stark resignation, the open acceptance of her plans, the selfless generosity of wanting her and Melody to have the very best . . .

Are. You. Out. Of. Your. Tiny. Little. Mind?

A small laugh burst from Laurel's lips.

I think I am a bit mad.

I think I am mad for that strange, complicated scoundrel of a man!

She felt the ship lurch beneath her feet. They were moving! She ran to the deck, Melody fast behind her. There were already fifty yards of water between the ship and the docks!

Jack stayed where he was and watched the ship move out from the docks. The wispy fog gradually came between himself and everything he loved best in the world, reducing the ship to a ghostly outline. How appropriate. That was what his life would be like from this day forward, nothing but a ghostly outline.

"It's gone, Papa. Why are you still looking?"

Jack's heart stopped at the piping voice at his side. He looked down in shock to see Melody standing beside him, her finger firmly in her mouth as she looked up at him. She pulled it out and pointed it out to sea. "I waved bye-bye. So did Mama."

Jack jerked his stunned gaze up to see Laurel standing a few feet away, her trailing wisps of hair not able to hide the wide smile on her face.

His breath left him in a burst. "But . . . I saw you go—"

Her smile widened. "I've never owned a ship before. Did you know you could order a sailor to bring you back in a dinghy even after the ship already set sail?" She leaned closer. "I promised him fifty pounds. It's a shameless ransom, but then again, I'm a very rich woman, aren't I?"

Jack could scarcely breathe. "Then, you'll stay in England? I can see Melody sometimes?"

Laurel snorted. "I should say so. I'm not going to be the one emptying the blasted kitten's litter pan every morning!"

The world went very still around Jack. Even the choppy river waves froze. Did she . . . was she—

Laurel moved close to him, then closer still. She went up on tiptoe to whisper in his ear. "Ask again."

His heart thudded once. Then again. Then, for the first time in years, it beat in a normal, happy rhythm.

"Will you wed me, Bramble?"

"No," she said with a brilliant smile, "but *you* may wed *me,* if you like."

Jack felt a little monkey hand tugging at his coat. He looked down to see Melody gazing up at him.

"Papa, can we get merry now?"

Epilogue

Jack rolled over and wrapped his arm about his wife. Laurel melted into the curve of his body. "Hmm."

Jack kissed her bare shoulder. "Good morning, my lady."

"Is it morning already?" She turned her face into the pillow. "It can't be. I declare that morning won't start until I've completely recovered."

Jack chuckled. "Oh, come now. It wasn't that bad."

Laurel turned her head to shoot him a grumpy glance. "I'm absolutely throbbing."

"Hmm." He ground his body into her bottom gently. "I know the feeling."

Slapping at him, she laughed. "There is more to life than can be found in bed, my lord."

"True, but why bother? Bed is wonderful. I wish I could live out the rest of my life in bed with you."

She snorted. "A short life."

"Yes, but I'm willing to make that sacrifice." He gnawed gently on that same shoulder and enfolded a warm breast in his large hand. "Wouldn't you like to go out in flames with me?"

He could tell by the way she started to writhe to his touch that warm, wet delights were soon to be his once more.

Rolling her atop him, he brought her mouth down to his, wrapping his hands around her jaw. She spread herself upon him, all heated and soft and marvelously Laurel.

A great crashing sound came from the next chamber.

"Ignore it," Jack murmured into Laurel's mouth.

Indignant yowling cut the sleepy morning air, followed quickly by happy, high-pitched barking.

"Bad puppy! Bad!"

"I don't hear a thing," Laurel sighed back.

"Mama! Genghis broke the china!"

Jack felt Laurel's snicker start deep. Smiling in resignation, he let his head fall back when she began to howl with laughter into his neck. Listening to Laurel laugh was every bit as satisfying as making love to her.

She rolled her warm, lovely body from his. "We might want to consider moving to Strickland House."

Jack went up on his elbows, so as not to miss the entertaining view of Laurel dressing. "You say that every morning and then you always say—"

"I just can't imagine leaving Brown's." Laurel smiled at her handsome husband. His dark, tousled hair was still too long, but happiness had filled in his hollow cheeks and driven the shadows from his eyes. The nightmares came rarely now, and when they did she held him close until they passed.

"I had a thought," she said casually as she tied the bow at the neck of her chemise. She glanced sideways at him, gauging her tone. "I wondered . . ."

Jack sat up. "Speak, Laurel."

Giving up her casual pretense, she climbed back

onto the bed and took his hand. Gazing into those dark eyes that had finally learned to laugh again, she took a deep breath.

"I thought that perhaps you ought to seek out the men who you saved that night, the ones you led back over the line."

His eyes darkened at the memory and she rushed on. "I just thought . . . if you could see them now, alive and well, that you could see that you had to do it and—"

He kissed her words away. Then he drew back and smiled sadly at her. "My love, I know that already." He lifted a hand and cupped her cheek. "Even if I could turn back time, I would still make the same decisions. What had to be came to be."

She blinked back the dampness in her eyes and smiled her pride at him. "Then you have no regrets?"

"No. We had to travel the road that led to here." He traced her bottom lip with the tip of his thumb. "Have you regrets? You lost so much—"

She bit his thumb to stop him. "I gained so much." He kissed her and she lost herself in his mouth, as she always did. Then another feline yowl assaulted their ears. She drew back with a rueful smile. "Although I think Colin and Pru might owe us a new set of china."

Jack sighed. "I just wish Melody and Evan were able to get along better. Ever since Evan decided to go off to Eton next term, Melody has been so upset. I don't think she'll ever forgive him."

Laurel smiled knowingly. "Oh, I don't know. Women tend to forgive the men they love."

Jack started. "Love?"

Laurel laughed and left the room.

"Laurel?" Jack scrambled up, forgetting his nakedness. "Laurel? What do you mean, *love*?"

Melody dabbed at her eyes. "They went through so much to be together! Evan and I didn't have to suffer nearly so much!"

Button finished adjusting the veil upon her head and stepped back. "Perfection," he stated serenely. "Of course."

Melody blew her nose violently. "It's so romantic!"

Button took the handkerchief away and handed her a clean one. "Your own tale is romance personified, pet. At this moment, Evan is downstairs, waiting to stand with you at the altar, willing to vow his love forever and ever. What do you say? Shall we join him?"

Melody smiled, like the sun emerging after a storm. "Oh yes. Let's."

A knock came at the door. Button opened it and swept a bow. "My lord, she is ready!"

Melody sniffed. "I am?" She blinked at herself in the mirror. From the elegantly beaded slippers on her feet to the miles of veil that began at her brow, she was completely and entirely ready.

The Marquis of Strickland stepped into the room. Tall and lean, dark hair handsomely edged in gray, his eyes widened at the sight of his eldest daughter. "You look just like your mother," he whispered.

"She does?" The marchioness bustled into the room, carrying a bouquet of fresh pink roses. She stopped and gazed at Melody. Then she let out a long, damp sigh. "Oh damn. When did you grow up?"

Melody held out her arms. "Mama!"

The marquis stood to one side, manfully containing

his own tendency to leak while his wife and daughter embraced and sniffled.

Then Button stepped in. "Yes, lovely, how nice to see you, my lady, shall we fix this veil?" Having repaired Melody to his satisfaction, he cleared his throat. "I have a gift." He held out his hand.

Melody blinked. "Button, you needn't—"

It was a handkerchief, a square of stained linen, carefully hemmed and trimmed in lace. The cloth was brown with age and rather nastily smudged.

Melody frowned at it. "Goodness. Er . . . thank you?"

Button's face creased in a smile. "I know that you thought she fell to bits years ago, but there was a piece I saved, from inside the knot—"

"Gordy Ann!" Melody gasped, then threw her arms about Button's neck. "Gordy Ann will be at my wedding!"

Button patted her gently on the back. "Something old, you know."

Sniffling a little, Melody drew back and carefully stuffed the grubby cloth into her beaded bodice, close to her heart.

Then she lifted her chin and smiled at her mother and father and dearest Button.

"Come along, then," she said brightly. "Let's get merry!"

The romance never ends...

Look for these other series from
New York Times bestselling author
CELESTE BRADLEY

THE HEIRESS BRIDES
Desperately Seeking a Duke
The Duke Next Door
The Duke Most Wanted

THE LIAR'S CLUB
The Pretender
The Impostor
The Spy
The Charmer
The Rogue

THE ROYAL FOUR
To Wed a Scandalous Spy
Surrender to a Wicked Spy
One Night with a Spy
Seducing the Spy

...and don't miss her latest series

THE RUNAWAY BRIDES
Devil in My Bed
Rogue in My Arms
Scoundrel in My Dreams